Reader Reviews for *Snap Decision*

"Riveting does not come close to describing this book! Holly does an amazing job of painting a clear picture in your mind of what is happening in every situation. I could not put this book down and I never saw the ending coming...the mark of a great author! A must-read for thrill seekers and murder mystery lovers!"

– Cheryl, reader

"Holly Spofford has done it again in a totally new storyline. Snap Decision weaves a plot with her usual twists and turns slowly building to a suspenseful and unexpected ending. You won't be asking for your money back."

– Ed, reader

"After reading Holly Spofford's trilogy of the mystery and suspense adventures of Daisy and NT (Nick), I looked forward to her introduction of new characters and hopefully many new adventures. Holly did not disappoint in her new book Snap Decision. From the first page where we meet Lindsey Johnson, the smart Tiparillo-smoking female tugboat captain of the Boston Babe, who pulls a body from the New York Harbor, Holly starts us on a mystery that just doesn't let up as each page is turned. I was completely gripped by the story and identifying everything happening, but most of all I was enthralled by the characters Holly created in this new book. Paige Buckley and Fina (Serafina) Manzetti, two young women from the Philadelphia area making their way as roommates in NYC, came to life as I read the book. Holly continues her strong character development as well as her attention to detail to create a mysterious thriller that held me in suspense and had me binge reading to the final page."

– Nancy, reader

Other books by Holly Spofford

A Letter for Hoot
Hot Ice, Cold Blood
The Even Game

For Lynn with love

CHAPTER 1

For a fourth morning in a row, ominous, dense fog crept over the New York Harbor. It overspread the docks in a treacherous, slippery sheet. Water swirled around the algae-covered pilings. An inky black sky revealed no cracks of sunlight.

Longshoremen coiled thick lines into neat, damp circles. A woman stood on one of the slick docks wearing a black wool captain's hat atop her spiky dirty-blond hair. Her red, all-weather coat laid over heavy yellow fishing coveralls. The woman, Lindsey Johnson, surveyed the conditions, her lined, bright blue eyes scanning the horizon. Smoke from the Tiparillo cigar clenched between her teeth swirled into the black sky.

Gazing out at the ominous morning, she felt her scalp tingle and an icy shiver ran through her. *Tired of this fuckin' fog. Makes my skin crawl. But me,* Boston Babe, *and the boys got a job to do.* She pushed aside the unease, took one last drag of the Tiparillo, and tossed it into the trash.

Pulling her hat down over her ears, Lindsey sent a silent prayer for a safe and successful day. As was her custom, she kissed her left hand and patted the starboard side of the *Boston Babe* before boarding. Lindsey had bought the boat over thirty years ago and cared for it like it was her child. As the only woman tugboat captain in New York, Lindsey had earned the reputation of one of the most skilled and knowledgeable captains in the maritime field. Many a cargo ship's captain requested her and hoped she would be assigned their captain to guide them to port.

In the tight galley, her four beefy crewmen sat around the round white table, sipping coffee.

"Mornin' boys," she said.

The Fab Four—Brett, Jeb, Leon, and Geo—grunted a good morning.

"Is my Fab Four ready? It's gonna be a tough one today, gents, so I need you all focused."

"Yes, Cap'n Tips!" Leon used the nickname only the crew called her in a nod to her love of Tiparillos. "We're ready."

Three of the four men had spent over two decades with Lindsey. Geo was the relative newcomer at three years. Word among the crews of all the tugs was that no one respected and revered their captain more than they did. Attempts to lure Lindsey's crew away by other captains promising higher pay always failed. They loved her like a sister and expertly performed their jobs.

"Damn fog is thickah than yesterday. We need all eyes shahp when we pull out. You know the drill." She nodded at them and retreated into the wheelhouse.

The four crew members tossed amused looks at each other. After rinsing their mugs in the tiny sink, they ducked up the three steps to the main deck and took their positions.

After radioing the harbor master for clearance, Lindsey fired up the engines. The familiar, comforting vibration from the twin diesel engines emanated up through the main deck, and the churning of the water fueled by the powerful engines broke the stillness of the morning. Jeb and Leon undid the lines and tossed the sodden ropes back onto the slippery deck. Geo and Brett manned the bow and pushed off from the dock. Lindsey gripped the helm, turned the tug into the cold morning, and chugged into the darkness.

* * *

Up in the wheelhouse, Lindsey slipped on her glasses and alerted the captain of the idling Chinese cargo ship waiting in the Hudson, "This is *Boston Babe* heading out to point 34J. Do you read?"

The response was quick and clipped. "Yes, roger that. We are approaching 34J now. Fog lights running."

"Roger. ETA is twenty-two minutes," she replied.

Away from the docks, the fog thickened like a bowl of overcooked oatmeal. Wipers going at full speed, Lindsey double-checked that all running lights were on, and the bow was manned. Her eyes lasered in on the fog-covered water, Lindsey gripped the helm with experienced hands and steered the *Boston Babe* toward the imposing, fully loaded cargo ship. *Damn stuffy in here*, she thought and opened the small side window. Crisp, cold air whooshed into the wheelhouse. Inhaling deeply, Lindsey filled her lungs and opened her ears. After thirty years on the water, the churning of the engines, the slap of the water on *Boston Babe*'s hull, and voices of her crew were Lindsey's lifeblood.

She hummed one of her favorite Irish drinking songs as the tugboat chugged into the morning. A low rumble from the starboard side made her stop. Stealing a fast look over her right shoulder, Lindsey saw nothing but fog. The rumble grew louder. *What the hell is that?*

Seizing the radio, she called down to the bow. "Jeb, you guys hear or see anything down there? Starboard side?" Lindsey doubted they would. The noise from the engines drowned out all other sounds.

"No, Cap. Why?"

"I heard a rumble on the starboard side. Please check."

"Aye aye. I'll radio back."

"Roger." As Lindsey hung up the radio, the rumble swelled to a roar. Caught off guard, she was temporarily blinded by a powerful light filling the wheelhouse. "What the *fuck*?"

Jeb's panicked voice replied, "Jesus, Cap! From what I can see, it's another boat headin' straight at us!"

"How far out?"

"Only about fifty yards!"

Lindsey's heart hammered in her ears. Steering the tug aside was out of the question. She reached for the horn and blasted it—one long, loud blast. *Please God! Let them hear it!* The blazing bow light of the unidentified boat illuminated the entire starboard side of the *Boston Babe*.

"Seek safety *now*!" she barked at her crew into the radio.

Closer and closer the boat sped, slicing through the fog-covered water. The space between the two vessels shriveled by the second. From the potent roar of the engines, Lindsey knew it was a new, powerful boat. She blasted the horn again and flashed her running lights. Fear gushed through Lindsey as she watched the boat bear down on them. Lindsey shrank back from glaring light. Blasting the horn one more time, she braced herself for impact.

Just as the bow of the rogue boat was about to T-bone the *Boston Babe*, the boat cut sharply away, but not before briefly sideswiping Lindsey's vessel. A tall, wide wall of spray shot overboard the *Boston Babe*, obscuring Lindsey's ability to identify the vessel. She pulled open a cabinet and yanked out a pair of binoculars. All that was visible were two enormous outboard motors retreating into the dark. *Son of a bitch!*

Seizing the radio, she checked on her crew. "Jeb! Everyone okay?"

No answer.

"Jeb!" She waited a few more seconds. "Please respond!"

"We're okay, Cap."

Thank God, Lindsey thought. With shaking hands, she lifted the radio to call the port authority.

"Captain! Something's stuck on us!" Jeb yelled. "I think it's from that boat!"

"What? You gotta be kiddin' me! What is it?"

"Tough to tell. Maybe some trash, can't tell. It's kind of latched on the bumper!"

For fuck's sake, she thought and throttled back the speed. From the wheelhouse window she saw the crew pointing over the starboard side.

"Cap, it's stuck in front. What do you want us to do?"

Lindsey had seen enough water pollution in her day. *I'm not leavin' any more shit in the river.* "Use the poles and grappling hooks and hoist it up." She watched while the crew lugged the object on board. It thudded onto the deck. Water slid from it and trickled around the crew's booted feet.

Jeb's head snapped in her direction. He urgently waved her to come down on deck.

"Ah shit!" she muttered and put the tug on autopilot. Lindsey marched out of the wheelhouse.

On the deck lay something, roughly five to six feet in length, wrapped in black plastic tarp and knotted at both ends. Slick rope resembling a large stretched-out slinky was wrapped around the middle.

Yanking on her gloves, she reached down to feel the object. The churning in her stomach grew to a tsunami of fear. *Oh no. That doesn't feel like a log.* A tightness formed in her chest as her stomach churned like an angry ocean.

"This is not good."

Lindsey saw the anxious glances bounce between her crew. The fear she saw in their eyes pulled at her.

"Everything will be fine, fellas. But I need your help. Put your gloves on and use the poles to roll this against the base of the wheelhouse. Grab some extra lines and secure it to the cleats."

"Yes, Captain," they answered, but no one moved at first until Jeb stepped forward.

"Thanks fellas. I'll go call the port authority."

As she waited for the port authority boat to arrive, Lindsey pulled out a Tiparillo. Cupping her hands around her mouth, she lit up and inhaled deeply. *I don't want to look, but it's hard not to.* She blew the smoke into the wind. Her instincts told her the undeniable, awful truth: Inside the black plastic tarp was a body.

The blue and red lights from the port authority boat grew closer. *Thank God.* She inhaled deeply and took a tentative step toward the tarp. She knew it had been submerged for a long time as the once-white ropes were slick with green algae. Based on the diminutive size of the object, she deduced it was a woman. *God forbid it's a kid.*

"Permission to come aboard?" a voice called.

Lindsey waved to her colleague from the port authority, George Peck, and a female police officer with him. They came aboard and exchanged abbreviated pleasantries. The officer, who introduced herself as Captain Carol McLoughlin, agreed it was in the shape of a body. She squatted down, and with gloved hands, untied the top rope and placed it in an evidence bag.

Lindsey briefed Peck and McLoughlin about the rogue boat. She added, "I think the boat stirred this up from the bottom."

McLoughlin nodded. "I need to see our victim to start procedures."

Carefully, she folded back the tarp to reveal a body. Dark,

matted hair covered the woman's face. As she reached to carefully push back the hair, Lindsey's heart throbbed and her stomach sloshed. Prickles of trepidation dotted her skin.

Captain McLoughlin gingerly brushed the woman's hair aside and sighed.

"Oh my God," Lindsey gasped.

"Do you know her?"

Lindsey glanced down at the blue, bloated face. Everything stopped. The question was not processed. Lindsey felt the blood rush from her face. Her knees threatened to buckle.

She swallowed bile and nodded.

CHAPTER 2
1983

Paige Buckley and Serafina "Fina" Manzetti locked eyes over the white line taped to the gym floor. Fina smirked at Paige who shook her head in defiance. Five other kids crouched in the back of the court, waiting like racehorses in the starting gates for Mr. Price to blow the whistle. Eight red playground balls sat on the line down the middle of the court. Eyes squinted and shot daggers at one another. Trash talk floated in the air. For the two teams of sixth graders at Whitemarsh Elementary, winning Dodgeball Day was almost on par with winning Field Day.

The atmosphere in the large gym swelled with an impenetrable, invisible undercurrent of competition. Mr. Price hoisted his middle-aged, corpulent body onto the metal folding chair and took the black whistle from beneath his black and white referee shirt. Flicking his eyes back and forth between the two sides, he barked, "Everyone know the rules?"

"Yes!"

"All right then! Let's get this party started!" With grand ceremony, he lifted the whistle.

BLEET! BLEET! BLEET!

Twelve pairs of feet raced to the balls; hands grabbed at them. Over the white dividing line, balls flew through the air like hand grenades. The slap and smack of the rubber balls hitting exposed flesh accompanied the shrieks of joy and moans of defeat.

Paige and Fina had been best friends since Fina stepped into Paige's classroom as the new girl in September. One day after they were paired up in Mrs. McKevitt's music class taking turns playing the xylophone, Fina told Paige, "You're really pretty and nice. Thanks for helping me." Paige knew they would be best friends—except when they were on opposing dodgeball teams.

Dodging right, left, backward, and forward, they soon were the only two left who had not been smacked by a ball. From the back court jail, teammates screamed encouragement while the enemies hurled barbs. Circling the court like hawks over a field dense with fat mice, Paige and Fina stared at each other across the dividing line, tossing the ball back between their own hands, daring the other to toss. As much as they adored each other, they also loved beating one another.

"Okay ladies!" Mr. Price called from his chair. "It's on you! Time's ticking down! Thirty seconds!"

Paige ignored him and as Fina turned her head ever so slightly in his direction, Paige juked to the right, cocked her arm, and let fly the ball at Fina's knees.

SMACK! The ball hit Fina's shin. Paige's team went wild to the point that a bystander would have thought they won Olympic gold.

Glancing up at her friend, Fina smirked and threw the ball at Paige, who ducked out of the way.

"Game's over, Fin!"

"For now."

* * *

Throughout their middle school and high school years, Paige and Fina widened their circle of friends, yet their bond was unbreakable. Lots of history was shared between them: mixing their blood in a pinky promise after slicing their fingers, getting drunk and puncturing more holes in their earlobes, turfing the neighbor's yard in an '84 Chevy wagon while wearing Russian hats. Boyfriends came and went. Drivers' licenses were attained.

Both were raised by working-class parents who taught them the value of earning their own spending money. For three of four of their high school years, they worked in the Plymouth Meeting Mall: Fina got a job in a kids' clothing store owned by the father of a friend, and Paige worked at the Twisted Pretzel as a baker and assistant bookkeeper. On the days when they shared the same break, they would sit on the edge of the sizeable fountain built into the middle of the mall, its tiled floor covered in sunken, wished-upon coins. Shoppers often rested on the edge and added to the bank lying on the bottom of the fountain.

One day during their senior year on a break, Paige and Fina perched at the edge of the fountain, backs turned to the gushing water to avoid the spray.

"Ready?" Paige asked, running her thumb over a penny.

"Yup!" Fina answered. "One! Two! Three!"

At the soft kerplunk of the pennies, they turned around and shared their wishes with one another. After a bit, Fina spoke up.

"Paigey, I'm feeling sad. You're gonna be so far away in Virginia and I'll be in upstate New York. We'll never see each other!"

Paige patted her friend's arm. "Fin, we will see each other over Thanksgiving and Christmas. Plus, we can talk all the time!"

"I know, but I'll miss you so much. We've always done *everything* together."

"I feel the same way. But you'll be so busy with classes, boys, and acting in plays that you won't miss me that much."

"Bullshit on *that.*" She stared at her friend for a beat and picked at her nails. "I don't know if I'll be able to handle all that plus keep good grades. Dad loves to tell me how much money he's shelling out for my education."

"I know. I hear it too. Four years will fly by and one day, we'll live together—just like we always planned." Paige reached over and squeezed her friend's delicate hand.

"I know we will. I can't wait."

CHAPTER 3

JANUARY 2001

The orange and pink fingers of a frigid winter morning crept between the white blinds of the small Cape Cod and spread across the linoleum kitchen floor. They inched up the taped boxes stacked on the square pub table and tried to stretch to the threadbare rugs lying across the boxes. Stacks of pots and pans towered on the chairs.

From the depths of the brisk, serene morning, a strident, high-pitched howl slid under the crack of the bedroom window and into Paige's subconscious. Her eyelids fluttered.

The howl came again, followed by an ear-piercing shriek.

Paige's blue eyes flew open at the heart-stopping din. Throwing the quilt aside, she ran to the window to see the source of the horrifying ruckus. A blaze of orange shot across the back lawn, a squirrel thrashing in its mouth.

Nothing like a National Geographic moment to start my day, she thought and watched the fox leap into the woods, the squirrel still screaming. From the back of her desk chair, she lifted a sweater and jeans, dressed, and headed into the kitchen. She cast her blues eyes on the stack of boxes and the pots and pans. *God, I hate packing.* She started the coffee maker, and soon, the machine gurgled to life. Placing a mug to catch the dark brown brew, Paige's nose tingled with the tantalizing aroma.

Paige savored the coffee and glanced around the living room of the recently sold house. *Fina and I had some serious fun in this place.* Her full lips pressed into a small, sad smile thinking of the wine-soaked dinner parties, questionable overnight guests, raucous game nights, and quiet movie evenings. *Four years we lived here, hard to believe. Time to move on, though.*

    She shuffled through the barren living room down the hallway back to her bedroom. She glanced at her clock radio, whose red numbers glowed 7:47. The movers were scheduled to arrive within two hours. *That gives me plenty of time*, she thought and pulled open the double doors of her closet. Inside hung several pairs of pants, a handful of blouses, cowboy boots, flats, and an entire shelf of colorful handbags—Paige's weakness. She draped the clothes over her forearm and placed them in a packing box. On top of them, she lay all ten of her handbags. The footwear was tossed into a duffel bag.

    The last item in the closet was a box containing her diaries from sixth grade to her mid-twenties. On her tiptoes, she hauled down her memories, crushes, first-time things, and placed it on her bed. *This will go with me to my grave*, she thought, smiling at the box. She chose a diary from the top of the box, one from sixth grade. At thirty years old, Paige still laughed at what was inside: *Dear diary, today I ate ice cream. Dear diary, J.O. has really pretty eyes but he likes that bitchy L.S. Dear diary, I got an A on my Amelia Earhart report!*

    Diary in hand, Paige lowered herself down. She reread the entry about Amelia Earhart. The words, penned in fat, loopy twelve-year-old girl handwriting, brought her back to her sixth grade classroom. Books about her hero, Amelia Earhart, spilled from her front-loader desk. Whenever Mrs. Purcell declared it was free-reading time, Paige could not lunge for her book fast enough. Reading allowed her to become lost in the world of everything aviation, a world that included very few women.

She still remembered, as an elementary school student, the swell of reverence she held so tightly for Amelia Earhart. Tucking a loose strand of blonde hair behind her ear, she found herself taking a trip down memory lane. *God, I wanted to be a pilot so bad, especially after that asshole Al Vassil said girls were too dumb to be pilots. He's probably still an asshole.*

Recess was the perfect time to watch for planes. Above her school was one of the many flight patterns for Philadelphia International Airport. Paige could still feel the heat of the sun and the chill of the winter on her upturned face when she watched the majestic planes cutting paths through the endless blue sky. The thrilling thundering of the jets rattled her bones. Her friends laughed at her when she waved at the jets.

Her dreams of soaring seven miles above the earth in a sleek jet loaded with souls came to a crashing halt on July 4, 1988.

* * *

Paige remembered that sticky July night as if it was yesterday. Her best friend Fina was hosting a Fourth of July party. Fina's parents were abroad, giving her and Frankie, Fina's younger brother, free reign of the two-acre property.

Paige and her then-boyfriend spent the afternoon preparing for the party: picking music, buying cups and snacks, and setting up the volleyball net in the Manzetti sprawling field. Fina busied herself hooking up speakers, sticking tiki torches around the pool and mixing her "special" Fourth of July punch. Paige could still hear the *clank, clank, smash* of the grain alcohol bottles Fina hurled into the trash can.

"Here, try some!" Fina's brown eyes glowed as she shoved a cup into Paige's hand.

Paige dipped a cup into the bowl and sipped. She spit the lollipop-red liquid back into the cup. "Are you trying to kill people? This is *so* strong! Try it!" Paige spluttered.

Fina skimmed a cupful and downed half of it. "I think that's pretty tasty!" She smacked her pouty lips.

In the early evening, hordes of red, white, and blue-clad teenagers—eager to celebrate America's two-hundred-twenty-first birthday—descended upon the Manzetti property. They dragged in coolers stuffed with drinks. Music pumped from the speakers and floated down to the field. Shrieks and splashing from the pool filled the night. The smack of the volleyball and shouts of team domination filled the air. The partygoers ate and drank until the sun disappeared.

"Time for fireworks!" Fina slurred. She ran in a zigzag to the garage and returned with a wheelbarrow overflowing with pyrotechnics. "Hey Paigey! Get over here and help me light these!"

Paige and her boyfriend were lounging on pool chairs, sipping warm beer. Laughing, Paige glanced at him. "Fina's so demanding when she's drunk." She clinked her beer bottle down on the pool deck. "Be right back."

She stumbled over to Fina who had dumped the wheelbarrow upside down. "Come on everybody! Time to light up the sky!" Fina yelled to the cheering crowd. "Here Paige, hold this while I light it. Then throw it up in the air and it'll go BOOM!" Fina cackled. Weaving, she lit the match and touched it to the fuse.

Nothing.

She lit another match. Still nothing.

"What the fuck?" Fina yelled over the chorus of boos

from the drunk, impatient crowd. "Hold it up higher," she said to Paige.

Acquiescing, Paige held it higher. Fina scraped the match across the top of the matchbook. The flame danced in the darkness. Paige leaned in to make sure the tiny fuse was lit.

White hot flame exploded from the firework. Paige's screaming silenced the cheering crowd. She frantically smacked at the heat burning her face.

The damage was done. And so was her future career as a pilot.

* * *

"Paigey! Where're ya at?" Fina's voice echoed down the hall. "We gotta get goin'!"

Paige snapped out of her trip down memory lane and tossed the diary in the box. If Fina saw her with the diary, she would instantly know what Paige was reliving. For months after the accident that stole most of the vision from Paige's right eye, Fina apologized. Every day. Guilt-filled sobs racked her body when she first visited Paige in Children's Hospital. No matter how much Paige reiterated it was an accident and she was forgiven, Fina could not accept Paige's forgiveness. Until the night after senior prom atop the roof of a hotel.

In those hushed, post-prom sunrise hours, Paige stood next to Fina on the black roof of the hotel, silently marveling at the palette painting the sky. Neither one had slept. Fina put down the bottle of vodka and took her friend's soft hand. Looking out at the rising sun, Fina whispered, "I accept your forgiveness and I love you." Fina wiped the tears streaming down her face.

"I love you too," Paige whispered. "Thank you."

***

"I'm back here!" Paige yelled. "Did you and Matt have a nice romantic evening after bar hopping?"

Fina leaned on the door frame, cracked her cinnamon gum, and snorted. "Kinda. Halfway through the night, he got called and had to go in. Some idiot on a Harley wrapped himself around a telephone pole." She yawned broadly. "Thanks for the coffee. I needed it." She took an enormous slurp. "Almost done?"

Fina, always wrapped in the latest fashion, wore strategically ripped designer jeans, chunky two-inch sneakers, and a Burberry quilted coat. Her thick, shiny dark hair was tightly pulled back from her finely boned face in a bouncy ponytail. Her deep brown eyes were perfectly lined like a runway model's.

"Yes. I was packing up my closet"—she pointed to her purses—"but got sidetracked deciding whether to keep all these purses or not," she lied.

"Keep 'em for now, but the moving van will be here in like an hour. You need to get off your skinny ass and drag this stuff to the living room. I'll help you."

"Yes ma'am!" Paige saluted her friend. "Right away!"

***

The living room was flooded with clear sunlight. Paige handed sticky pieces of tape to Fina who slapped them onto any open boxes. They stood and scanned the piles of boxes.

"I think we're done. Don't you?" Paige said. "How did we gather so much stuff?"

"Who knows. On the way out of town, we'll drop the donations at St. Thomas."

Paige nodded and said she could not look at the boxes any longer.

Back in the kitchen, they leaned against the counter and reminisced about the years at The Cod, their nickname for their house.

"Remember that party where someone broke the toilet seat? And you came skipping through the middle of the party with it around your arm like a bracelet?" Fina choked on her own laughter. "I can see it like it was yesterday!"

"Oh my God, yes! And who was that crazy British guy? Tall, skinny? Was he a friend of Duff's?" Paige said.

"Oh, you mean Tin Man? He's the guy who always had that little tin full of pills. Drank gin?"

"Yup!"

"Yeah. He hit on me once. And that was it." Fina scowled. "I went all-out Serafina on him!"

"I also—" Paige was interrupted by the squeal of brakes and the halting cough of a truck.

Paige and Fina glanced out the window and saw two burly men leap down from the cab, open the back of the cavernous truck, and pull out blue moving quilts.

"Damn, he's *hot!*" Fina eyeballed one tall, strapping mover. "I wonder if he has a girlfriend?"

Paige turned to her friend. "Jeez Fina, you have *the most* devoted boyfriend in the entire world! And he's an ER doc, no less!"

Fina curled her full lips into a smirk. "Yeah, I know. I'm gettin' a little bored with him though. And that pager going off in the middle of the night? Ugh, who needs it? Plus, we're moving to the big city and you know how *fine* New York guys are!"

"We're not exactly moving *to* New York, Fin," Paige reminded her.

"I know *that*. Hoboken is damn close enough to those

hot city boys, though." She snapped her gum even louder and gave Paige a wicked grin.

Paige rolled her eyes and went to answer the door.

* * *

After a week of unpacking, setting up checking accounts, and sorting out other housekeeping duties, Paige and Fina stood in their tastefully furnished living room. They clinked wine glasses and admired the Twin Towers from across the Hudson River. The early evening sun bounced from the river and splashed onto the buildings, drenching them in glorious light. In the corner of the room, the ancient radiator banged against itself and pushed heat into the air. Paige and Fina sat down on the deep red three-seater couch. On the table in front sat a calculator, a pad of paper, and a pencil.

"Oh no, not this!" Fina groaned. "I haven't had enough to drink to face doing a budget!"

"Too bad," Paige said and started the number crunching. "We both can save some money each month if we don't buy coffee every day, limit dining out to once a week, and bring our own lunches to work at least four days a week."

"Are you saying I can't go to Starbucks every day? I'll die!" Fina moaned. "I'll be the only person at the magazine who *isn't* sipping on a Starbucks!"

"Maybe you'll start a new trend in your department—drinking *office* coffee!"

"Very funny. I'll miss it."

"You *can* still drink it, but it won't help you to save any money. Do the math. At two bucks a day, five days a week, four weeks a month," Paige explained. "All that money for something you can get at the office."

An exasperated sigh escaped Fina. "*Office* coffee? I'd

rather drink rotten milk!" she joked. "Your new firm won't know what hit them when you start work on Monday! Their accounts will be perfectly balanced."

"Thank you, you are correct." Paige sipped her wine and continued. "You do what you want. But if you want to save *any* money, then cut back."

From the rectangular, knotted pine coffee table, Paige lifted Fina's wine glass. She filled it with the last drops of the pale Chablis.

"And you knew when we took these new jobs we'd have to be on a budget. It's a whole lot more expensive to live up here than in Philly. I know we both got a pay raise, but still. Can't hurt to save." She took a sip. "Not too terrible."

Fina cocked a fine penciled eyebrow at Paige. "For boxed wine, it'll do. But when I *own* my own magazine, we'll drink nothing but the best stuff!"

CHAPTER 4

Maksim Petrov Dovic's squeezed his intense ice-blue eyes shut as he listened to the message. *Son of a bitch! How could this happen?* Snatching up the office phone, he barked to his assistant, "Franklin, get Marty and Stu in here now!"

"Yes sir! Right away!"

Max slammed the phone down. The pain in his neck woke up with a vengeance. He placed his large hands under his chin and twisted his jaw to the right and left. *Pop! Pop!* went subluxations in his neck, releasing only an iota of the tension. *Not enough.*

He hoisted himself from his desk chair and walked over to the mini refrigerator. From it, he retrieved the bottle of tequila. Gripping the chilled bottle generated a sense of calm. Max unscrewed the lid, put the bottle to his lips, and took a swig.

The golden liquid did its job, filling his veins and clearing his head. He gazed out the office window from Tower Two and watched taxi cabs fifty-eight floors below race around Lower Manhattan like tiny toy cars blurring into yellow streaks. People were only identifiable by woolen hats pulled tightly over their heads, bobbing quickly to avoid being in the cold.

Max did not turn around at the quiet knock on his door. "Enter," he commanded.

"You wanted to see us?" Marty asked.

"Sit down." Max heard them sit. Not turning around, he addressed them. "I received a distressing phone message just now. Apparently, number fifty-four did not receive all of his shipment. As a result, he is only going to pay half. Which means *you*"—he turned to face them—"screwed this up."

Stu and Marty exchanged a bug-eyed expression. Stu cleared his throat before addressing Max. "We delivered what was on the list; one package was there."

"Fifty-four was to receive *two* packages, not one. Do you understand?"

"But—" Marty tried.

"Is this clear?"

Marty and Stu nodded.

"You two need to fix this. I am due—as you two are—a *significant* payment for this exchange. Fifty-four expects the rest of the delivery. The business is flourishing. We cannot afford any missteps. If one occurs, we're finished. I worked extremely hard to broker this deal. Get it done the *right* way."

Marty and Stu shot from their seats. "We will call you when it's done," Marty said.

Max heard his door shut, his eyes not leaving the bleakness of the winter day.

Winter always brought visceral memories of the orphanage, ones he wished he could rip from his mind. Max exhaled and tried to push away the palpable memory of the cold that seeped through the orphanage walls, which bit through his flimsy winter coat and lodged in his bony chest. Memories of Polina, the pinched-faced, gray-haired nurse who administered medicine, surfaced from the recesses of his mind. He remembered the pain of her filthy fingernails raking across his scalp.

"This will stop your *horrid* coughing that keeps the babies awake and crying!" Polina shrilled as she yanked back his head and jammed purple cough medicine down his raw throat.

Max shook his head of thick dark hair. *Stop! You must stop! You are better than this!* He glanced down at Lower Manhattan. Filthy snow lay in piles. Gaunt trees reminded him of malnourished prisoners of war. Everything was blanketed in icy depression. *You are a successful man now. You are not that helpless child in the orphanage.*

Turning away from the window, he strode across his office and dropped into the leather desk chair. He logged onto his computer, pulled up the spreadsheets, and studied the numbers staring back at him.

A thin-lipped smile crept across his angular face. *Despite the mistake, these are nice. Very nice indeed.*

* * *

Gut-tearing hunger pangs reminded Max he had not eaten for several hours. The tiny cup of plain yogurt he ate six hours ago had long burned off. Feeling dizzy, Max swigged some water before hustling to the elevator to head down to Liberty Avenue where numerous food trucks offered fare from all corners of the globe. He made a beeline to the truck serving the best Mexican cuisine. *Screw the diet, I'm eating a burrito!*

Max could not wait until the elevator climbed the fifty-plus floors to his office. As soon as the doors slid shut, the tantalizing aroma wore away any shred of self-control. *What the hell. I'm so low on fuel.* He unwrapped the shiny foil and chomped on the burrito. Eyes closed in pure food ecstasy, he sighed and savored every flavor. So caught up in the burrito, he was not aware the elevator stopped a few floors before his. As he took another massive bite, the doors opened.

Flicking his eyes above the burrito at the *ding* of the

opening doors, he saw a stunning woman hustling toward the elevator.

The doors began to close when she called, "Please hold the door!"

Max hit the hold-door button with one hand. She flashed him a bright smile.

On her way in, she tripped into the elevator and pitched hard into Max. The half-eaten burrito flipped onto his chest, splattered his coat, and tumbled to the floor. The doors slid closed and the elevator started its climb.

"Jesus Christ!" Max barked at a gaping Paige. "Look what you did!"

Paige clapped a hand over her mouth and uttered, "Oh no! I am so sorry!" She glanced at Max and then at the floor where the burrito lay on the floor in a sad, half-eaten heap. "I'm so sorry!" She pulled a tissue from her bag. "Here, let me clean your coat off!" She tried to scrape cheese and sauce from him.

Anger flooded his entire body. Glancing at his soiled cashmere coat, he snapped, "Like a flimsy tissue will help? Just stop! You're making it worse!" He pushed Paige's hand away and picked off pieces of shredded lettuce.

Paige flinched at his touch and stepped back. Heat flooded her face. *Oh my God. It's my first week and this happens.* "Again, I'm really sorry. It was an accident. I'm not used to wearing heels." The words tumbled out of her mouth.

Max cut his eyes to the floor. His heart skipped a beat at what he saw—on her feet were three-inch red and black high heels. Slowly, he moved his eyes up Paige's muscular calves exposed by a black pencil skirt. He admired how her black and white silk blouse set off her dark blonde hair. His gaze came to rest on her deep blue eyes. Something inside melted away the anger. He could not tear away his gaze. Her eyes reminded him of the frigid, darkly beautiful, white-capped Baltic Sea. Months of back-breaking work hunting for cod instantly rushed back to him.

"Again, I'm really sorry. I'm a klutz sometimes."

Yes, you are. But a beautiful klutz, he thought. Softening his tone, he said, "It's okay. Stop apologizing. Accidents happen. I'm sorry I yelled."

Paige tucked the pack of tissues back in her bag. "Yeah, I know that better than anyone. Trust me," she laughed. "Can I please pay for your coat to be dry cleaned? I insist."

Those eyes, Max thought. *Wow.* "If you insist. But I—"

Ding! The elevator stopped on his floor and the doors opened.

"This is my floor. Step out with me and we can discuss your offer." He pointed down at his coat.

They exited the elevator and Paige pointed at the coat. "We don't need to discuss. Please hand me your jacket and I'll take care of the rest?"

"I can see I don't have a choice!" Max laughed. He acquiesced and shrugged off his coat. "You really don't have to do this."

Along with his piercing light blue eyes and full head of dark hair flecked with hints of gray wisps at his ears, Paige admired how his light blue button-down shirt lay on his lean, broad torso as if custom made. The blue highlighted his smooth, healthy complexion and high cheekbones. *This guy is gorgeous.*

"I know. But I was raised to stick to my word. So hand it over." She flashed him a smile when he folded the coat over her outstretched arm. "Thank you."

"You're welcome."

Oh no, I don't know any dry cleaners. "Another thing. I'm

new to the city. Maybe you can suggest a certain dry cleaner you prefer who's near here?"

Max's eyebrows rose in interest. "New? You certainly know how to make yourself known!"

"I guess I do." She laughed.

He flaunted his expensive smile. "Two blocks down on the right—Stanley's Kwik Klean. Great guy. Older, bald, bushy eyebrows. Tell him I sent you."

"Thanks. I will. Do you have a card?" Paige asked.

"Yes. Always." He reached into his pocket and produced a business card.

Paige read it aloud. "*Maksim P. Dovic. WHS Shipping Brokerage.* Thanks."

"Max, actually. And you are?" he asked.

"Paige Buckley. Nice to meet you, Max."

"You as well, Paige."

They stood outside the elevator door, politely smiling at each other until Max spoke. "I have a conference call in a few minutes. I'm sorry to have to run."

"I understand. Go ahead." She gestured to the elevator. "I realized I got—or tripped—on the wrong one."

Max chuckled. "Is that right? Maybe it was fate. Tripping into someone eating a burrito is one way to meet people!" He laughed. "And cut yourself some slack. It's difficult being new."

"Fair enough. But I want to make sure I get on the *right* elevator this time. I need to go down several floors...well, like twenty floors!"

Max pointed her in the right direction. "To where?"

"The CDS Firm."

"Ah, yes. Several floors below." He punched the elevator button. When the doors slid open, he asked, "I'll talk to you soon?"

Paige smiled at him. "Yes. I will call you when I have your coat."

Returning the smile, he replied, "I look forward to that."

The elevator opened and Paige stepped in. "I do too." The doors closed.

* * *

Paige hustled down the sidewalk, carrying Max's coat over her forearm. His handsome face lingered in her mind. *He sure was pissed, but he knew it was a mistake.* Careful not to miss the store, she glanced up at all the storefront signs when she stepped onto the second block. Glancing up, she saw the sign for Stanley's Kwik Klean exactly where Max said it was located.

A buzzer sounded when she stepped inside. The store smelled of spray starch and funnel cake. A worn, faded reddish rug covered the small floor. Hissing sounds and steam filled the back of the store. Fifties music played from a portable radio perched on a shelf. A white Formica counter ran from wall to wall; on it sat a cash register and a hand bell. Next to the bell was a cardboard sign that read, *Please ding-a-ling if I'm not here.* A smiley face drawn in blue marker grinned underneath the request.

Paige dropped the coat on the counter, picked up the bell, and rang it. Nothing. She rang it again and peered over the counter. She saw no one. She rang it for a third time, becoming impatient.

"Here I am! Here I am!"

Paige turned all the way to the right and saw a man step from behind the carousel of clothing hanging in shiny plastic wrap. His gait reminded Paige of the Leaning Tower of Pisa.

"Hello! Dropping off?"

Paige saw his name tag read *Stanley*. "Hello and yes I am." She showed him the coat.

Stanley scrutinized the coat and tagged the stains with small pieces of red tape. "This certainly is a fine coat." He ran his hands over the item. "Best cashmere money can buy."

"Really?"

"Oh yes. This coat probably cost close to a thousand bucks."

Paige gaped at the smiling little man. "Did you say a *thousand* bucks?"

"Yes."

Oh my. "So it'll cost a lot to clean it, right?"

Stanley's eyebrows drew together as he studied her. "I haven't seen you before, right? If you're a new customer, you get a ten percent discount."

"Truth be told, I'm actually getting this cleaned for someone who recommended you."

As Stanley punched the numbers into the cash register, he said, "Oh yeah? Who?"

"Max Dovic."

Stanley nodded. "Ah, yeah, Dovic. I shoulda figured it was his coat. I've only seen him maybe a handful of times in the years he's been coming here."

"He's been a customer for a few years, but you've only seen him a few times?"

"That's right. He usually sends in his, I don't know what you call him... Driver? Valet? Assistant? Guy's name is Andreas."

Paige rolled this around in her mind. "This guy Dovic has a *personal assistant*?"

"If that's what you kids call it, then yeah, sure."

Paige tucked that information away. "I wonder what that's like!"

"Who knows, but I know Dovic will want this back ASAP." He printed out the pick-up slip. "Since you're new and friend of his, I'll give you fifteen percent off."

"That's very generous of you, but not necessary!"

"I know, but I like to think of myself as a generous guy!" He printed a receipt and handed it to her. "See you in two days."

"Thanks so much. Bye, Stanley."

CHAPTER 5

Paige hustled back to her cubicle. She thought again of the debacle in the elevator and what Stanley told her about Max. *A personal assistant? A thousand-dollar coat? Gobs of cash can buy anything, I guess.*

A bottle of water sat on her desk. She took a swig and it was as if the icy cold water ran through her veins, calming her down. Sitting back in her chair, she chuckled as she imagined Fina's reaction when she told her what happened: "Oh my gawd! You fell on a guy *eatin'* a *burrito*? That's a riot!" Fina's rich laughter would control them until their sides hurt.

Inside her three-walled cubicle, she studied Max's business card. "*Maksim Petrov Dovic, WHS Shipping Brokerage,*" she read aloud and ran her finger over the shiny embossed black letters etched into the cream-colored card. *Nice card*, she thought. *All right, enough about this. Time to focus on work things.* She tossed the card into her drawer.

In front her of sat a stack of papers she needed to sign as part of her new job as an auditor. When she first told Fina she wanted to be an auditor, Fina looked at her like she had eight heads and asked, "Why *that*?"

"Because I'm really talented at finding discrepancies with numbers. Numbers are clean, and they're either right or wrong—nothing abstract. Remember how much money I saved Bud and Marian, the owners of the Twisted Pretzel? They were getting so ripped off by those guys who sold them the dough."

"Hey Paige, everything going okay?" a friendly voice came from behind.

Paige turned in her seat to see her supervisor Todd leaning on the partition, an orange mug in his hand.

"Hi Todd, yes, everything is going well. Thanks for asking. I'll get these papers back to HR before the end of the day."

"Sure thing."

Paige finished her work before six and was eager to get home and tell Fina about her day. She called her and left a message. "I have a great story to tell you! See you at home." After straightening up her cubicle, she slung her bag over her shoulder and pushed her chair under the desk. She hoped to catch the 6:23 subway which would get her home by seven.

Walking to the elevator, she felt her face flush again at what transpired earlier in the day. She punched the silver button and when the doors slid open, Paige scanned the five weary faces, wondering if Max was among them. He was not.

Paige was surprised at the unexpected flash of disappointment she felt.

* * *

Commuters jammed the subway car, and Paige was forced to stand. She tried not to feel self-conscious that her body, specifically her midsection, was in such close proximity to those commuters lucky enough to be seated. *I'll get used to this.* She focused her gaze on a ripped railway poster hanging by a shred at the front of the car.

A deep cramp formed in her shoulder and crept up her neck. *I have to pack less stuff,* she thought and shifted the bag to her left shoulder.

Soon, the stuffed car rolled to a stop and a blast of cold air shot through the open door. A volume of commuters hustled out, leaving several hard plastic seats vacant. Paige did not hesitate and plunked down next to a woman who held a folded newspaper. Tucking her hair behind her ears, Paige sat back in the seat and let her mind go blank. She closed her eyes and felt herself melt into the rocking rhythm of the subway.

"That's fuckin' lame!"

Paige's eyes shot open. It was the woman next to her.

Curious, Paige looked over, but could not clearly see what caused the exclamation. Since the woman was on her right, Paige had to fully turn in her seat to see. A middle-aged, cropped-haired woman was muttering while working on a crossword puzzle. She tapped a pen against her cheek.

"Dumb answer?" Paige ventured.

The woman glanced at Paige and snorted. "Yeah. This guy"—she slapped the paper by the puzzle maker's name—"puts in some ah the dumbest answers."

Paige laughed. "I get it. Dumb answers *are* annoying, especially when the double entendres are *really* stupid."

Friendly, lively green eyes peered at Paige from behind round tortoiseshell glasses. "You do puzzles? At your age?"

She nodded. "I love them. My grandad and I used to have races to see who would finish first."

"Huh," the woman grunted. "I think you're the first person undah fifty I've evah met who liked crosswords!"

"Been doing them for most of my life. I read a lot which helps to answer the clues."

She laughed. "Yeah, me too. Books beat most ah the crap on television."

"My parents say the same thing!"

"They're right!" A crease appeared between her perfectly arched eyebrows. "So, what's a five-letter word for silly?"

Paige scowled and ran through words in her mind. "Five-letter word for silly? Absurd?"

"Nope, that's six letters," the woman replied, chewing on her pen.

"Inane?" Paige suggested and noticed small laugh lines around the woman's eyes and mouth. She guessed her to be in her late fifties or early sixties.

The woman counted the letters on her slim fingers. Paige admired several silver bands stacked on her middle finger. "Yep, that's it!" Into the small squares she printed the answer in perfect capitals. "You're good at this! I may need some moah help!" A throaty guffaw filled the subway car.

"Sorry, but the next stop is mine."

The woman cast the puzzle aside and gave her full attention to Paige. "Yeah? Mine too! Where do you live?"

"Hudson Towers."

"Yeah? No shit! I live two blocks away!"

"Really?" Paige smiled. "My best friend Fina and I just moved in. We love it."

She tucked the pen behind her ear and thrust her hand at Paige. "Welcome! My name's Martha."

Paige grasped her hand, which felt soft and warm. "Hi, I'm Paige. Nice to meet you and to know someone on the subway and a neighbor as well."

"You too. You work in the Twin Towahs?" Martha asked, her attention back on the puzzle.

"Yes, for an accounting firm. Do you?"

"Yep. I'm head of security. Prior to that, I was a cop for many years in Boston. I got tired ah the BS goin' on in law enforcement and the lack ah respect for cops. Plus, we were forced to take all these ridiculous classes. At my age, who the hell wants homework? Not me!" Martha folded up the crossword puzzle and placed it into a backpack placed between her feet. "Next stop is ours, kid."

"You work in the same building as I do." *What a relief*, she thought and smiled at Martha.

"Correct. Looks like we'll be seein' each othah. I usually work every day, eight to six."

The subway rumbled to a halt and the doors slid open. Paige and Martha exited and walked up the steps together into the darkening evening. The cool bite of air was refreshing after the long ride in a stuffy subway car.

"Wintah's brutal!" Martha commented, zipping up her coat higher.

Paige dug her hands into her coat pocket. "Yeah, I like winter. I wonder if we'll get any snow?"

"I hope so. Nothin' beats wintahs in Bahston, though. Shit, we'd get tons of snow. Play all day till we froze."

"You grew up in Boston?" Paige asked.

Martha nodded. "Yeah, my whole life. Where'd you grow up?"

"Philly...well, outside of the city."

Martha sliced her eyes at Paige. "You one of those crazy Eagles fans?"

"You know it! They're struggling now, but always a fan. I assume you're a diehard Pats fan?" Paige laughed.

"Oh yeah. Nobody plays like Bledsoe. And I love lookin' at Brown's tight ass in those pants," Martha cackled.

The wind picked up. Leaves cartwheeled over the sidewalk onto the street. Soon Paige found herself outside of her building. She turned to Martha. "It was great to meet you. I hope I see you at work."

"Oh you will. My desk is the first one to the right when you enter the building from Liberty. I also patrol my floors.

What floor are you on, kid?"

"Thirty-fifth."

"One of mine." She turned her head and coughed loudly. "Sorry 'bout that. Cold weather does that to me. Time to go home. Great meeting you. See you around, kid!" She turned and walked up the sidewalk.

"Nice meeting you. See you soon!" Paige turned and the gush of heat from her building wrapped around her.

* * *

When Paige opened the door to the apartment, the spicy aroma of arrabiata sauce hit her square in the face. *Yum! Fina's famous arrabiata!* She tossed her coat onto a chair and yelled hello as she walked into the kitchen. Fina was busy at the stove, stirring a pot and singing along with a Queen song belting from the radio.

"Yo roomie!" Fina called and shook her hips to the beat as she stirred the homemade sauce. "Hope you're hungry! Tonight we're carb loading!"

"Sounds like a plan. I'm starving." Paige taste-tested the sauce. It was heavenly mix of rich tomato, spicy red chilies, a dash of salt, and a touch of basil. "Be right back." Paige changed out of her work clothes into her usual sweatpants and returned to the kitchen to help Fina.

The normal small talk ensued over dinner, as did the bottle of red wine.

"I love red wine." Fina finished her glass.

"So do I. It's almost as good as sex," Paige replied, at which Fina snorted.

"Let's not go *that* far. Nothing beats sex, well *good* sex."

Paige raised her glass and clinked in agreement with Fina.

"So what's this great story you want to share?" Fina asked.

Paige giggled. "Wait until you hear this. But first you need a refill."

By the time Paige finished telling Fina about the debacle in the elevator, streams of black mascara streaked down her face.

"You fell on a guy eatin' a fuckin' *burrito*! In an elevator! Oh my God! Classic!"

"Well, you of all people know how klutzy I can be!"

Fina dabbed at her eyes with the cuff of her sweatshirt. "Oh I do!" She fell back on the couch. "And I can just see you using *a tissue* to try to clean it off!" Tears rolled down her face.

Paige added how she took his coat to the dry cleaner. "I felt like I had to do something! I was mortified. I felt so badly too."

"I'm sure! Was he pissed?"

"At first, I'd say yes. He kind of slapped the tissue away."

Fina's eyebrows shot up. "He *slapped* it away? That seems aggressive."

"Agreed. Maybe he was having a crappy day already. I was so embarrassed I could barely think. In retrospect, it *was* pretty stupid to think I could clean it with a tissue!"

"I can't argue with that. Did he act more normal afterward?"

"Oh yes. He apologized for getting angry."

"As he should have. More importantly, is he good looking?" Fina winked at Paige.

Paige recalled Max's arresting eyes and inviting smile. "I wouldn't say cute, but he's really handsome."

"We can work with handsome."

"I can tell he works out. He's lean, but not skinny. Thankfully, he doesn't have a pot belly. And I'd guess he's a little older."

"How so?"

"He has a few flecks of gray hair—very sexy."

"Of course you think that. You've always liked older guys."

"True. They tend to have their act together. And I think this guy is obscenely rich."

Fina poured more wine. "Really? How do you know?"

"Stanley, the older guy who owns the dry cleaner, said that coat cost close to a thousand dollars."

Fina spat out her wine and stared at Paige. "What the hell? Are you *serious*? Who is this guy?"

"His name is Maksim—Max—Dovic. He does something in shipping."

"Whatever he does, it sure pays well. Who spends that kind of money on a *coat*?"

"Someone who has a boatload of money, that's who!"

"Girl, you better pursue him because if you don't, I will!" Fina said.

Paige laughed and continued telling Fina about her day, including when she met Martha. "She lives two blocks from us."

"That's cool and it's great you met someone who lives near us. Do you know what she does?"

"She works in Tower Two. She's head of security and used to be a cop."

"Wow, I'd love to meet her. What a powerful woman. She'd make a good story for the magazine." Fina rose from the couch, stretched, and announced she was going to bed. "Speaking of work, I have to be in early for a meeting."

"Something important?"

"Yes, actually. A story is in the works about women

breaking the glass ceiling and my department will be organizing the layout of the articles and pictures of the women we're featuring."

"Exciting! When will the story run?"

"I think in the next few weeks, probably in the early spring issue." With an enormous yawn, she bid Paige goodnight and entered her bedroom.

"Night, Fin."

CHAPTER 6

While she waited on the platform for the subway, Paige glanced around for Martha. She did not see her anywhere. *Oh well. Maybe she went in already. Hopefully I'll see her later.*

Once settled in her seat, Paige flipped open her planner and ran through her day: meeting from ten o'clock to noon, lunch with Todd, call JLS and Company, pick up coat. The last item brought Max's face to mind. A hint of a smile crept onto her slightly flushed face. She shook her head and glanced out the window. *You're like a teenage girl! Someone as good-looking as him probably has a girlfriend—or several.* She sighed, looked down at her planner, and mapped out the rest of the week.

Todd droned on and on about the new software and when the training would commence. After he finally wrapped up the meeting a few minutes later, he called Paige aside and told her he had to cancel their lunch.

Relieved, Paige ambled back to the area where she and her colleagues worked. Glancing at her phone, she saw the message light blinking. Listening to the message, Paige smiled when she heard Stanley's voice informing her Max's coat was ready early. "Come get it when you like."

No time like the present.

Outside Tower Two a cool breeze blew, an invigorating welcome from the stuffy office. Paige walked down the sidewalk, filling her lungs with the mid-winter air. *This feels so good. I wonder if Todd would mind if I took a mid-morning walk a few times a week? It's worth asking him sometime.* She soon she found herself in front of Stanley's Kwik Klean. As she entered, Paige heard him.

"Good afternoon, young lady. How's your day so far?" A welcoming smile spread across his thin face.

Paige smiled. *What a cute little old man.* "Good afternoon to you. My day is busy, just how I like it. You?"

Stanley beamed at her. "I got up this morning, so it's a great day!" He chuckled. "You're here for Dovic's coat, right?"

Paige nodded.

He turned and hit the button for the carousel. After the plastic-covered clothing looped around once, Stanley hit the stop button. "Bailey, Belcher, Blair, Bloomberg," he mumbled as he checked the tags. "What's the name again?"

"Buckley."

"Ah, further down the alphabet." Tearing the tag from the coat, he brought the garment forward. "I don't know what the hell was on here, but it took two tries to get it all out."

Paige rolled her lips inward. "Well, if you want *really* want to know, I'll tell you."

Stanley's light blue eyes twinkled. "I'm all ears!"

Paige took a deep breath. "Here goes." She relayed the story of the fiasco in the elevator.

His jaw fell open. "You ain't shittin' me, are ya?" He broke out in peals of laughter. "A burrito?"

"Guilty as charged!"

"I'm sure Dovic was not too happy about that! He likes things just so."

Paige tossed him a look. "Really? I don't know him well at all. In fact, this"—she pointed at the coat—"is how we met."

"Is that so? I doubt he'll forget you now!" He guffawed.

"Pretty damn picky, though, about how he likes things done. Given his position, it doesn't surprise me."

Paige frowned at the man. *Position?* "What do you mean?"

"He's in shipping. Don't know exactly his position, but considering this coat? He's done well."

Paige thought of Max's heavy, well-crafted business card, the expensive clothes. "Impressive."

Stanley agreed. "Yeah, he's an interesting guy all right. *Always* pays in cash, the kind of customer I like!"

Paige pulled out her wallet. "What do I owe you?"

He told her.

"Are you sure? That doesn't seem like much," she said, handing him her card.

Stanley smiled at her and nodded. "You're just starting out in an unfamiliar city. I like to help. I hope you to see you again—and remember, the newbie discount will stand." He winked at her.

"Sold on that! Thanks, Stanley. Have a good day."

"I will."

* * *

Outside, Paige slung the coat over her forearm and walked back to her office. She glanced up at the shiny Twin Towers, which seemed to soar without end into the azure sky. A shiver of reverence ran through her. She sighed. *Architecture in Philadelphia is beautiful, but nothing there is as powerful and commanding as these beauties*, she thought and entered.

At her desk, she called Max's office but was told he was not in. "Is it okay if I drop something off for him?" She was told yes and made her way up to his floor.

At the front of Max's office, a bearded young man looked

up from the computer. "Can I help you?"

"Hi. I called a little while ago about dropping something off for Max Dovic."

He stood and looked down at Paige. Assessing Paige with probing eyes, he replied, "Yes. I spoke to you. You must be Paige."

Paige was caught off guard. *Max has mentioned me. Weird—but also interesting.* "Ah yes, I am. And you are?"

"I'm Stu. I work for Max." He extended his hand.

Paige grasped it and shook it firmly. "Nice to meet you."

"You as well. I see you have—"

He was interrupted by a male coming from behind.

"Stu, are we going to..." It was another man, roughly Paige's age. "Sorry, didn't know you were with someone." The man's eyes crawled up and down Paige. A curl of a smile turned up one corner of his barely existent top lip as he asked, "Who do we have here?" His gaze roved over her once again, and she cringed inwardly.

Really? Have you never seen a woman before? Paige folded her arms across her chest, cocked her head, and threw knives with her gaze. "Well, what you *have here* is a woman returning a coat for Max Dovic." Paige held out the coat and dropped it on the desk.

The man's eyebrows shot up. "Ooh!" He waggled a finger at her. "You're the burrito woman, right?"

Stu spoke up, "Marty, come on man. Have some couth. Her name is Paige." He looked at Paige and rolled his eyes. "He's like an eighth grader sometimes."

Paige did not disagree.

"Sorry. I'm Marty. Me and Stu work together for Max."

Paige glanced at both men. Inwardly she winced at Stu's butchering of proper grammar. "Good to know. Please let him know that the *burrito woman* returned his coat."

CHAPTER 7

Panting, heart racing, Max doubled over the leg press machine. Sweat dripped from his forehead onto the black faux leather seat. He sucked in a deep lungful of air. *I can't do anymore.* It was leg day in the rotation of his exercise regime. After punishing his quads, hamstrings, and calves, he headed into the locker room to immerse himself into a much-needed ice bath. Nothing gave him clarity like a soak in frigid water.

Stripping off his dripping shorts and T-shirt, Max unfolded a towel and wrapped it around his waist then went to wash his hands. Admiring his taut half-naked body, he grinned at the six pack of muscles rippling his tight torso. *Pretty damn good for forty-one. Many men would kill to look like this. But I suppose to some it's easier to be overweight, slovenly, and not give a damn.*

Deep inside the locker room sat three ice-bath tubs. Stepping into the middle one, as he always did, he allowed a quick gasp at the shock. *Get in. You need this.*

Blocking out the needles of cold, he picked up a pitcher of ice cubes and poured them in. *Plop, plop, plop* they splashed into the metal tub and found a place among the other floating cubes. Settling in, he reached for his kale-heavy protein drink and took a long sip. Another long day lay ahead of him, but he knew his energy level would be high due to his workout and the ice bath.

He closed his eyes and found his thoughts wandering to

Paige and his coat. *My coat should be ready today. Maybe I'll see her when she drops it off. What are the odds a woman as stunning as her would cross my path? I need to ask her out without seeming like it's a date. The advantage I have is she's new to New York and doesn't know the city like I do. Score one for you, Max.*

The icy water transported him to another world. Each time he soaked, he pushed himself to soak longer than the previous baths. Practicing control of his mind and body was an art he planned to perfect.

Glancing at his fingertips, he saw they were on the verge of turning blue. *Thirty seconds and I'm finished.* He held his breath and slid underwater until time was up.

* * *

Back at his office, the redheaded woman behind the desk greeted him. "Hello Mr. Dovic. When I was out for my break, Stu said some woman came by with your coat. Shall I retrieve it for you?" She leaned forward, allowing him to see and admire her ample breasts wrapped in a tight dress.

Damn, I missed her. "Ah, yes please Tina. And her name is Paige." He took his coat from her. "What time was she here?"

Tina pressed her lips together. "Late morning. Around ten or ten thirty, I was told."

He grimaced when he checked his watch. *Damn, I missed her only by a few minutes.* "Thank you." He walked back to his office where he put the coat in his closet and fell into his desk chair. *It's the polite thing to call and thank her. Maybe she'd like to have lunch one day.* He glanced at his computer to see his inbox was crammed with emails. *I'll take care of this first and then call her.*

By early afternoon, Max finally had free time to call

Paige. He had Franklin, his immediate office assistant, track down a phone number for her office. He was pleased when he heard Paige's voice.

"Hello Paige, it's Max. How are you?"

"Oh, hi Max. I'm doing well—busy, though. How are you?"

"I'm doing well also. I'm calling to thank you for dropping off my coat. I'm sorry I was not here."

"Don't even think about it. We're all busy people."

"Very true." *I like how relaxed she sounds.* "I recall you saying you were new to New York. Which would mean that you are unfamiliar with where to eat."

Paige laughed. "You are correct."

"I can help with that. If you're free for lunch tomorrow, we can meet at one of my favorite more casual spots."

"I *think* I'm free. But I need to check the time of a meeting."

Max scowled. "I see."

"I'll ask my boss and call you back later today, okay?"

I guess I'll have to settle for that. "Of course."

"Talk to you later on today. Have a good rest of your day."

"Likewise. Bye, Paige."

"Bye Max."

I guess I have to be patient. She obviously has her priorities set straight; I understand that. He pressed a button on the phone—his direct line to his office assistant. "Franklin, can you please tell Stu and Marty that I need to see them?"

"Yes sir."

Within a few minutes, Stu and Marty were seated in Max's office.

"I wanted to double-check with you two about the plan for this evening."

Stu spoke first. "Yes sir."

"We will meet in the lot at eight thirty. You two will have secured the package, and from there, I will take it to the boat."

Marty glanced at Stu. "Yes, Max. That's what we had planned."

"Excellent. You will—"

Franklin's voice floated through the speaker phone. "Sir, there's a Paige Buckley on line one for you. Shall I tell her you're in a meeting?"

Max's head snapped to the phone. "No!" *Calm down.* "Sorry, Franklin. I did not mean to yell. I'll take the call."

Taking their cue, Stu and Marty rose from the chairs.

"Don't be late," Max warned. "These things can't wait."

"We know, and we'll be on time," Marty responded.

Max waited until they left and picked up the phone. "Nice to hear from you, Paige."

* * *

Later, after work, they sat in their living room, watching television. During an ad, Paige hinted that she had a lunch date.

Fina grabbed the remote and silenced the television. Her wide, dark eyes shimmered. "Do you?" She placed her beer on the table and rubbed her hands together. "Well?"

Paige told her Max called and asked her to lunch for the next day.

"I'm so impressed! Where are you going?"

Paige swallowed a sip of beer. "To one of his favorite low-key places, some diner. So in other words, I have no idea!" She laughed.

Fina set her eyes on Paige. "Did he sound anxious or nervous?"

"Not at all. He sort of has this soft but deep tone to his voice; it's almost too smooth."

"Sounds kind of sexy."

Paige cocked her head. "I would agree with that. And his voice *definitely* sounds as if it was meant to match his looks."

"How observant! I'm glad you're excited for this date." Fina clinked her bottle against Paige's.

"Date? Not sure I'd go that far. He knows I'm new and he's being friendly. That's all." Paige turned and glared at her friend.

"We'll see."

* * *

After a busy morning of running audit reports, Paige hopped into the elevator a little before noon and headed out into the cold, windy, sun-drenched day. Always a planner, she wanted to get to the diner early to secure seats.

She hailed a cab outside and gave the driver her destination. She watched the world whizz by through the cab window until her thoughts turned back thirteen years to that life-altering day of her diagnosis.

The pity in Dr. Brandt's eyes that day was seared into Paige's memory, as were the words the doctor whispered: "I'm sorry, Paige. But your condition is permanent." The nausea and fear she felt that day were buried deep, yet still very much alive. She remembered her tears. The air pulled from the small examination room. The hollow of disbelief and the clutch of fear.

"I'm so sorry," Dr. Brandt sighed.

"But I can sorta see out of this eye! Doesn't that mean I'll get more vision back?" Paige cried.

"No, Paige. I'm afraid not. I know your injured eye is not

fully void of vision. However, too much damage was done. It can't repair itself and neither can we."

"So, I'm always gonna have like this, this blurry fog in my vision?"

"Yes." She rubbed Paige's shoulder. But nothing stopped the flow of tears running down Paige's crumpled face.

Paige stuffed that awful memory in a box and focused on her lunch date and "safe" topics to discuss, especially with a stranger: New York City, restaurants, museums, sports, movies. When the cab stopped in front of the diner a few minutes before twelve thirty, her heart rate shifted into high gear.

Inside the brightly lit, jam-packed diner, silverware clinked against plates, the hum of laughter, and conversation mixed with the aroma of grilled bread and bacon. Shouts of "Order up!" accompanied the clank of plates loaded with towering sandwiches being thrust through the serving window.

Paige waited at the host stand and turned so she could see the entire diner. A row of four-seater booths pressed against a large window. Each one was occupied. About twelve tables sat in the center of the diner; all of those were occupied as well.

"You waitin' for a table?" a gruff voice barked from behind.

Paige turned back to the stand. There stood a boney black-haired person with skin so pale all their veins and blood vessels resembled a road map. They tapped a menu in their milky-white hand. A thick silver hoop hung out of their elongated nostrils and reminded Paige of a door knocker. "Ah yes, I think."

"Whadda ya mean, you *think*?" the person groused.

"I *think* she means that we'd like a table for two. It's fairly obvious."

Paige felt as if a thousand butterflies fluttered in her empty stomach. She looked over her shoulder and Max beamed at her. *Oh wow, he's more handsome than I remember.* Clearing her throat, she said, "Yes, like I said earlier. A table for two please."

The person snatched two menus from the stand and ordered Paige and Max to follow. "*Enjoy* your lunch." The sarcasm seeped from the first word.

"I don't think that person majored in customer service, do you?" Max joked.

Paige laughed. "Absolutely not," she said and opened her menu. "Maybe they're having a bad day."

"Or they hate their job."

"That's entirely possible. I'd bet money on that," Paige responded.

"Me too. I assume you've not eaten here before?" Max took her in, admiring her slender, strong hands and soft pink nails.

"No. Someone in the office said the food is excellent." Paige glanced up and smiled at Max. Never had she seen such a perfectly symmetrical face. A small, yet noticeable white patch in the middle his right eyebrow stood strikingly white against the brown of his brow. The crinkle of smile lines around his eyes added to his allure. His full mouth softened a sharp jaw and square chin. *He's definitely a hottie*, she thought and looked down at the menu before her face flushed. "I'm starving."

After perusing the decadent and delicious lunches, she settled on blackened tuna sandwich with pepper jack cheese and avocado. Max ordered a large chef salad with extra Russian dressing.

"You sure you don't want a burrito?" joked Paige.

Max smiled. "I only eat them when I'm in an elevator!"

"When we were little, we used to love to make Russian and French dressing," Paige commented. "I'm pretty sure it wasn't my parents' favorite, but they ate it anyway."

Max smiled at her. "Do you come from a large family?"

"Kind of. I have three siblings: one sister and two brothers and I'm the baby. It was chaotic at times, as you can imagine. But fun. How about you? Do you have siblings?" Paige sipped her drink and studied his face.

The vibrancy in Max's voice dulled. He shifted in his seat. "Regrettably, I..." he began but was interrupted by their server.

"Here you go folks! One chef salad and one blackened tuna sandwich!" He plunked down their lunch. "Enjoy!"

"As I was saying. I don't know if I have biological siblings. I never knew my parents. I was born in Russia to young, unwed parents who could not afford me. I considered the other orphans where I grew up to be my siblings."

Paige picked up on his subtly sad undertone. *He grew up in an orphanage. How horrible.* She met his gaze. "Oh wow. I'm so sorry. I hope I didn't upset you."

"I'm not upset. Plus, you didn't know."

"True. I assume you grew up in Russia then?"

"Until I was seventeen. After all those dark years, I fled the cold, cheerless orphanage. I worked on a fishing boat on the Baltic for four years." He picked up his knife and carefully cut the large circles of pinwheeled turkey, ham, and cheese nestled on Romaine leaves. "Fifteen years ago I met a man who offered me a job at a shipping company here in America."

"Growing up in Russia *and* working on the Baltic? That's impressive. I've never even been to Europe, as embarrassing as that is. Not to mention seeing the Baltic Sea."

"It's quite a striking body of water. It's a glorious shade

of blue I had not seen until that day in the elevator."

Paige scowled at him and blotted her mouth. "What do you mean?"

Max laid his fork down on the edge of the bowl. He leaned in close enough for Paige to catch a scent of his sandalwood cologne. "Your eyes, Paige. Without sounding too forward, allow me to explain." He dabbed his full mouth and swallowed. "When you gazed up at me after ruining my burrito, my world stopped. The blue of your eyes is the same magnificent and captivating shade of my beloved Baltic Sea," he whispered.

A red flush inched up her neck and settled in her cheeks. The butterflies in her stomach morphed into waves of heat. "Thank you. I ah, I've never been told that before." She laughed nervously, reached for her iced tea, and took an enormous gulp. *Why's he staring at me like that? Like he's never seen blue eyes before.*

"I hope I did not cause you embarrassment or seem too forward."

"No, not at all," she lied. *This guy is intense.* "I guess I'll have to get to the Baltic someday then, right?"

"Oh yes. It's a strikingly stunning part of the world. Very different from New York City."

"I can only imagine."

Max drizzled the extra dressing on his salad. "Going back to the day in the elevator, that was your first week of work?"

"Yes, the first week. And when I learned you worked in the same building, I was so mortified."

"Frankly, I'm glad you fell on me. I always enjoy meeting new people, especially when they insist on buying me lunch!"

As they ate, they discussed Paige's move to New York and the wonderful cultural life of the city, including restaurants and museums.

"Is there a significant difference between living in Philadelphia and New York?" Max asked.

"Well..." Paige dabbed her mouth. "I actually live in Hoboken, and from the short time I've lived here, I've learned the culture is different from Philadelphia—not to mention much more expensive!"

"Oh, I didn't realize you were in Hoboken. Is it a long commute for you to get to Manhattan?"

"No, not too bad. I used to take the subway to work when I was in Philly."

"Tell me again. What do you do?" Max folded his napkin and gazed at her.

"I'm an auditor."

His eyebrows shot up in surprise. "How interesting. You enjoy working with numbers then?"

"I do. I think of my work as an enormous numerical jigsaw puzzle. Pieces don't always fit at first until I work my magic."

"You don't mind the long hours, especially during tax season?"

"I'm used to it. I've always worked—since I was fifteen. I remember the thrill of earning my first paycheck and how liberating it was to earn my own money." Paige sipped her drink. "How about you? I'm sure you pull long hours being in shipping. What exactly do you do?"

Max grimaced and chuckled. "Oh I do. I'm a shipping broker. Which means I bring the importers, carriers, and exporters to the table to broker the best deal. While it's very rewarding, it can be a complex business. Often I have to temper stubborn personalities and rely on variables outside of my control, something *I do not like.*"

Paige wasn't sure how to take his last four words. *Do I make a joke? Switch topics?* She went with the former. "I suppose you're a bit of a control freak then?" She laughed.

His eyes cut to hers. In a low voice he replied, "Control freak? I'm not one hundred percent sold on being labeled *quite* that way. However, I will admit, Paige, I do prefer and expect things done *my* way." His eyes lingered on hers. "After all, I have a lucrative number of accounts as well as a large staff working for me, so I suppose I am guilty of being a bit of a *control freak.*" A tight-lipped smile spread across his mouth.

I hit a nerve. She prayed he did not see the hot-red embarrassment flush her cheeks. "In certain ways, I'm one too. I think we all have that propensity." *What else can I say?*

When their server reappeared, Paige sent up a silent prayer of gratitude. "Anyone for coffee or dessert?"

They both declined and the server placed the check on the table. They both reached for it and Paige jumped at the spark when their fingertips touched. Max placed his hand over the check. A corner of the bill stuck out from underneath his large, smooth hand. "I am happy to split this with you."

Paige slid the check from under his warm hand. "You will do no such thing. But thank you anyway." She set cash on the table and removed her coat from the back of the chair. "Shall we?"

Outside the diner, the air had taken on a bitter chill. They stood on the sidewalk as the brisk wind blew papers and other discarded items. Max joked, "I'm glad we met, as messy as it was. Thank you again for lunch. It was a nice break from my regular routine." He could barely restrain himself from pushing her hair away from her face as the wind swirled.

"You're welcome. I'm glad to have met you as well." Paige looked at her watch. *Damn, I need to go.* "Have a good rest of your day, Max." She smiled and walked to a waiting cab. A tingle raced from her toes to her scalp. *He can't take his eyes off me.*

"Paige! Wait!"

Leisurely, she turned around. "Yes?"

"Ah, I know we just met. But would you like to have dinner sometime?"

Paige regarded him for a moment. He stood, hands in his pockets, teetering back and forth on his heels. "Sometime, sure. You know how to find me."

CHAPTER 8

"What the hell is the point?" Max mumbled, rubbing his clean-shaven face. Three tries to focus on shipping contracts resulted in absolute failure. Only one thing was on his mind and her name was Paige. Since their lunch, Max has found his mind wandering to Paige.

What is it about her? I've had countless women in the past willingly throw themselves at me. But Paige is different. She's not going to be that easy—she's smart. I think I will enjoy this challenge.

Absentmindedly, he fiddled with a pencil. Thoughts of their lunch filled his mind.

I'm impressed with her assertiveness to pay for the dry cleaning and lunch. What a lovely breath of fresh air; a woman who is confident and beautiful. I'm sure there are lots of other men who want her. I can't let that happen.

He glanced at his phone. He toyed with breaking his code of never appearing too enthusiastic when it came to seeing a woman. Max stood and wandered to the window, fifty-eight floors up from the vivacious metropolis of Lower Manhattan. From this vantage point, he did his best thinking.

Screw it. He picked up the phone and called Franklin. "Bring my schedule for the next week."

Franklin sauntered in a few minutes later with a black date book in his hands. Making himself comfortable in a plush leather chair, he opened the book and ran down the week.

Max shook his head. "I have engagements *every* night this week. I need to reschedule one of them, the lowest priority engagement of course."

Franklin ran a slim finger over the pages. "On Wednesday, you're scheduled for a call with a startup consulting firm, an unfamiliar one. Reschedule that?" He flicked his eyes at Max.

"Possibly. I may need to keep that though. What else?"

"On Thursday, you have a brokerage dinner. On Saturday evening, you're scheduled to attend the opera."

Max scowled. "The opera? What was I thinking?"

"Actually, it's an old Christmas gift from a former, ah, lady friend of yours."

"I see. Give away my ticket, or you may have it."

"Thank you, sir. I'll take it. Is there anything else?" Franklin asked.

"Yes. I need you to find the office where a woman named Paige Buckley works. I believe she is several floors under here."

"Ah, I see." Franklin gazed at his boss and understood Max's tone; it was loaded with undeniable insistence that Franklin was to find Paige. Now.

Max nodded and Franklin rose. "Yes, sir. Give me a few minutes."

* * *

Paige was knee-deep in crunching numbers when Millie, the office assistant, shrilled through the speaker on her desk phone.

"Paige, you have a call on line one." *Click.* Millie was always very direct.

"Hello, this is Paige."

"Hello Paige, it's your lunch date."

A triumphant grin spread across Paige's face. *That didn't take long.* "Hello, Max. What's going on?"

"I was calling for two reasons. One, I thoroughly enjoyed myself at lunch, and two, at the risk of being too forward, I was wondering if you were free on Saturday evening for dinner?"

Paige sat back in her chair. "Yes, I enjoyed lunch as well. And Saturday..." She paused, not wanting to answer right away, "I'm not sure. I'll have to check and get back to you."

A pregnant pause. "Oh, I see."

"You sound disappointed," she teased.

"Not disappointed. Curious as to how long you're going to make me wait to hear about dinner?"

That's a little pushy, she thought, *but I like his tenacity.* "Can you wait until tomorrow? My roommate and I made tentative plans. It's not definite yet."

"If I must wait until tomorrow, yes I can."

"Good. I appreciate your patience." Testing the waters, she added, "Something, though, tells me you're not always so patient."

"You're starting to get to know me," he laughed. "I've been told patience is a virtue and I need more of it. However, when it comes to waiting to hear if I will be spending the evening with an intelligent, lively, beautiful woman, my level of patience grows significantly."

Paige let his words sink in. *Oh, he's good. I wonder if he's this way with all other women?* "Is that so? I'm very flattered." *Rich, good-looking, and successful usually adds up to a guy being a dick.* "Thank you."

"You're welcome—and it's the truth, Paige." He sat up in his chair and continued, "Anyway, if you *are* free, I will make reservations at my favorite Italian restaurant, Alfredo's. I assume you enjoy Italian cuisine?"

"Oh, I love Italian food. I could eat pasta every night."

"Let me assure you, Alfredo's serves homemade pasta dishes and other entrees that never disappoint."

"I take your word for it. When I get home tonight, my roommate and I will talk and I'll call you tomorrow."

"I'll be in and out of the office tomorrow with meetings. I hope I don't miss your call."

She cut her eyes to her calendar and assessed her day. "Turns out I'm really busy all morning, so I'll call you after lunch. Okay?" *He won't say no.*

"Yes, that's fine. I look forward to hearing from you."

"I'll talk with you tomorrow then. Have a good rest of your day," Paige said.

"I will, and you do the same."

* * *

Before she knew it, it was past six in the evening. Her eyes felt like a cracked, waterless riverbed thanks to hours of reading the new tax codes. *This is when having good vision in only one eye really sucks*, she thought, sitting back in her desk chair. *Time to get outta here.*

Paige trudged to the subway in the dark. *How many more months of darkness coming at four in the afternoon?* Pulling her coat up around her neck, her thoughts turned to Max and a possible dinner date. She hustled down the empty steps to the subway platform. The strident squeal of the brakes reverberated in Paige's head and blocked out all other sound. As she stepped from the last step, someone grabbed her bag from her blind side. Caught off guard, Paige stumbled, but managed to keep her balance.

"Get off me!" Panicked, she fought back and scanned the

area for help, but no one paid attention.

"Shut up, bitch!" the pockmarked, greasy-haired woman screamed and pulled even harder.

"I said get *off* me!" Paige wrenched the bag back with enough ferocity to propel the woman forward like a ragdoll. "Stay the hell away from me!" As Paige turned away from the woman, the woman leaped to her shoeless feet and charged.

Lunging, she shoved Paige, forward who fell hard on the platform. With snake-like quickness, the woman grabbed Paige's bag. Staring down at Paige, she shrieked, "This is *my* bag! It has my car and kids in it!" The woman pivoted and dashed for the stairs.

Paige scrambled to her feet and raced after her. People turned at the high-pitched scream; no one helped even though Paige shouted for aid. The woman charged up the steps, taking two at a time.

"Stop her! She has my bag!" Paige hollered and sprinted up the steps.

The woman skittered up the stairs and was almost free until someone body-blocked her. The woman bounced off the person and landed with a thud on the top step.

Relief flooded Paige when she saw Martha reach down and snatch the bag away from the shrieking woman.

"Martha! Thank God!" Paige gasped when Martha yanked the woman from the floor and shoved her. "Stay the fuck outta heah! Got it? Next time I won't be so nice!"

The woman flipped the bird, spat at them, and scuttled down the steps.

"You okay, honey?" Martha asked and gently rubbed Paige's arm.

Paige's voice shook as she said, "I think so. Thank God you showed up."

Martha rubbed her quivering shoulders. "Me too. You

sure you're okay? Did she take anything?"

Paige rummaged in her bag. "Everything is here." Her heart battered against her ribcage and she noticed a trickle of blood from her finger. "I never saw her. Then again, only having one good eye doesn't help."

Martha stared at her. "One eye? What's that all about?"

Paige gave her a brief explanation. "She came at me from my right side, so I never saw her."

"I'm so sorry. Those two-legged cockroaches are usually harmless and crawl out later at night—unless they need a fix."

"Should I file a police report?" Paige asked.

"Oh yes. Right when you get home. I know she probably won't be caught, but at least your attack will be recorded."

Small talk with Martha on the subway helped to calm Paige's frayed nerves. She walked Paige through how to file a police report and offered her help if more was needed.

"Thanks, but I think I get it. I can't thank you enough for helping me. I owe you a drink, or coffee if you don't drink, as a thank you," Paige said.

"Me *not* drink?" Martha let out a throaty laugh. "Sure kid, a drink sounds good! But you don't have to do that."

Paige faced her and stared intently. "I know, but you stopped something potentially horrible from happening to me. Please, I insist."

Martha saw the seriousness in Paige's look and heard it in her voice. "Well okay, if you insist."

"I do and I'll defer to you where to go since I'm new around here. I'll bring Fina, my roommate, okay?"

"Sure. I know lots ah places." Martha opened the paper to the crossword puzzle and took a pencil from her bag. Soon a furrow between her perfectly arched eyebrows appeared and the pencil scratched across the paper.

A heartfelt ripple of gratitude came over Paige. *Thank God she appeared*, Paige thought. The rest of the ride was quiet aside from Martha uttering disparaging comments about the puzzle.

CHAPTER 9

A tangible stillness greeted Paige when she entered the apartment. No singing from the kitchen, no wafting aroma of dinner. *Fina's still at work.* Paige sighed. *I wish she was here.* Before throwing her coat and bag on a chair, she took her phone from her bag. She called Fina, who did not answer. Paige tried to keep her voice level, as she did not want to alarm her.

"Hey Fin. It's almost seven and I forgot to get something out for dinner. Will you pick up some cheesesteaks on the way home? See you soon."

Paige gathered her thoughts before calling to report her assault. She jotted down her memory of the woman's appearance and other details in case the police department asked for a description. Double-checking she had the correct information, she dialed the police station and reported the assault.

* * *

Fina bustled into the kitchen holding two grease-stained bags. The tantalizing aroma of the cheesesteaks filled the kitchen, making Paige's mouth water.

"They smell so good and I'm *starving*," Paige commented. "I'll get plates and wine if you want to go change."

"Perfect!" Fina disappeared into her bedroom and reappeared in her favorite post-work outfit: a bubble-gum pink

Juicy Couture sweatsuit.

"How was your day?" Fina asked. "I meant to call you during the day to see what you wanted to do for dinner, but work got crazy. I had to trash an *entire* photo layout and redesign a whole new one." She took a swig of wine. "And my boss sort of hinted that I might be going off-site."

"Oh yeah? For what?"

"I'm not really sure. Something about New York Harbor."

"Sounds fun and interesting."

"Something different is always good. But I want to hear about your day."

"I think we should sit down before I tell you about my day," Paige replied and took the chicken cheesesteaks and fries to the kitchen table.

"Ah, okay." Fina was alarmed by the seriousness in Paige's tone. "What's going on?" She took an enormous bite of the gooey, oniony cheesesteak and rolled her eyes in delight.

"Do you want to hear the good or bad first?"

Mouth full, Fina mumbled, "Bad."

Paige nodded and shared what happened in the subway and how Martha came to her rescue.

Fina's mouth dropped open. "Are you effin' serious? God Paige, are you okay?" She rubbed her friend's hand.

"Yeah, I'm fine. Scared the crap out of me, but I'm fine. She didn't get anything, thank God."

"Martha sounds like a badass. I'm so glad she was there. Not that you couldn't have taken that bitch."

"Oh, I would've pulled out the old karate moves I learned as a kid, but lucky for her, I didn't have to!" Paige joked.

"So, what was the good part of your day?"

Paige put down the half-eaten cheesesteak and took a sip of wine. "Well, a certain *hottie* called me today," she started. "And he asked me to dinner on Saturday night."

Fina's eyes widened. She choked on her wine. "Wait," she sputtered. "You just had lunch!"

"So? He's *obviously* dying to see me again!" Paige batted her eyelashes.

"What did you tell him?"

Paige sighed. "I told him we—meaning you and me—may have plans."

"To do *what?*" Fina narrowed her eyes. "You *know* we don't have plans."

Paige sighed and slumped back in her chair. "I know we don't." She folded her arms across her chest. "I guess I lied because I don't want him to think I'm too…I don't know… available, eager?"

Fina shook her head. "Paige, the fact that *he* invited *you* to dinner tells me he's the eager one, right?"

"I guess. I also got the vibe that he's very used to getting what he wants, especially from women," Paige replied. "And I don't want to be just another conquest."

Fina scowled. "So you think he's a player?"

"I don't know for sure if he is or isn't. He sure looks it. But there's something about him, Fina."

"Like what?"

"I can't quite place it. Mysterious? Guarded? He seems open, but I can't quite tell. Maybe I feel that because he grew up in an orphanage."

Fina stopped mid-dunk of her cheesesteak in a blob of mayonnaise. "*What?*"

Paige relayed how Max never knew his parents and how he grew up. "Sad, right?"

"Very. I can't imagine. No wonder why he has an edge." She then asked about lunch.

"Lunch went well, even though I tried to joke about being

control freaks. He didn't appreciate my humor. Anyway, I definitely felt a connection between us—as cliché as that sounds. I know we both felt it. And it's been a *really long* time since I've had a jolt like that, and I liked it."

"Then what the hell is stopping you from saying yes to dinner?" Fina rose and took the cheese-smeared plates to the kitchen sink.

Paige called after her, "He strikes me as a little pushy and expects to get everything he wants. But on the other hand, he was very polite and open about how hard he has worked to be so successful. He also seemed very interested in my career and life. I guess I'm hesitant because he's rich, handsome, and successful—usually they're the perfect ingredients for a guy to be a prick."

"God, Paige! Are you listening to yourself? You don't know he's a prick!" Fina yelled over the running sink and clanking of dishes. "Go out with him again! That's the only way you'll find out."

***

A knife could not slice through the invisible cloud of Paco Rabanne and oniony body odor in the poorly ventilated, cramped weight room of GET FIT gym. Beefcakes flexed and admired their glistening, bulging biceps in the mirror-walled room. Nirvana's latest hits pumped from the black corner speakers. Grunts, groans, and shouts peppered the air.

On the tattered brown bench press, Stu exhaled through gritted teeth and grunted as he lifted the two-hundred-pound bench press.

"Ya got this, man! Come on! Push!" Marty encouraged from above. Sweat dripped from Marty's face onto Stu's forehead.

Arms quaking, pecs screaming, Stu groaned and pushed the weight back into the rack over his head and sat up. His massive chest heaved under the gray tank clinging to his damp torso. He looked up at Marty. "Come on man, use a fuckin' towel!" He wiped his head with his shirt.

"Sorry man, it's hot in here!" Marty wiped his face. "Plus, it's only sweat!"

Stu shot Marty a glare that made him wither. "Sorry!"

Stu snorted and left the weight room. He glanced at the blue digital clock on the wall above the men's' locker room. The blue numbers glared 7:43. *Plenty of time to shower before the meeting*, he thought. Leaning against the wall with one hand, he stretched his powerful quads and gazed into the spinning room. A dozen people, mostly women, were mounted on spin bikes. He smiled at the display of tight asses on some of the women who stood and pedaled as if their lives depended on it. Stu heard the instructor clapping and offering encouragement to the spinners, most of whom shone with perspiration and huffed heavily.

"Not a bad view, huh?" Marty came up behind him.

"Depends on what you like to view," Stu replied, fixing his gaze on a woman pumping hard and breathing even harder.

Marty followed his gaze around the room and gestured to three men struggling to keep up. "What guy in his right mind would want to sit on a hard bike seat smaller than a brick? That'd crush your balls, right?"

"Amen to that," Stu replied. He swigged from his bottle. "We're meeting at eight thirty. Don't be late."

"I won't."

* * *

Snap Decision

At precisely eight thirty, Stu and Marty arrived separately at the church parking lot. Inky blackness covered the lot. Moonlight fought to push through the clouds. Each man stepped out of their car and glanced around. A chill hung in the air.

Motioning to the white steeple standing sentinel in the night sky, Marty quipped, "The irony of why we're meeting and the place we're meeting can't be lost on anyone."

Stu said nothing until sweeping headlights from the opposite side illuminated the darkened parking lot. He held up his arm to shield his eyes from the blinding light. "Showtime."

The driver held open the back door for the passenger, who slid silently from the vehicle.

"Good evening, gentlemen," Max said.

Stu and Marty nodded at Max.

"I—" Max stopped abruptly at the forceful slam of a door. They froze. All eyes cut to the church.

A figure emerged from a side door. The person shuffled toward the street in front of the church, muttering, and disappeared around the corner.

"As I was saying, I assume you have the package?"

"Follow us." Stu turned and walked to the car. "In here."

Marty popped open the trunk and pointed.

A satisfied smile crept across Max's face. "Excellent work, gentlemen. This will do *very* nicely. This should be enough for the foreseeable future." He turned to Andreas, the driver. "Please pop the trunk. I'll help move this to my car."

After filling the trunk, Max asked Andreas to retrieve his briefcase. "Thank you." He opened it and handed one wrapped bundle of cash each to Stu and Marty, who slid the stack into their pockets.

"Thank you, Max. Shall we follow you to the boat?" Stu asked.

"No. That'll be enough for tonight. See you tomorrow," Max replied and slid back into the car.

"That was easy," Marty commented.

"Agreed, and a whole lot easier than driving around to bus stops and things like that," Stu said.

They stood and watched the car's red taillights shrink into the dark night.

CHAPTER 10

At six the next morning, Paige awoke and stumbled to the bathroom. *Thank God it's Friday.* Yanking the shower on, she turned the handle far right and stepped in. Frigid bullets pounded onto her head and face. She stood under the icy cascade until her skin was numb.

Sleep had eluded Paige the night before, the conversation she and Fina had about dinner with Max bouncing around in her head most of the night. Under the stone-cold shower, the same questions swirled in her mind like the water swirling down the drain.

Why am I reluctant? He appears to be a nice guy, and it's not as if it's a marriage proposal. Lunch went well. But something about him makes me feel wary—maybe it's because he has a ton of money. And I'm not used to that. It's intimidating. Like Fina said, I don't even know him, so what's holding me back? You're thirty years old. Grow up, Paige, call him, and go out to dinner.

Decision made, she stepped out and got ready for the day.

* * *

"Max Dovic, please. It's Paige Buckley." She was put right through when she identified herself.

"Hello Paige, how are you?" Max greeted her.

"I'm fine, a little tired after a long day."

"I understand that. My day has been busy as well, and regrettably, it's far from over." Max sighed.

"Oh? But it's almost six at night."

"The shipping world doesn't care about East Coast time. Plus, I have a dinner engagement."

"Understood. Speaking of dinner, Saturday night works for me, as long as it does for you too."

Max smiled broadly into the phone. "It certainly does. I'll make reservations for seven thirty. Does that suit you?"

"Yes, it does." *I wonder if this place is dressy*, she thought. "Max, without sounding terribly naïve and, since I'm new to New York, is Alfredo's a fancy place or more hole in the wall?"

"Not naïve at all. You're wise to ask. Alfredo's is a small, off-the-beaten-track place. No need to dress up. But not sweatpants either!" Max laughed.

Given their schedules, they agreed to meet at the restaurant.

"Great. I'll see you tomorrow. Don't work too hard, it's Friday!" Paige joked.

"I'll try not to. I'm looking forward to it."

"So am I."

* * *

Paige and Fina stood in front of Paige's closet. "Fin, I need your help. The restaurant is casual, but not sweatpants casual. Any suggestions?"

"Definitely wear a dress." Fina slid hangers across the metal bar. "You have this really cute black wrap-front one. It's basic, flattering, and easy to take off!" Fina laughed.

"Get your head out of the gutter!" Paige replied. "Basic black, simple. Can I borrow a pair of earrings? The pink teardrops?"

"Sure, what's mine is yours and vice versa. I'm so excited for you!"

"I am too. A little nervous, but I'll get a workout first. Want to join me?"

Fina shook her head. "I can't. Mom called a little earlier and asked me to come home for the weekend. Nana is on a downward slide and Mom...well, you know how she gets."

Paige rubbed her friend's arm. "I understand. And I'm so sorry."

* * *

Paige entered Alfredo's a few minutes past seven thirty and was immediately enveloped in the tang of sizzling garlic, simmering marinara, and fresh basil. Glancing around at the sturdy wooden chairs, gray ceramic floor, and close-set tables, she was transported back to her teenage years to her family's favorite restaurant. Seldom did she and her family dine out. When they did, however, Sorrento's was where they went. Since it was a bring-your-own-booze place, it was one of her parents' favorites. Sorrento's was where Paige was schooled in the difference between Chianti and Cabernet.

"Mr. Dovic is waiting for you," Paige heard from her right side.

Turning halfway to see, Paige saw a young, porcelain-skinned hostess smiling at her. "Oh, hello. Thank you."

"He's in the back. Right this way." The hostess led Paige through the crowded restaurant to the back where only three tables sat. Max rose from the table and beamed at Paige. He leaned down and gave her a quick, warm peck on the cheek. She caught a subtle hint of the same sandalwood cologne from the other day. *Not only does he smell good, he looks great.* She admired his royal blue, semi-fitted shirt tucked into gray pants. An alligator-skin belt encircled his tight waist.

"You look radiant." His gaze traveled over her and came to rest on her eyes. "I'm glad you and your roommate did not have plans." Max walked behind her and pulled out her chair. "Please take a seat."

"Thank you. It's nice to be out and not at home eating cereal!"

Max laughed. "What would you like to drink? Wine? Cocktail?" he asked and from the shadows behind Paige, a waiter appeared.

"I'll have a Tito's club soda and splash of grapefruit juice, please," Paige said.

"And I'll have an Angel's Envy, neat. Thanks, Oscar."

"My pleasure," Oscar responded and disappeared to the bar.

"So how was your dinner last night? You sounded like it had been a long day," Paige asked.

"Thank you for remembering. It was tedious, but lucrative in the end."

Oscar put the drinks down and sashayed off.

Max raised his glass. "Cheers and happy Saturday!" He raised his glass and locked eyes with Paige.

"Cheers and happy weekend for that matter!" Paige held his eyes, and the butterflies returned.

* * *

Oscar brought a bottle of red wine and poured for them before dinner was served. Over steaming bowls of osso bucco, baked pasta, plates of hot, buttered Italian bread, and a garlicky pile of broccoli rabe, Paige and Max ate and talked. And talked.

Paige offered Max a hunk of the bread.

"Oh, no thank you. Bread and I, ah, don't get along," he said.

"You sure? It's delicious."

"Yes, I am. Tell me more about where you grew up."

Paige grinned as she told him about growing up in a small suburb outside Philadelphia where she attended a large public school, Plymouth Whitemarsh. "And I've worked since I was fifteen. I had a job at the Twisted Pretzel at the Plymouth Meeting Mall all through high school. I baked pretzels and learned from Bud, the owner, how to balance books."

"So you became interested in numbers while baking pretzels? What a fascinating combination," Max said.

"I also loved my accounting class in high school, even though the teacher was a real pervert."

Max was intrigued. "What do you mean?"

"Well..." She swallowed a bite. "He told me he loved the coral-colored lipstick I wore. If that wasn't bad enough, he also said he was going to take me to the islands and buy me pearls."

"*What?* That's completely unacceptable."

"Looking back, yes it was. But I also took several computer science classes which I loved."

"You've worked your whole life then. Were you always interested in working with numbers and computers?"

Paige sipped her wine. "Sort of. I actually wanted to be a pilot, so I took those classes to help build some type of scientific background to study aviation."

Max's dark eyebrows rose in surprise. "A pilot?"

"Yes—and no pun intended here—but that dream crashed and burned." She recounted the events of that

Fourth of July night.

Max gaped at her; a cloud of sadness hovered over his face. "Oh, Paige. I was not aware. I'm so sorry."

"It's fine. How could you know?"

"How horrifying for you, though. I'm sorry you went through that." He reached over and placed his hand on hers.

Oh, his skin is so warm. "Thanks, but that's nothing to how you grew up. You never knew your parents. What's that feel like?"

Max sighed and sat back. "For many years, I was conflicted with feelings of anger, self-pity, and other things. I hated the orphanage. I hated and blamed my parents for abandoning me, yet when I learned of their young age and lack of money, I tried to understand their decision, which was the right one." He paused, sipped his water. "And when I worked on the cod boat, at roughly their age, I realized that I was responsible for my life. I held my future in *my own hands.*"

"I understand the self-pity part. After this"—she pointed at her right eye—"I threw the best pity parties ever. As I slowly began to realize how lucky I was that I didn't lose vision in *both* eyes, I changed my thinking. I appreciated the fact I could and would have a very normal life."

"Perspective is everything, isn't it? I knew that if I worked hard enough, met the right people, and saved money, I would be successful."

"Perfect plan for success." She sipped her water. "Remind me again how you wound up in the United States?"

"In my last year on the Baltic, I met a man who asked me if I would be interested in working with him in the States. He needed someone to help run his fledgling shipping brokerage business, and since I was young enough with no family, I said yes. I moved to New York and under his tutelage, I learned a great deal. Other men in the company were in line to advance, but they seemingly disappeared."

Paige frowned. "Disappeared?"

Max laughed. "Perhaps disappeared was not the best word. They seemed to have left New York. I don't know to where or why. That left only me, and since I was hungry, I worked my fingers to the bone and soon I had enough money saved to join forces with WHS Shipping."

"The American Dream, right?"

"Yes."

"Cheers to that!" Paige raised her glass.

Oscar appeared holding a small white plate upon which sat a slice of cake. "Compliments of the chef. Her tiramisu cake. Enjoy."

Max took a small taste as Paige devoured most of the dessert and decaf espresso.

Soon, the restaurant staff was stripping tables, vacuuming, and wiping down tables.

"I guess they're dropping a subtle hint," Paige commented.

"I quite agree," Max replied.

"Thank you for a wonderful evening, Max. My dinner was delicious." Paige reached over and put her hand on his.

"You're most welcome." He turned his hand over and caressed her palm with his thumb. "I'm glad you're here with me." He took her hand, kissed it gently, and placed it on the table.

The butterflies she felt earlier exploded into fireworks. Heat spread throughout her body. "I am too."

*　*　*

Outside the restaurant, the street was deserted aside from a cat sitting in a doorway, licking its paws, paying no attention to Paige and Max.

They walked aimlessly in front of sleeping storefronts. Paige ruminated about the evening. *He's very easy to talk to.* "Thank you again for a wonderful night."

Max stopped and turned to her. He lightly gripped her forearms. "Paige, I have not had this enjoyable of an evening in a *very* long time. *I'm* the one who should be thanking you." Without warning, he leaned down and kissed her.

Paige melted at the softness and warmth of his mouth, his kiss full of intensity. Surprised, she stepped back. "Max, I..."

He stammered, "I'm so sorry. I shouldn't have done that. I just—"

"Max, it's okay. You surprised me is all."

He took her hands. "That was too forward of me. Please forgive me for being brash. I must admit, you *do* have a certain, powerful effect on me."

As you do on me, she thought. "Thank you." She looked down at her feet. "I, ah, haven't dated in a very long time."

Max's eyebrows rose and he lifted her chin. "Really? I find that hard to believe."

"Really. And without being too forward, are you dating anyone right now?" Her lips pressed into a line, she stared at him.

"I'm not."

"Well, we have cleared that up!" She laughed. "But, how about we take things slowly. After all, this was only our first *real* date."

He squeezed her hands. "Of course we can go slowly. You're pragmatic, I like it." He laughed. "And you're right, it *is* our first date."

They walked a few blocks in silence, his warm hand clasped around hers.

"It's late. I need to catch a cab to the subway if I want to get home," Paige said.

"No cab for you. Allow me." Max took out his phone and placed a short call. "See you in a few minutes."

"Who was that?"

"My driver. He'll drive us to the subway." Glancing at his watch, he said, "The last one leaves in twenty minutes. Plenty of time."

"Your *driver*?"

"Yes. I can't stand driving in the city. Andreas is much more skilled than I."

Of course you have a driver. Paige saw headlights illuminate the street and turn toward them.

The car cruised through the few quiet streets. Andreas killed the ignition when they arrived at the subway. Max got out and held open Paige's door. The night was a deep black, with a sliver of a moon smiling down on them.

"You'll be okay getting home?" Max asked.

Paige hesitated. She thought of when she was almost mugged. *He doesn't need to know about that.* "Yes. I've done this before. Plus, there are other people around." Paige indicated others heading down the brightly lit steps.

Max eyed a few stragglers on the street. "I'll walk you down." He linked his arm through Paige's and they descended.

CHAPTER 11

On the filthy subway platform, Paige and Max stood, cautiously observing the People of the Night who shuffled and scuttled in and out of the shadows. Unidentifiable sounds floated from under the stairs. Max protectively entwined his warm hand into Paige's and held it. She gave it a squeeze. Within minutes, the subway ground to a halt.

Max turned to her. "You'll be okay from here?"

"Yes. It's not a long walk from the subway to my apartment."

Max took her other hand. "Please call me when you're home, okay?"

"Of course." She squeezed his hands. "Thank you again for tonight. I had a great time."

"I did too. Perhaps we can do it again. Is it okay if I call you next week?"

The squeal of the subway doors opening delayed Paige's response. "Yes." Quickly, she stood on her tiptoes and gave Max a peck on the cheek. "I'd like that."

She stepped into the sparsely occupied car. The doors slid shut. As she glanced out the windows, Max kissed his hand and waved. She held his gaze until the subway sped off into the night.

* * *

Despite the fact it was late and a bottle of Chianti was consumed, first-date vivacity ran through Paige's veins. She sat on the couch in her quiet apartment and flicked on the television. The eleven o'clock news was about to begin. Paige gazed at the female reporter, but her thoughts were pulled to what Max shared about his early life. *What a sad way to grow up, in an orphanage. I can't imagine not having a family. He seems so normal for growing up that way.*

A buzzing grabbed her attention. She glanced around and realized it was her phone. "Where is it?" *In my bag in the kitchen.* Jogging to the buzzing, she knew it would only be one of two people: her mother or Fina. *Oh crap! I forgot to call Max.* She let the phone go to voice mail as she shot a quick text to him.

It was Fina who called. Paige called her back.

Music pounded in the background. "Well, how was it?" Fina barked. "Sorry! It's kinda loud in here!"

"It was really low-key and we talked endlessly. I have the feeling he eats there frequently."

"What do you mean?"

"Well, it seems he has his own *private* table. And the waitstaff fawned all over us."

"Lucky you! Are you at our place? Or his?" Fina laughed.

"Of course I'm at home!" Paige poured herself a glass of water. "Where are you? It's really loud!"

"After visiting Nana at the home, Frankie needed a drink. So we're at Flanagan's. I feel like I'm the oldest one here by five years!"

"You might be! How's Frankie?" Paige asked about Fina's younger brother.

"He's fine. Nothing new to report. In his fifth year at Temple. Thinks he wants to be a PT." Fina swigged her beer. "Enough about Frankie. Tell me more about Max and your date."

Paige inhaled. "Well, like at lunch, he was attentive, polite, and kind. We never ran out of things to talk about. And the food was so good."

Fina sighed. "Jesus Paige, it sounds like you went on a date with my dad!"

"It was our *first* date! But...he is a really good kisser!"

Fina squealed with middle-schooler delight. "Is he now? Good girl! It sounds promising you'll have another date. Tell me more."

"He fished on a boat on the Baltic Sea for many years, which is how he got into shipping. He's lived in New York for a long time and works as a shipping broker. Oh, and I asked him if he was dating anyone else."

"Did you? And?"

"He's not and I believe him."

"Good. Sounds like he told you a lot. If I had some successful, older guy fawning all over me, I'd love it! Does he have any single, rich friends?" Fina laughed.

"Maybe. Like I said, it was *one* date."

"I know, but maybe you can ask! You should research him and see what else you can find. Go on Yahoo or something like that."

Paige pursed her lips. "Not a bad idea. I will when we hang up."

"Speaking of that, Frankie's waving at me. Gotta go. See you Sunday!"

"Have fun and be careful!"

Paige mulled over Fina's suggestion. Albeit she learned some compelling things about Max at dinner, she wanted to learn more. *Why not?* She rose from the couch and sat at the desktop computer in the dining room.

In the dark, with only the glow of the computer illuminating her face, she typed in Max's name and waited. A few hits came up with the information being sparse, but there were links to his business page. Paige twitched her lips back and forth and clicked on the first link. Knowing it could take a few minutes, she rose and went to the bathroom.

Upon returning, she saw the computer screen turned black. When she hit enter, she was pleased to see there was more information about Max and his company. Her eyes popped in shock as they moved down the glowing screen. *Oh my.* She read again to be sure she read it correctly. Her jaw hit the floor.

CHAPTER 12

Paige was roused from a deep sleep by heavy rain battering her bedroom windows. She lay on her side and watched wet streaks paint the glass and blur the world outside. *So much for a morning walk.* Rolling onto her back, she lay thinking about her date the night before and how comfortable it was to be with Max. Her thoughts switched to what she read about Max and WHS Shipping company. *Wait until I tell Fina.* Reaching for her phone on the nightstand, she saw it was past ten. *I need to get up.*

She made coffee, heated a sugary cinnamon roll, and stared at the gray rain until the caffeine lifted the Chianti fog enough for her to fetch the newspaper on the ground floor. She was getting used to reading the local paper, but she did miss the *Philadelphia Inquirer*, especially the local section.

She extracted the crossword puzzle and folded it to fit on a clipboard. With a sharpened pencil, she attacked the crossword puzzle for an hour. She made a mental note to bring it with her tomorrow to work on it with Martha as they rode the subway.

As she was getting dressed, her phone rang. It was her boss. *This can't be good.*

"Morning Todd, what's up?"

"Good morning, Paige." He sighed. "I hate to do this, but I need you to come in today for a few hours. Apparently, some reports were not backed up so we need to start from scratch." He sneezed. "As you know, tax day coming up."

Paige rolled her eyes. "Bless you, and I understand." She glanced at the clock on the wall. "I can get there by one or so."

"Perfect. Thank you so much. I need your expertise and tech savviness. I'm sorry about this."

"It happens. I'll see you soon."

* * *

The few riders of the subway sat, heads resting on the windows, facial expressions ranging from fatigue to joy to disdain. Paige sat alone. In her datebook, she scribbled a grocery list and some to do's. She flipped the pages of her datebook back and saw the green star which indicated the date on which she and Fina moved from Philadelphia. After the green circle was the first purple circled date, her first date with Max. *I hope to draw more purple circles.* She leaned her head against the window and replayed their date from the night before. *Something about older men. They have their acts together and are more mature, but they're not old. Max is easy to be with and I like how he seems sincerely interested in me and my life. We'll see where it goes.*

She walked through the sprawling lobby of Tower Two to the rows of elevators. The space always sent a shiver up Paige's spine because it felt so sacred. Others felt that way since it was meticulous, pristine, and shiny.

"Hey! What're you doin' heah?" Martha's voice shot through the empty lobby.

Paige pivoted to see her walking across the lobby. Keys jingled at her hip; a walkie talkie clung to her black belt opposite the keys. A paper coffee cup in hand. A broad smile stretched across her face.

"Hey Martha. My boss called and he needs some help today."

"That sucks. It's Sunday!" She shook her head.

"It's fine. I didn't have any real plans anyway. Plus, I'm dragging a bit from last night."

"Big night?" Martha laughed. "You do look a little tired."

"I am. I went on a date and we *definitely* imbibed."

"Good for you. Glad you're gettin' out. Who's the lucky guy?"

"You probably know him. He works in this building."

Martha chuckled and mentioned the thousands of people who work in Tower Two. "But hey, it's worth a try. What's his name?"

"Max Dovic."

His name hung in the air, heavy. Martha's eyebrows shot up. She cocked her sharp jaw to one side, and her eyes narrowed and slid sideways to Paige. "Oh really? Yeah…I know him—not well."

Her brooding, ominous expression and tone sent a chill through Paige. "You don't look very happy about that."

Martha sipped the coffee and motioned to a bench. "You got a minute?"

"Um, sure." Paige followed her to the bench, accompanied by a stinging pinch of insecurity.

Martha sighed and turned her bright eyes to Paige. "Look honey, I don't wanna crap on your love parade, but I've heard some shit about him that's not real pretty."

"Like what?"

"Apparently, he can be a real dick. Supposedly he made heaps of money and I truly admire that. But just because he's rich as hell doesn't mean he can treat people the way he does."

Paige's eyes grew wide. "Oh, that's disturbing. He's always been respectful to me and treats me like royalty." She was hesitant to ask the next question. "What have *you* seen or heard, if anything?"

"Well, I've seen him rip people new assholes, *right in this lobby,* for whatevah reason. And my friend Lindsey, who works on the docks, has seen the same thing. Said he goes fuckin' nuts if one of the loaders makes a tiny mistake."

How do I respond to that? "Maybe because he has a stressful job with lots of people relying on him. And he expects *a lot* from people."

Martha sipped her coffee. "I get that. But there's a way to go about getting the best and most from your workers. Berating them isn't the way." She slid back on the bench and quietly added, "I also heard that he's a bit of a ladies' man. I've seen him come and go with lots of, ah, women on his arm."

A hot flash of jealousy lit up Paige's face. With more of a sharp tone than she meant, she replied, "I can see that. Come on Martha, he's hot, rich, and single. I'm sure his phone is *exploding* with women's phone numbers. I asked him outright if he's currently dating anyone. He said no, and I believe him."

Martha saw Paige's face cloud up in anger and tried a stab at humor. "Sorry. I didn't mean to rattle your cage. But don't worry honey, my number ain't in his book! Not my type!" A guttural laugh echoed throughout the lobby.

Paige could not help but laugh and countered right back. "Then you're one less woman I need to fight off!" She stood. "I need to get upstairs. Duty calls."

Martha put her hand on Paige's arm and gazed up at her. "Paige, I'm sorry. I'm only looking out for you. I don't want to see you gettin' hurt, especially with all the men out there who would kill to go out with you."

Startled by Martha's emoting, she gripped her friend's hand. "That's kind of you to say. I promise I will keep in mind what you told me." She turned to go, but something stopped her. "I'd be a liar if I said I didn't feel that something..." She pulled for the words. "...is, um, unusual? Unique maybe, about Max."

"I'm sure you'll find out more about him as time goes by. Keep me in the loop."

CHAPTER 13

Fina arrived home early Sunday evening after being in Philadelphia all weekend. *I'm so tired. I hope I can make the walk home.*

She stepped off the subway and began the trek to their apartment. Her weekend had been exhausting; being around family for two days and nights wore her out. The *clack clack clack* of the small wheels of her portable suitcase on the pavement cracks matched the rolling of her thoughts.

Mom is so stressed about Nana and freaking out on everyone... Dad's shoulder is killing him again... I can't babysit Frankie anymore when he's drunk. He's old enough to do that.

She was eager to tell Paige about her family-infused weekend. *She'll understand what's going on with them*, she thought. No one understood her family's dynamics like Paige. *Thank God we've been friends forever.*

Fina wanted to hear more detail about Paige's dinner date. *I'm glad she had a date with someone who sounds normal.*

Fina lugged her bag onto the elevator of their building and hit the button.

"I'm home, honey!" Fina shouted into the apartment.

Quiet answered her.

"Are you here?" Fina tried again.

Again, silence.

"Weird." She put her bag in her room and called Paige's phone. "Where are you?"

"Oh hey Fin. Sorry, I forgot to tell you I had to go to work today. I'm just leaving and will be home soon."

"On a Sunday? That sucks!"

"I'll explain when I get home."

"Okay, see you in a bit."

Over a dinner of hot buttery grilled cheese, tomato soup, and salad, Fina asked Paige more about Max.

"Are you physically attracted to him?"

Paige grinned. "Oh yes. And it's very mutual."

"Oh really?"

"Unexpectedly he kissed me—on the mouth! I kind of pulled back and I think he was embarrassed. I wasn't expecting it, but that's not to say I didn't *want* him to. But as I told him, it was only our first real date and I wanted to take things slowly."

"I understand. Smart move, too."

Paige shared with Fina what she read about Max on the internet. "According to what I read, he's the broker who secures enormous, lucrative contracts between many transportation companies and WHS Shipping. It sounds as if Max wasn't the 'go-to' guy, WHS Shipping wouldn't be so successful."

"Hmm, kind of like a real estate broker. And since it's New York Harbor, that means a lot of ship traffic. I'm sure he's made a ton of money."

"That seems to be the case." Paige giggled.

"What's so funny?" Fina leered at her friend.

Giggling again, she replied, "He also has a *driver!*"

Fina's dark eyebrows practically reached her scalp. "A *driver*?! Damn!" She twitched her lips side to side. "He's gotta be worth a boatload of money, then, right?"

"Apparently."

Fina's observation made Paige think of her conversation

with Martha earlier that day. Paige knew how fiercely protective Fina was of her. *Do I tell her or not? I'll wait. No need.*

"When are you going out again?"

"Not sure. He's going to call me next week." Paige stood and cleared the table. "Enough about me. What's going on in the Manzetti family?"

"Oh boy. We may need to open another bottle."

Paige reached into the refrigerator for the unopened bottle of Pinot Grigio. "Coming right up."

CHAPTER 14

March

Fina's alarm shrieked at five thirty. She stumbled through the dark to the bathroom, careful not to wake Paige. Leaning on the bathroom sink, she looked in the mirror and flinched. "I can't terrorize the public with this face."

Thirty minutes later, a showered, heavily made-up Fina closed the apartment door quietly and headed to the office. On the ride in, she thought about how she and Paige had developed a comfortable routine and settled into a new city. *The few months we've lived here have flown by. It's almost spring.* She smiled thinking about them hunting for the cheapest grocery store, liquor store, and hair salon. Even though winter still gripped the East Coast in an arctic fist, they delighted in wrapping themselves in blankets and sitting on the mini balcony of their apartment. She recalled Paige's observation of how lower Manhattan glowed even in the depths of winter. *I'm a lucky girl.*

A blast of cold air shot through the subway car jolted Fina from her musings. *Time for work.*

* * *

Fina rubbed her mouth in concentration. Her eyes danced over the photo layout splayed on a large desk. "I think this picture should go *here*." Fina pointed a pale pink fingernail to a corner on the table. "The model's dress really jumps out here instead of at the top."

"I think you're right," Leigh, her boss, agreed. "And this other picture," she said, pointing, "can go at the bottom here so the article is split evenly."

Fina admired the layout. "I like it. The balance is perfect."

Leigh turned to Fina. "Fina, you have done a great job on this layout highlighting this woman's struggle to establish her fashion line. Solid work. Well done."

Redness flamed across Fina's face. She basked in the compliment. "Thank you, Leigh. I really appreciate your words and I hope I can keep producing for this great magazine."

"Oh you will, I know it. I think."

Leigh was interrupted by a knock on the door. A shiny, bald head peeked around the door. "Knock, knock. I hate to interrupt your work, but I need to steal Fina." Peter was the magazine's editor-in-chief.

The women exchanged a knowing look that said when Peter needed something, he usually got it.

"Fina, go with Peter. I can finish this up."

* * *

Peter closed the glass door of his office and asked Fina to take a seat.

This can't be good. Fina sat on the edge of the leather chair. "Is everything okay?" She chewed the inside of her lip. "Am I being fired?" she blurted.

Peter's bushy eyebrows shot up. He laughed and adjusted his rimless glasses. "Certainly not! You're not in trouble nor losing your job. As a matter of fact, your work is outstanding."

Fina felt her insides release and her heart slow down.

"Phew!" She sat back and asked why he wanted to see her.

"I need you in the field. Both of our photographers are ill, and we have a scheduled photo shoot of one of the top shipping companies in the world—WHS Shipping. With your keen eye for detail, I'd like you to shoot photos."

"When?"

"Tomorrow, two o'clock. And then later in the week or next week, you will interview the top broker."

"An interview? It's been a while since I've done one. Will you help me prep questions?"

"Of course. You should know that WHS Shipping is one of the largest importers of high-end restaurant equipment used by all the five-star restaurants in NYC. As well, WHS is the number-one exporter of civilian aircraft parts and cars to countries all over the world."

"That's impressive. I can't wait to start," Fina commented.

"What's truly impressive is the backstory of their top broker, Maksim Dovic. A true rags-to-riches story."

Holy crap! The name clicked. *Paige's Max?* "My roommate is dating him. Small world and I'd be honored to interview him. Thank you so much for this opportunity."

"Grand. WHS Shipping will be the featured story in next month's edition. One of your pictures could end up on the cover, which would be a feather in your cap."

Fina frowned. "Feather in my cap?"

Peter sighed, "Oh yes. That's an idiom of days gone by, one lost on younger generations. Pity." He explained the meaning of the archaic idiom and the details of her assignment. "Any questions?"

"I don't think so." She rose and headed to the door.

"One last thing Fina. At the risk of sounding forward, those heels you have on are not dock-friendly, if you know what I mean." He laughed. "Plus, they may, ah, *distract* the dock workers."

Fina glanced down at her three-inch black heels. "Good point. I'll be sure to wear something more comfortable. Thanks for the head's up."

"You're welcome."

"Thanks again for taking a chance on me, Peter. I won't let you down."

* * *

Fina stepped out into the forceful wind whipping around the New York and New Jersey port. Her hair blew across her face until she found a hair tie in her bag. Food wrappers, paper coffee cups, and other trash was tossed about. For early spring, it was cooler than usual. Pulling her coat up around her neck, she was doubly glad she changed into jeans, sneakers, and a heavy sweater. Out on the deep East River, she saw a handful of enormous cargo ships, tugboats nudging or pulling them to their appropriate docks.

This place is humungous, she thought. *I want a better look before I go down there.* She leaned over and placed her bare hands on the frigid metal railing. She snatched her hands away, wishing she had gloves. "Damn that's cold!"

Diesel fumes and cigarette smoke rose from below. The cry of seagulls flying in the blue sky reminded her of the beach. Workers of all shapes and sizes barked orders and directions. *Not the cleanest place*, she thought and walked down the maze of ramps to her assigned area. "Time to go to work."

Gazing up and down the enormous, intimidating port, Fina felt like an outsider and her frustration started to surface. *Hopefully my contacts know to come and find me*, she thought. Peter told her their names—Marty and Stu—

but she had no idea they looked like. *Stop standing around looking stupid and helpless. Go ask someone.*

She scanned her surroundings for someone who appeared to be somewhat helpful. The longshoremen who stopped their labor to ogle her were her last choice. From her left, she thought she heard a woman's voice.

At the edge of the port a woman stood facing the water. The black walkie talkie in her hand crackled as she spoke. Fina heard the conversation as she approached.

"Jeb, I need you and the crew to thoroughly clean her up," Fina heard in a raspy, yet friendly voice. "*Babe* is not a fan of being dirty. Thanks, over and out." She jammed the walkie talkie into her heavy coat pocket.

"Excuse me, sorry to bother you. My name Serafina Manzetti and I'm hoping you can help me."

The woman turned to Fina and gave her the once-over. "Yeah? With what?"

"I'm looking for Marty Merlany and Stu Wallis. Do you know them?"

"Yeah I do." She took out a Tiparillo and lit up.

"Um, thanks. Do you know where they are? I have no idea what they look like."

The woman took a deep drag and blew smoke from the side of her mouth. "Hang on, I'll find them for you." From her inside coat pocket, she took her phone and dialed. "Yeah, it's me Lindsey. There's a woman heah lookin' for Marty and Stu. Know where they are?" She ambled away from Fina and continued the conversation.

She returned a few moments later. "They'll be here in a few minutes."

"Thank you, Miss...? I'm sorry, I didn't catch your name."

"Lindsey Johnson. What do you want with those two?"

"I work for *What's Hot* magazine and my boss assigned

me to take pictures of container ships. And interview a higher-up. Marty and Stu work in the PR department and they're my contacts."

The woman, Lindsey, narrowed her blue eyes as she finished her Tiparillo. "Huh. What ship?"

"I don't know the exact name, but the company is called WHS Shipping. Know it?"

The woman belted out a thick laugh. "Who the hell doesn't? WHS is one of the bigger companies around. One of the most prolific importahs and exportahs in the whole world. I pushed in one of their ships last month."

Fina had no idea what she meant. "*Pushed* in a *ship*?"

"Yeah, in my tugboat."

Her tugboat. Fina tried not to laugh as she imagined a toy boat in a bathtub. "What do you mean?"

"I'm a tugboat captain, have been my whole life."

Fina stared at her. "Really? That's *so* cool. Are there many women captains?"

"Nope. I'm a rare breed, as they say. That's my boat over theah." She pointed to the right where the *Boston Babe* was situated. The tugboat shone red in the afternoon sun. Fina saw the crew hosing her down and scrubbing the deck.

"*Boston Babe.* Cool name. I'm assuming you're from there?" Fina asked.

"Born and bred. Moved here in the eighties."

An idea started to percolate in Fina's mind. "Captain Lindsey, would you like to be interviewed sometime? Since you're a rare breed, as you said, I'm sure your story of why you wanted to be—and how you became—a tugboat captain is fascinating, especially as a woman."

Lindsey chuckled. "I'll think about it. It really isn't anything spectaculah, but I'll think about it."

"If I may be so bold, that's *your* opinion, Captain

Lindsey!" Fina laughed and drew a business card from her bag. "I'd love you to think about it. My number is on here if you're interested."

Lindsey scanned the card and looked at Fina. "I'll let you know." Over Fina's shoulder she saw a golf cart approaching them, two young men in the seat. "Looks like Stu and Marty are here." She gestured to them.

Fina pivoted around. The men appeared to be around her age, give or take a few years. Sizing them up, she said to Lindsey, "Hmm, they're kind of cute—especially the one driving."

Lindsey squinted at them and a slight, sardonic smile crossed her lips. "Not really my type."

The golf cart stopped a few feet short of where Fina and Lindsey were standing. The driver waved and both men slid out and approached the women. Fina noticed the driver's shock of thick blond hair and he was at least a head taller than his passenger. His athletic saunter oozed confidence. The other man's buzzed hair, creased pants, and ramrod posture screamed military to Fina.

"Well, it looks like Marty and Stu have arrived," Lindsey said.

"I guess so." Fina turned to her. "Thanks again for your help. And I sincerely hope you'll consider doing an interview."

Lindsey eyed the card. "We'll see."

CHAPTER 15

"Hello, I'm Marty and this is my partner Stu." Both men stepped from the golf cart and extended their hands.

Fina introduced herself and why she was there.

"We're looking forward to helping you. It's not every day WHS gets exposure in a magazine," Marty said and beckoned toward the golf cart. "Stu, climb on the back so Fina can sit. Here, put your bag back here." Marty pointed at the basket behind the seat.

"Thank you." Fina slung her camera bag into the basket. "I really appreciate you guys helping me out. I think it's best to defer to you for what you think will highlight the enormous success of WHS Shipping."

"Our pleasure, that's what we do for the company. We run public relations," Marty said.

Fina turned to Marty. "In the cab over here, I researched the company and saw your names. I also read that your immediate boss, Max Dovic, is quite a success story, isn't he?"

"Oh yeah, he sure is. You want him brokering any kind of deal. He knows how to bring people together. He's one tough SOB too. Do you know his story?"

"No, not really. But I have plans to interview him."

"That'll be interesting," Marty replied, and steered the cart toward an enormous, towering cargo ship. In massive white letters, *WHS* was painted on the starboard side, standing out against the deep blackness of the ship. Fina guessed the vessel to be close to a thousand feet long. Containers of all colors were stacked on top, reminding her of a Legos set.

"Pretty impressive, huh?" Marty remarked.

"Oh my, yes. I've only ever seen container ships at a distance, but up close is a whole other story." Fina could not tear her eyes away from the vessel. Camera in hand, she snapped away.

"Wait until you see the inside," Stu said.

"Let's do it."

Inside the cavernous interior, types of cargo of all kinds were piled from the floor to ceiling. Each pile was positioned to keep their weight evenly distributed. Ear-splitting beeps shrieked from the forklifts buzzing around the floor. Fina was reminded of worker bees toiling inside of a hive for their queen.

"How about you get several shots of the interior being loaded and unloaded?" Marty yelled and gestured at the forklifts. "Gets loud in here! Put these in your ears and you have to wear this safety helmet." Stu handed Fina earplugs and a yellow helmet.

Fina nodded and lifted the camera and shot away. Moving closer to the stacks, Fina was impressed with the speed and accuracy at which the drivers of the forklifts completed their jobs.

Marty tapped her shoulder and gave a thumb up. She nodded and he drove the cart to the corner near a door with steps.

"Let's go up to the deck," Stu said.

A frigid, powerful blast of air hit them as they exited, propelling the helmet from Fina's head.

"Oh no! My helmet!" Fina watched it somersault down the dock. Marty sprinted after it and handed it back to her. She brushed a few wayward hairs behind her ear and placed the helmet back on. "Thanks. What happens up here?"

"On this deck, we load and unload the containers. Needless to say, the crane operator must be highly trained to lift the containers and place them perfectly on the dock or ship's deck. Our biggest concern is too much swing, which can easily happen on windy days like these," Stu said, rubbing his hands together. "I'm freezing. Does anyone but me want a cup of coffee?"

Marty and Fina said they would.

"I'll be back in a bit."

"Thanks man," Marty said.

"What do the other men do?" She gestured to a crew on the other side.

"Those crewmembers strap down the container to make it immobile. They're fast and efficient and can load this ship within a day. It's amazing to watch them," Marty replied.

"I'll take some pictures of them working, if that's okay?"

"Sure, but don't get too close. With this wind the containers swing around quickly. I wouldn't want you to get hurt. Scoot back here."

She let Marty gently take her arm.

Stu returned with three steaming cups of coffee.

"Thanks Stu." Fina took the paper cup and asked if she was permitted access to the dock to capture the crane operators in action.

After twenty minutes Fina announced she was finished with the photoshoot. "But I need the workers to sign a release so I can identify them in the photos. Doing work like that, those guys deserve recognition."

"We can help you with that. I'd love to see the pics first, though. Why don't we go somewhere and look at them?" Marty flashed her a smile. "There's a cool bar a few blocks away. They have great happy hour deals."

"Who could say no to good happy hour deals? And I'd like to get some information about you two."

* * *

In the course of the three-block walk, Fina, Stu, and Marty talked about WHS Shipping and Fina's job at the magazine. As they crossed a busy street, Stu and Marty veered from the sidewalk to a set of steps which, from the sidewalk, appeared to lead to a black abyss. Not a crack of light was visible from the bottom of the steps. Fina stopped short, unsure where they were going. *Am I going to end up in someone's basement?*

"Hold up, guys." She did not budge one step further. "I thought you said we were going to a bar," she said. "*That*"—she pointed down at the darkness—"looks like somewhere you get taken when you're being kidnapped."

Marty and Stu glanced at each other and broke out in laughter. They reassured her there was a bar at the bottom of the steps.

Stu jogged down the steps and held open the door. Music wafted up. "See? Nothing to fear!"

Fina's squinched up shoulders immediately relaxed. Together, they descended the well-trodden brick steps. As she stepped down, a flash of *Cheers* crossed her mind. Above the door in white-frosted letters she read the name: SURGE'S. *Cool name*, she thought and entered.

Inside, the atmosphere was warm and welcoming. A tall, blonde bartender joked with her patrons; a group of men hooted and hollered over a pool table.

Stu glanced around and saw an empty table by the bar. "You two go get drinks; I'll get the table. Marty, grab me a Stella please."

Returning with drinks, Fina and Marty joined Stu, who asked to see the pictures. Holding the camera, he scrutinized each shot. "These are great. You really captured life on the docks for all the workers," he complimented her. He handed Marty the camera, who agreed with Stu.

"Thanks guys. Cheers to that!" Fina held her glass up. "Hopefully your boss will like my work as well."

"I think he will," Marty replied.

"What's he like anyway?"

Stu and Marty traded a look before Marty replied. "He's driven, very serious, and incredibly demanding."

"But if you work hard for him, he recognizes that and is generous," Stu added.

"Generous?" Fina asked. "How so?"

"He gives a healthy bonus at the end of the year, or extra time off, things along those lines," Stu said.

"Nice. How long have you guys worked for him?"

Stu glanced at Marty. "A couple of years."

"And you like working for him?"

"Most of the time. But when he's in a bad mood, watch out." Marty laughed. "Right, Stu?"

Stu shot Marty a hard look. "Whatever you say." He drained the rest of his beer and rose from the table. "Time to go."

Outside, Fina thanked them for their help and the drinks. "I'll need to attain the signatures of the WHS employees to sign releases," Fina said to Marty, who handed her a card. "Thanks. I'll call you," she said. "I very much appreciate the tour today. Container ships are incredible vessels. Thanks again for your time."

* * *

At home that evening, Fina examined the pictures again. "Damn," she muttered. She tossed the camera on the couch.

"What's wrong?" Paige asked, putting down her magazine.

"Some of these pictures are blurry. Peter put his trust in me and some of these are crap." She slumped into the couch.

"If that's the case, go back down and shoot more. Right?"

Fina brightened. "Right. I'll go later this week. I don't need to mess up this chance of a promotion."

Paige heard the microwave beep and hopped up. "Popcorn is ready. I'll get it. Will you start the movie?"

"Sure." Fina picked up the remote and loaded *Mystic Pizza*, their favorite movie. "Wait! How could I be so dumb?"

"What?" Paige returned, and the aroma of hot buttered popcorn filled the room.

"I can't believe I forgot to tell you! I'm interviewing your *boyfriend* for the magazine!"

Paige fell onto the couch. She chuckled. "No way! Max? When?"

"Soon, like two days from now? Whenever Peter says."

Paige glared at her friend. "And Fin, he's not quite my boyfriend...yet."

Giggling, Fina replied, "That can mean only one thing: You haven't gotten down and dirty...yet!"

Paige picked up a pillow and playfully jabbed her friend in the ribs. "It's only been a few months!"

"What're you waiting for? If he's as hot as you say, get goin'!"

Paige shook her head. "Hush up and watch the movie!"

Fina snickered and dug into the popcorn.

CHAPTER 16

Gulls circled and shrieked overhead, their eyes roaming the docks for discarded scraps of anything edible. Fina watched them against the darkening sky and wondered what it would be like to see the world as sharply as birds do. She walked a few steps down the bird crap-splattered dock toward the looming cargo ship, the *WHS* staring at her from its portside. Lifting her camera, she quickly snapped several pictures of the vessel. She turned to her right and snapped a few more pics of the dinosaur-like cranes that stood idle against the evening sky.

"What're you doin' down heah?" a raspy voice came from Fina's left.

Startled, she turned to see Lindsey. "Oh hi! I, um, needed some better pictures." Fina struggled to remember her name. "It's Lindsey, right?"

Lindsey nodded. "And you're Fina, right?"

"Yes, nice to see you again, Lindsey." Fina almost did not recognize Lindsey in civilian clothes. She wore a long-sleeved white T-shirt with *I tug, do you?* scrawled across the front. Her faded jeans hung loosely on her hips. A red baseball cap with *Boston Babe* stitched into the front sat on her head, wisps of short, thin dark blond hair peeking from underneath. Small gold hoops pierced her upper ears; gold studs sat in her lobes.

"You were here before takin' pics. You didn't like those?" Lindsey asked.

"Not really. I'm dissatisfied with some. I thought I'd come back to snap some better ones."

"At night? Man, you got a good work ethic." She shook her head. "But, someone like you shouldn't be down heah at night, alone."

Fina shrugged. "It's not night yet and there are some people around, right?" She glanced around and realized the docks were almost a ghost town.

Lindsey held firm. "Look Fina, I've been tuggin' heah long enough to know this isn't a place you want to be at night and alone."

Fina felt a chill as Lindsey's words sunk in. "That sort of sounds like a warning."

Lindsey pulled out a Tiparillo and offered one to Fina, who declined. Lindsey lit up and through narrowed eyes, she said post-inhale, "It is."

Fina's scalp tingled. Caution signs flashed through her head, but she pushed further. "I'd like to know why."

Lindsey blew smoke into the air. "I've been heah since dawn. There's a good spot—Chub's—a few blocks away." Lindsey gave Fina the address.

"See you there." Fina walked to the parking lot.

* * *

Low lighting made Fina squint when she opened the door to Chub's. She stood in the door and scanned the bar for Lindsey, who sat at the corner, sipping a beer.

"What'll ya have?" the bartender asked Fina.

"Same as my friend here."

"Cheers." Lindsey tapped Fina's bottle with hers when the bartender placed it down.

"That's good. Anyway, back to the dock. Why are you

warning me? The pictures were for work. Why would that make people suspicious?"

"Because you're taking more pictures of Dovic's brokered boats—and he has people everywhere. People who report to him about everything that goes on down heah."

Fina fiddled with the label glued on the bottle. "He and his company are highlighted in a story my magazine is going to run. I got clearance the first time."

Lindsey finished her beer. "I know that. But you bein' down theah twice may raise some eyebrows." She signaled for another beer. "Need one?"

Fina declined. "Why and for who?"

"Because he doesn't like strangers sniffin' around. He holds his cards close to his chest."

Fina twitched her lips and tossed out an off-the-cuff comment. "Is he a bad guy or something?"

Lindsey glanced up at the television. "I don't know about that, but anything's possible. I've worked for him and he pays well, but there's something about him. He's guarded and I've seen him treat people like they're dogshit stuck on his freakin' Gucci loafer."

And my roommate is dating this guy. "Really? My roommate's dating him. She said he's the nicest guy."

Lindsey chuckled. "That's 'cause he probably wants to get in her pants."

"Don't all guys want that?" Fina laughed.

"I guess. Not my bag."

"Sounds like I need to warn her, right?"

"I would. I hear he's slept with half of Manhattan; then again, that's hearsay." She tilted the bottle to her thin lips and cast a sideways glance at Fina.

Fina understood and logged it away. "You said you've worked for him, so obviously you know him."

Lindsey snorted and lowered her voice. "*Everyone* knows him." She glanced around and whispered, "He's the fuckin' Godfathah of the docks and many container ships."

"What do you mean?"

"In a nutshell, he brokers deals between the owners of shipping companies and the carriers ah goods. He also has to make sure that freight arrives on time."

Nodding slowly, Fina answered, "I understand. But what I don't understand is if he's such a dick, why do you work for him?"

Lindsey cocked her head and glanced at Fina. "Come on Fina, you're smarter than that." She tapped the stack of cash sitting on the bar.

"Ah. Got it."

"To be clear, he's not my boss. I work for the port authority, but when I get assigned to one ah his carriers"—she patted the cash again—"it's a great payday." Lindsey went on to explain the erratic schedule of cargo ships arriving and departing. "All kinds of shit can screw up the schedules: weathah, illness, supply chain issues."

"How well do you know Stu and Marty? They told me they're in PR."

"Not very, but I've heard when Dovic says jump, they fuckin' *jump*. I do know he hired them to be extra pairs of eyes and hands. Also, they tell Dovic about what goes on down on the docks when he isn't theah." She paused and continued. "He's always rubbed me as the shady type to cheat the IRS or have some kind of illegal but profitable side business."

Fina digested that. "You think he's doing criminal stuff? He'd risk all of that, including the potential of getting himself in legal trouble?"

"It wouldn't surprise me." She drained her beer and ordered another.

Fina's blood chilled. "If that's the case, he sure sounds like very unlikable."

"If you enjoy playing in a pit ah cobras, then you'll like him."

CHAPTER 17

Fina arrived fifteen minutes early for her interview with Max. The day before, she spent three hours researching WHS Shipping, writing questions and editing them with Peter. Jitters rattled in her stomach in the elevator. *Please let this go well*, Fina thought of her impending interview. *It's been so long since I've done one. Luckily, we have a common connection: Paige.*

Fina introduced herself to the receptionist, who announced her arrival to Franklin.

"Franklin will be right out. Please, make yourself comfortable." The woman pointed to a velvet couch opposite her desk.

Franklin? "Thank you." Fina lowered herself onto the lush couch.

Only a few minutes passed until Franklin appeared. Fina admired his pink-and-white-checkered shirt. The pale pinkness highlighted his light brown, perfect complexion. He extended a slim hand when Fina stood. "Hello Miss Manzetti. Welcome to WHS Shipping."

"Thank you," she said, shaking his hand. *His skin feels like he just gave it a sugar scrub.*

"Please follow me." He turned and strode down a long hallway, all the way to its end. Fina trotted to keep up.

"Max will be here in a minute. We'll wait in one of the boardrooms," Franklin said.

Her breath left her when she stepped into room. *Holy*

shit! This is the size of our apartment! Admiring the glorious light pouring in through the spotless windows, Fina felt like she was in a glass bubble floating above the city. At her feet lay a massive, intricately patterned dark blue, beige, and sea-green carpet, in her mind the colors evoking a beach. A long, rectangular chestnut table spanned the length of the carpet. Two cream-colored leather chairs were placed under the window.

From behind, Fina heard, "You must be Fina. Hello, I'm Max Dovic."

Snapping out of her trance, Fina whirled around and felt her breath leave her again. *Holy Mother! He looks like an older Christian Bale!* She feared her heart could be seen pounding through her blouse. Fighting the urge to stare, she cleared her throat and thrust out her hand. "Ah, yes I am. Hello Mr. Dovic, it's... It's so nice to meet you."

He gently shook her hand. "Please, call me Max." The lines around his eyes deepened when he flashed Fina a million-dollar smile.

"I will. Thank you for seeing me. I know you're a busy man, so I won't keep you too long."

Max held his eyes to hers before sliding his gaze to Franklin. "Franklin, perhaps Fina would care for a drink of some kind?"

Franklin smiled pleasantly at Fina. "Can I get you anything?"

"I'd love some water, please."

"Sir?"

"Lemon water please, Franklin. Thank you."

Franklin nodded and left.

"Please Fina, have a seat." Max gestured to the two chairs. He took his time examining Fina's assets as she sat down. "We may as well get comfortable."

Franklin returned. "Sir, don't forget you have a lunch meeting at twelve thirty."

"Thanks, Franklin." Turning his attention to Fina, Max asked, "Shall we?"

"To be sure we don't run over, I'm setting the alarm on my watch." She toyed with her digital watch.

Max laughed. "I'm not sure I'm that interesting!"

"Oh, you'd be surprised, trust me. Interviews fly by." She took a notebook from her bag. "Are you ready?"

For a little over an hour, Fina questioned Max about his childhood, and how he became interested in being a shipping broker. She decided to exercise prudence and not mention she and Paige shared an apartment until later.

"I spent many years on the Baltic Sea fishing for cod. Life on a boat was second nature to me. I saw firsthand the global importance of all types of maritime industries—not to mention how profitable they can be."

"It certainly sounds as if you're not afraid of hard work," Fina commented.

Max chuckled under his breath. "Hardly. I've only had myself to rely on my entire life. I've become successful because I've worked hard and been cutthroat at times. Lastly, I learned to surround myself with the right people."

Fina consulted her watch. "We have a few minutes left and I'd like to know—as would the readers—what Max Dovic enjoys doing outside of the office." Pen in hand, she sat ready to note his response.

Max smiled and ran his eyes all over Fina. "I enjoy spending time with lovely women like yourself."

Fina's head snapped up as if someone threw scalding water on her. She stared at Max. *Oh, he's one of these.* Ants crawled over her skin. Without missing a beat, she replied, "Yes, I know you do. You're dating my roommate, Paige

Buckley." She let that settle.

Max's brief yet sharp intake of air tightened the atmosphere. Clearing his throat, he shifted in his seat and flipped his tie. "Your roommate is Paige. How lovely."

Fina lay it on. "I know, isn't it? And I would hasten to add, what a coincidence to be sitting here *with you*." Her gaze bore holes into his face. "She's a great person and you're lucky. I can't wait to tell her I interviewed you."

"Ah yes, she is a charming, intelligent woman. I enjoy spending time with her."

"As you should." She glanced at her notes. "Let's get back to some questions. What do you enjoy doing in your off time?"

"That's the hardest question thus far." He tilted his perfectly styled head and twitched his lips side to side. "I work out regularly with weights followed by an ice bath. As far as sports, I enjoy watching soccer and various professional teams. As far as my own athletic preferences, I occasionally play tennis or squash, followed by a steam—nice and *hot*."

The ants continued their crawl. She consulted her notes. "I see. How about hobbies?"

"Aside from dining out? I enjoy wine tastings. In fact, I prefer to think of myself as a seasoned oenophile. I presume you know what that means?" He pursed his lips.

Oh my God, what a dick. Smiling sweetly she replied, "Yes, I do know. Other hobbies?"

"This should come as no surprise given my past, but I thrive on being out on the open water. It's very liberating."

"How do you mean? Fishing?"

Max chuckled. "No. I mean on my yacht."

"Yacht?" Fina's eyes popped. "How fancy."

"Oh, it is. Trust me." He folded his hands, a smirk

spanning his face.

And he brags. Focus. "Tell me—"

"In fact, I have a wine cellar on my yacht that holds over fifty bottles." He leaned forward in his chair, close enough for Fina to feel the heat from his knees. "In fact, I like to think of myself as having a seasoned, discerning palate, one that can taste all the flavors the world has to offer."

She noted his response. "Paige loves wine. Did you know that?"

"Of course I did. She especially loves Chianti."

Following several more questions, the alarm dinged. *Thank the Lord.* Fina tucked her notebook in her bag and rose. "Thank you for your time, Max. I will have someone from the magazine let you know when the story runs. I'll see myself out."

Max stood. "The pleasure has been all mine. Perhaps our paths will cross again sometime, Serafina. What an *exquisite* name, one not heard often. I just love how it feels to say."

The ants continued their crawl. *Weird.* "I'm sure our paths will cross sooner than later." *Get me out of here.*

A little too quickly, Max offered, "Perhaps we could go out on my yacht sometime. I think you would enjoy it."

"Paige and I would enjoy that. Does she know you own a yacht?"

"It has not come up in conversation. I will see her soon, so I'll set up a date."

Fina gazed at him. "We'd like that."

"Consider it done."

* * *

The train sped along, its speed matching Fina's racing thoughts. Her mind was crammed with thoughts about Max, his relationship with Paige, Lindsey's comments, and her own instincts regarding Max. She laid her head against the window and wrestled with what she was going to tell Paige. *I'll be guarded but tell her the truth. I know she'll ask me as I would her.*

She dragged herself up the stairs and opened the door to their apartment. Its placidity was not unexpected. *I'm glad I have some time to organize my head before Paige asks about the interview.* It was only a little past six and Paige was still at work. *She'll be home in an hour or so. Time for a bath.*

Fina dumped a few shakes of lavender oil into the tub and lowered herself into the hot water. Lying back, she closed her eyes and sank into the tub. She thought again about the interview with Max. *What is about him? He didn't flirt, but it wasn't not a flirt.* Fina decided he was drunk on his own money and power. *Nevertheless, he can't be that good of a guy if he kind of flirted with me.* She decided Paige needed to be warned, yet in a gentle manner.

Soon, the water turned tepid, chilling Fina. She pulled up the stopper and watched the oily water swirl down the drain.

* * *

At the kitchen counter, Fina sprinkled fajita seasoning on chicken tenders. A bright shiny pile of red, yellow, and green peppers sat on a cutting board. Slivers of onions peeked among the slices of peppers.

Paige had left Fina a message she was on her way home, concluded with "I can't wait to hear how the interview went!"

"I'm sure you can't," Fina mumbled.

Around seven Paige walked in and announced she

was starving. "I need to get out of these clothes. I've been wearing them for ten hours. Be right back." Her mood was cheery despite a long day.

Fina opened two beers and turned her attention to cooking and talking to Paige.

"Cheers!" she said when Paige returned. Fina took down half the bottle.

"I'm dying to know how it went with Max!"

Fina gazed at her friend. She rubbed her chin and smiled slightly. "He certainly made for an interesting interview. And you weren't kidding about his background—enthralling." Another swig of beer. "The info I gathered will make for a solid and compelling story."

"I know. Pretty interesting, right? And knowing he doesn't know his parents makes you feel kind of sorry for him, right?"

Not really. "He's a borderline workaholic, wouldn't you say?"

Paige leaned against the counter. "Yes, a hundred percent. As far as I've noticed, it has paid off for him rather well. He's taken me to some great restaurants—and he always pays. I try, but he says no."

And there's the segue. Tell her. "Paige, I got a...how do I say this..." She paused.

Paige frowned at her. "What, Fin?"

"A strange vibe from him. When I asked him what he did for fun, he said something like 'I like to spend time with lovely women, like yourself.'"

Paige cocked her head and rolled her lips inward, sucking her teeth. "Hmm. Did he? And how did you follow that up?"

Fina inhaled and exhaled. "I told him that I knew that because he's dating you, my roommate. And my best friend."

Paige took her beer and sat heavily in the chair. "I'm not sure what to say or think."

Fina joined her at the table. "I'm sorry, Paigey." She took her friend's hand. "I thought it was an unusual thing to say, especially to someone he'd just met. And you needed to know."

Paige looked at Fina and felt a burst of sisterly love and affection. "As hard as this may be to say, you're right. I would have told you too."

"I know. And on the other hand, he simply may have been nervous or trying to make me feel comfortable." Fina shrugged. "Maybe I'm reading too much into it. And remember, I don't know him well."

A lengthy sigh from Paige lingered between the two women. "Maybe yes, may be no. He does like to make people feel comfortable, though. I'll be careful too."

"Well, good." Fina stood to finish preparing dinner. "Oh, and you were right about one thing—he's *really good looking.*"

"I told you!" Paige laughed. "That he is. Oh Fin, are we really *that* shallow?"

"Not at all! Just look at him!" Fina laughed.

Over the fajitas, Paige thanked her friend for telling her. "We have plans for tomorrow night. Do you mind if I ask him how the interview went?"

"Not at all. I'll be curious to hear what he says."

Paige dumped salsa on her plate. "Me too."

Chuckling quietly, Fina could no longer keep it to herself. "Did you know Max has a *yacht*...with a wine cellar?"

Paige's eyes popped. "I do now! With a *wine cellar?*"

"He said he'd set up a time for *all of us* to go on it when you see him again."

"I can't wait! I'll see him tomorrow." Paige sat back down. "A yacht with a wine cellar. I'm impressed."

CHAPTER 18

The evening held a tinge of early spring warmth, even at nine o'clock. Paige and Max exited the gallery after viewing the opening exhibit of New York's newest, most sought-after artists. Paige inhaled deeply and commented on the loveliness of the early spring evening.

"In fact, I think it's so nice that we should have a celebratory drink now that spring is here." She linked her arm through his.

"Grand idea." He kissed her on the head as they walked to a brightly lit bar two blocks away.

Paige's stomach knotted up as she pondered asking Max about the interview. *Keep it light but ask the right questions.* "I understand you met a friend of mine recently." She saw him frown, then a flash of recollection in his face.

He stopped walking and exclaimed, "Yes, *Serafina*! How could I have forgotten? She's a lovely woman who's very good at her job, a real firecracker."

Paige felt the knots loosen up. "Oh she is, trust me. She enjoyed interviewing you. Your background fascinated her."

"I'm happy to hear she took pleasure in our conversation." He took a few steps and stopped. Turning to her, he asked, "Did she tell you *everything* we talked about?"

Paige hesitated. *That's a loaded question.* "Of course she did. She's my best friend." She did not imagine the flicker of uncertainty in his face. His Adam's apple bobbed like a yo-yo. *You need to talk about his interaction with Fina.*

He cleared his throat and began to walk again. "I see. Do you think she'd like to get together with us sometimes? Perhaps a day trip on my yacht?"

"She'd like that and so would I." Paige stole a glance down the sidewalk. *Before you get to the bar, you need to talk about what Fina said.* She took a deep breath. "Max, Fina said something else, something I don't quite understand."

"Hmm? What?" He kept walking.

"Please stop for a minute." She turned to face him. Lifting her eyes, she continued. "She said you mentioned something about 'enjoying spending time with beautiful women, like her.' What did you mean by that, Max? Were you hitting on her?" Her eyes were glue on his face. She did not fail to see the almost imperceptible tiny, lightning-fast puff of his cheeks. *He's grinding his back teeth. Not good.*

Eyes stuck to hers, he told her, "Yes, Paige. I did say that to her. And no, I was not hitting on her. In fact, I was trying to make her feel comfortable as she appeared to be nervous." He took her hands. "I meant it in the most complimentary way. I apologize if I made her—and more importantly *you*—feel as if I was hitting on her. That certainly was not my objective. I'm very sorry for making you question my intentions."

He sounds so sincere. I hope he means what he says. Smiling at him, she said, "Thank you for being honest."

A smile crept over his face. "It appears as if Fina is very protective of you." He continued walking.

"Oh, we always have been of each other. She's the best."

"She is also frank with you, it appears. Is that the only thing she said about me? I certainly hope she doesn't perceive me to be this lecherous, evil villain." He chuckled, but no smile accompanied it.

Is he guilty of hitting on her? It makes sense to make

someone feel comfortable. But in the way he did? He could have denied saying that, but he didn't. And he just apologized. "I'm sure she doesn't. Like you said, she was being protective; best friends do that for one another. And I'm sure she'll understand."

They stood outside the bar. "I hope so. Since we're going to be spending more time together, it's important for her to like and trust me." He took Paige's face in his hands. "Paige, I am a better man for having you in my life. No other woman..." He sniffed and looked away for a second. "...has made me feel like you do."

At his touch, Paige felt a jolt of electricity. She focused on the contour of his soft lips. *He sounds so genuine and he's never emoted like that before.* What Martha told her about Max being a womanizer poked at her out of nowhere. *If he is one, why would he say that about spending time together? And how I make him feel? She and Fina aren't the ones who have been spending time with him. I know him better than they do.*

"I like hearing that."

"Good." His lips were soft on hers. "I think about you all the time. I hope you know that. If I *ever* hurt you..." He stopped and wiped his damp eyes with the back of his hand. "...I would not be able to live with myself."

Oh my gosh, he's crying. She reached to embrace him, but leaped back at the strident scream of a car alarm from the vehicle to their left. Paige clutched her chest and laughed. "That scared the daylights out of me!"

"Me too!" Max put his arm around her. "Let's go have that drink."

At the bar, they clinked glasses and discussed the subtle erotica of the artists' work. "That one artist, Bernie Nation, captured emotion and desire so well without feeling like you're on the set of a porn movie."

Max laughed. "I almost felt like I was in the room with the subjects."

"Yes. It is a true gift to capture such pure emotion and desire." Paige caressed Max's hand with the lightest touch.

He turned on his barstool to face her. Max's eyes smoldered. "It is a true gift to not only capture desire, but to *feel* it." Her thigh was soft and warm under his hand.

Desire overcame any doubts she felt earlier. Paige leaned closer into his caress. "It certainly is," she whispered.

With his hand lightly inching up her thigh, he whispered, "Perhaps you will come back to my place to see where we can hang my new acquisition?" He tossed cash on the bar.

"Oh, I think that's a *wonderful* suggestion."

Max took out his phone and called Andreas.

* * *

Inside Max's penthouse apartment, they wasted no time. Clothing was flung haphazardly onto furniture. Shoes were kicked in all directions.

Paige traced down his chest and gently pushed him against the wall with her finger. Tilting her head up, she kissed him gently at first, until they were overcome with an insatiable desire. He wrapped his arms under her legs and carried her into the kitchen. He sat her on the granite counter, his mouth never leaving hers until she squealed at the cold countertop.

She wrapped her legs around him as he hoisted her from the counter and carried her into his bedroom, the arousal building.

Standing in front of his king-size bed, they kissed deeply and intensely. She fluttered her fingers up and down his heated, muscular back. He groaned when she slid her hand under the waistband of his boxers and caressed his backside, then eventually explored the front.

"I've dreamed of this moment." His voice was husky against her neck. He moved down to her breasts and kissed the top of each one. A soft moan escaped Paige.

"I know," she murmured into his neck; the light aroma of his sandalwood cologne enveloped her. She inhaled his scent, heightening her arousal.

Unhooking her bra, Max took her breasts in his hands and gently ran his tongue over them. Paige immersed herself in the pleasure and ran her fingers through his hair.

"Your body is an exquisite work of art," he murmured.

Paige lay back on the bed and Max gently lowered himself on top of her. He slid his arms under her back and held her tightly as he kissed her. She moaned and wrapped her legs around him. His lips were soft and hot on her neck. He slowly made his way down her body and slipped one finger under the matching lace panties and pulled. He leaned over and traced the muscle above her pelvic bone with his tongue.

Pleasure washed through her. She closed her eyes and lost herself in the perfect sensation.

Without warning, Max suddenly stopped his exploration. He leaned to the side; he moaned, "Oh no."

Paige's eyes flew open. She cast her eyes to Max and bolted upright. Her heart hammered in her chest as Max rocked back and forth, holding his head, moaning. He fell to his side on the bed.

She scrambled to him and placed her hand on his back. "Oh my God, Max! You're pouring sweat!"

He lifted his head. Paige's inner alarm system resounded throughout her body when she saw his colorless face.

"Oh my God, what's wrong?" She grasped his arm which was also covered with perspiration. But his skin was ice.

He closed his eyes and puffed out his cheeks. "I'm...I'm diabetic...and...my blood sugar is too low. I need something...right now," he whispered. "In the refrigerator...there is a...bottle...of orange juice. Can you please get it?" He fell back down on the bed, his body coated in a gleaming film of perspiration.

Paige shot up and ran to the kitchen. She yanked open the door, took the juice, and ran back to the bedroom.

"Here!" She thrust out the bottle to Max. He took two deep slugs and collapsed back onto the bed.

"Do you need more juice?" Panic was thick in her voice. "Max!"

Max's eyelids fluttered. He said nothing. Sweat glistened on his chest. He was still.

"Max!" Paige was on the verge of vomiting. She shook him.

Nothing. Seconds ticked by, turning into minutes.

Panic raced like a wild animal. "Max! *Say something!*" She smacked his face.

Slowly, Max opened his eyes.

Paige saw they were glazed; he frowned in confusion.

"What's going on?" he stammered. "Why am I in bed?"

"I think you passed out!"

Dazed, he frowned at Paige. "Did you...get me...this?" He gestured to the orange juice.

"You don't remember?"

He frowned and stared at the wall across the room. "I remember kissing in the hall and coming to bed. Then not feeling right."

"You seem better now. Are you feeling more normal?"

Max pushed himself up to a sitting position and took

Paige's hand. He kissed it and apologized profusely. "Yes, I am. I'm sorry I scared you. Sometimes my blood sugar has a mind of its own and takes a deep dive." He laid back on the pillows. He cast his eyes to the ceiling. "I feel awful about disappointing you."

"Max, stop. You didn't disappoint me at all. You did scare me to death, though."

"I'm sorry. It's been quite a while since my sugars dropped so quickly." He looked at her and added, grinning, "It's all *your* fault, making all the blood rush to the little head!"

Paige giggled. "I have that effect on men!" She rubbed his chest and added, "I don't know much about diabetes." She lifted the bottle and asked if he needed the rest.

"No, no. I don't need to go into hyperglycemic mode; hypoglycemic is enough for one night!" He laughed. "But would you mind putting the rest of the juice back in the fridge?"

"Be right back."

When she returned, Max had gotten under the covers and indicated for her to join him.

She lay down next to him and folded herself into his warm skin. He stroked her hair and joked, "I'm not as perfect as you think I am."

"Neither am I. Don't forget, I'm half-blind!" She pointed at her right eye. "We make a great couple!"

"Touché." A sleepy laugh came from him. He yawned. "I'm a little embarrassed."

She rubbed his arm. "It's not your fault. I'm glad I was here to help you."

"So am I. " He let out another enormous yawn. "Excuse me. When a sugar crash is so severe, it exhausts me."

"Then you need to sleep."

"Yes, I do. I will make this up to you, I promise."

Paige shushed him, turned out the light, and laid her head on Max's chest.

CHAPTER 19

Somewhere in her subconscious, Paige sensed water running. Sleep still held her brain in its clutch until the sound of water grew louder. Rolling over, she saw Max's side of the bed was empty. She flipped her legs over the edge of Max's bed and padded to the bathroom.

Outside the glass wall protecting a massive shower, she stood and watched Max through the steam. His eyes were closed; his face radiated health and serenity. She smiled as she watched the hot water run over his hairless chest, rippled stomach, and taut thighs. Her body was soon fully awake.

She removed her bra and panties and opened the door. Through the thick cloud of steam, she stepped into the shower.

Max cast his eyes to her and said, "I was hoping you were going to join me."

Sliding her eyes down his body, she replied, "I can tell. And I'm glad you're feeling better."

He held out his arms. She stepped through the steam into his dripping arms. Max kissed her intensely as hot water from the massive shower head cascaded over them. Steam enveloped them in a sensuous swirl. His low, soft moan floated through the splashing of water as she ran her hands up and down his slick back.

He turned her around and let the water caress her back. He kissed her shoulders, reached in front of her, and gently caressed her breasts with the grapefruit-scented body wash. A sigh slipped from her lips, originating from deep inside. Paige closed her eyes and rested her head back on his chest. She breathed heavily as she was swept into the head-spinning sensation of the slick body wash, warm water, and Max's hard body pressing into her.

His hands inched further down her slick body and explored all of her. She gasped at his light, gentle touch. Her heart raced; her body flushed with heat. She slowly swished her hips back and forth against him. Max held her hips and swayed with her. "I have to have you."

Paige turned around. His mouth was hot on hers. She pulled back. "Yes." She gazed up at Max whose eyes burned with desire. Locking her arms around his neck, he lifted her, legs wrapped around him. He carried her to his bed.

As one, they fell onto the rumpled sheets. The sensation of skin on skin, the scent of freshly washed hair intensified their longing. She stroked his hair, caressed his back. His moans excited her. Gripping him, she locked her legs around his waist.

Max wrapped his arms around her as he entered her. A soft intake of breath. A small, faint moan escaped from him. They moved together in heated, feverish rhythm. Paige gripped his tightened glutes and pressed him deeper into her. Their heated bodies meshed perfectly. He pushed himself up on his arms, the angle touching Paige with the perfect amount of pressure.

Breaths came in ragged pants; sensual moans echoed in the once-silent bedroom. Max collapsed on top of her, out of breath. She ran her hands up and down his smooth back. They basked in the warm blanket of sex.

She laughed. "Pretty damn good for our first time."

"I'll say. I'm sure we'll be better the second time, don't you?"

Paige rolled over on top of him. "There's only one way to find out."

* * *

They lay tracing one another's bodies, dreamy smiles on their faces.

"I don't know about you, but I'm glad we tried a second time," he said.

"As the old saying goes, 'practice makes perfect,'" she giggled.

"And we have plenty of time to practice!" Max flipped his legs over the bed and padded to the bathroom. A few minutes later he reappeared. "Hungry?"

"Oh yes."

Over breakfast, Paige asked him about being a diabetic.

Max sipped his coffee and replaced his cup on the fine saucer. "Medically speaking, it means that my pancreas does not produce insulin any longer. And since that's the case, I need to use this." From his robe pocket, he pulled what looked like a thick pen about eight inches in length.

"A pen?" She frowned and tilted her head.

"More or less. It's full of insulin which I inject before each meal. This is a short-acting type of insulin to break down sugars in the food. I take a longer-acting type every night which helps to keep my sugar levels steady, and the same in the morning."

Paige digested all this and silently added up the number of injections each day. *Five. Wow.* "So you inject *five times a day*?"

Max nodded.

"Is it painful?"

"At first, yes. But like anything else, you get used to it."

"I knew that diabetes was related to sugar, right?"

"In a nutshell, I basically don't eat sugars and carbohydrates—unless I have a crash."

Paige felt a stab of sympathy for him. She processed this. "Oh wow, there are so many foods you can't eat. Pasta, bread, cereal, *pizza!*"

"You are correct. But I'm happy to say that hard liquor is relatively carb and sugar free. I'll take it!"

"So there is a silver lining!" She laughed. "But last night, your sugar got really low. And the orange juice helped you. How?"

"When I'm that low, I need an instant sugar boost and anything like juice or soda will bring me back very quickly—or I could slip into a coma. Sometimes it just happens. And *any* physical activity I engage in—including what we did last night—affects my sugars too. It's all about keeping my sugar levels in check."

"I'm glad I know how to help if it happens again."

Max nodded. "Let change the subject to something more uplifting, such as planning for my birthday celebration on the yacht."

CHAPTER 20

M AY

"Oh! They're *beautiful!*" Paige exclaimed as the florists carrying the numerous potted orchids onto the *Baltic Blue* followed the directions of Captain Brennan. Paige marveled at the deep purple, creamy-white speckled with pink and shocking yellow shades of her favorite flower. *Perfect for an intimate birthday party.*

Paige boarded the yacht and headed toward the stern where Max's stateroom was located. Inside her bag was his birthday gift, one that she knew he would love. Opening the door to the room, she extracted the gift, a specially made crystal figurine of the yacht. Paige admired the detail. Its sharp edges and clean lines held light so that the figurine seemed to glow from within. She wrapped it carefully and signed his birthday card.

Where should I put it so he sees it right away? The bureau on which Max always placed his keys, watch, and money clip sat across from her, its top naked except for an old-fashioned clock ticking away the seconds.

Perfect. She placed the box on the bureau and slipped out. As she walked down the passageway, something protruding from under a cabin door caught her eye. Walking closer, she saw it was part of a runner from inside the cabin.

Sparing the cleaning crew Max's wrath if he saw it, Paige opened the door and saw she was right—a corner of the runner had somehow been pushed under the door.

Grabbing it, she slid it back in place. When she stood, she looked around the room and realized it was not like the other cabins. *I don't think I've ever been in here.* No bed. No dressers. Several recessed lights formed a circle around a large round light fixture embedded in the ceiling.

What looked like a mobile massage table stood in the center of the room, half of it draped in a white sheet. Having never seen this room, curiosity got the best of her. She closed the door and walked to the table. Lifting the other half of the sheet, Paige saw a slice of foam the same dimensions as the table resting on top. A corner of the foam was askew, exposing what lay underneath.

Paige reached down and touched it. Immediately she yanked her hand away. The chill of the table surprised her. *What the hell is this? Maybe Max likes a firm table?* Glancing around, she saw a small, rolltop desk sitting opposite the table. Nothing was placed on top of it. *What a cool little desk!* Grasping the two brass knobs, Paige rolled the top open. Pens, a blank legal pad, and pencils sat in neat rows inside. Opening a drawer, she saw a folder with *Baltic Blue* written on the front. *Owner's papers, I guess.* She closed the desk and exited the room to the passageway, but she did not get far. She yelped when she almost bumped into Captain Brennan.

He loomed in the passageway. "Miss Buckley. What are you doing in there?" He pointed to the cabin.

"Hi, Captain. I was just dropping off something of for Max, his birthday present."

From under the brim of his white captain's hat, his eyes bore into hers. "No. Not his stateroom. What were you doing in *that* cabin?" He pointed at the cabin door.

Paige threw a quick glance at the door. "Oh, there was something sticking out from under the door. I put it back."

Captain Brennan closed the ten-foot gap between them

with three strides. "And what was it?"

"Part of a rug was sticking out. You know how Max likes everything just so."

"I see. Miss Buckley," he said, his tone hushed, yet with a hint of warning, "please *do not* go into that cabin. Ever again." He took out a ring of keys and locked the door from the outside. Placing the keys in his pocket, he turned. "You don't belong in there."

Paige stared at him in disbelief. *What am I, a child being scolded?* "What do you mean, I don't belong in there?"

A scowl sliced across his brow. In his clipped, chilled manner of speaking, he replied, "This cabin is not for guests. Mr. Dovic—as well as his associates, including some of the crew—use it for business and personal reasons."

Personal reasons? She challenged him, "What do you mean, personal reasons?"

A cloud of anger slid over his face. He continued to stare at her, ignoring her question. "I advise you to stay out." He turned to leave, but before he did, he said, "Do I make myself clear?" Nodding at her, he turned and left.

A small shift in the air covered Paige in a heavy chill. Her stomach felt scooped out and acidic. Bewildered, she watched him disappear into the dark passageway. *What the hell was that all about? Why would he warn me not to go into that cabin ever again if it's an office? Is he hiding something?* She lingered in the passageway for a few minutes. Glancing back at the cabin door, she tucked away the warning from Brennan and returned to the party.

* * *

After an elegant dinner and endless champagne, Max and the remaining guests sat around the table discussing business.

Paige excused herself and took advantage of the moment. On the bow of the *Baltic Blue*, she took in the night air, hoping to clear her head of the champagne bubbles. The party was a success even though the warning from the captain played in her mind all evening. The stillness of the evening air was soothing, but her thoughts returned to that cabin. *What is in that room? After what Brennan said, I need to find out.*

Feeling emboldened by the champagne, Paige stole down to the room. Taking a longer route, she tiptoed past the bridge and saw Captain Brennan and the crew eating a late dinner. *Perfect.*

Removing her heels, Paige dimmed the light and skittered down the passageway to the cabin. Convinced the door would be locked, she was surprised to see it was cracked open. A thin strip of light spread across the passageway floor. *Who's in there?* Even more surprising was that she heard voices. Inching closer, she heard snippets of conversation floating from the cabin. The intense whispering continued. She closed her eyes to concentrate.

"The doc will...extra time..."

"...order needs to...soon! There's...ton of money..."

"Okay, calm down. I'll see her...yes...then..."

"...she's a perfect...so don't fuck this up."

"You need...bring her...boat."

"And it needs to be done here..."

"...Max'll freak if this..."

Paige suddenly sobered up as a chill ran from the base of her skull down to her toes. Her heart hammered in her chest. *That's Stu and Marty in there. What're they talking about and who is the "her"?* She crept closer to the door with the hopes of catching a glimpse of them. Peering around the door, she saw Stu and Marty standing by the folding table, their backs to her. Their conversation stopped.

What sounded like paper being brushed together filled the silence. She could see their hands moving and heard them quietly counting. When Stu stepped away from the table, Paige gasped at what she saw. Never had she seen so much cash before in her life. *What in the world?*

CHAPTER 21

Max's snoring was loud and guttural. Paige lay next to him, wide awake. *Too much champagne. The snoring won't stop and I won't sleep.* Glancing at the clock radio, she saw it was close to four o'clock. Sighing, she slid out of bed, took a robe from the chair, and walked up to the stern.

Night air wrapped her in its coolness. Stars danced and twinkled above. The white night lights of the *Baltic Blue* leaped out in bright contrast against the darkness surrounding them. *What a beautiful night.* She tightened the robe and relished in the serenity of the pre-dawn stillness. It did not last long.

Voices carried over the water. *What the hell? It's four in the morning.* She turned to the portside of the boat where she saw two men on the dock, roughly three slips down, speaking. Whoever it was spoke too quietly to hear properly.

She saw movement. *Is that a wheelbarrow?* She struggled to see who it was, and covered her right eye to help. *Having one good eye sucks!* She could not see a face until the person passed under a dock light. She inhaled sharply as the man's face was illuminated. It was Brennan. And he was pushing a wheelbarrow loaded with large white jugs.

What's he doing out here right now and what's with the wheelbarrow and jugs?

Brennan carefully placed the jugs in the bottom of the motorboat. He was joined by another person who turned the small motorboat in Paige's direction. She ducked behind an upright lounge chair and watched.

Without a word, Brennan and the man unloaded the white jugs onto the yacht. Afterward, Paige saw him nod and shake hands with the unknown person. Brennan produced an envelope from his jacket pocket and hand it to the other person.

Money? This is really strange. It's the middle of the night.

With one hand on the railing to help guide her back down below, Paige hustled back to the stateroom. Max's snoring was still deep and undisturbed. She crawled back into bed, knowing sleep was out of the question. Various scenarios ran through her mind trying to rationalize what she witnessed, but she kept returning to the same thing. She could only deduce Brennan was involved in drug dealing or smuggling.

What's in the jugs? Does Max know? I don't care what Brennan said, I need to tell Max what I saw. Tomorrow.

Closing her eyes, she breathed deeply and wished for sleep.

* * *

By nine the next morning, Paige and Max had roused from the dead. They lay in the warm king bed, eyes still closed, legs entwined. Paige reached out and stroked his stubbly face. She asked how he was feeling.

"As if a drumline was practicing in my head." Max moaned and rolled onto his back.

"I'm sure. I'll get you some water." Paige went to the bathroom and filled the crystal glass that sat on the sink.

"Thank you, love." Max sat up and sipped eagerly. "That helps. I haven't drank that much champagne in a long time. I now remember why I don't."

Paige laughed. "It was a wonderful party and everyone had a fantastic time."

"I'm glad to hear it. I remember most of it, but I don't remember going to bed. Thank you for helping me."

"You're welcome." She rose and began to dress. "What you need is a big, greasy breakfast. I'll tell Chef."

Max turned adoring eyes onto her. "You're an angel."

* * *

After plates of eggs and bacon and countless cups of potent coffee, Max and Paige enjoyed a day on the super yacht. Clear blue skies and calm waters were forecasted. Only the two of them were aboard, aside from the crew who only surfaced when summoned.

As the sun started its journey to the other side of the world, Max and Paige stood on the bow and absorbed the beauty of New York City and her landmarks. Since they were alone, she knew it was the best time to talk to Max about Brennan.

"Feeling more human?" she asked him.

"Oh God yes. How're you feeling? You seem quiet."

"I'm tired, but not because of a hangover." She turned to him. "Max, I saw something kind of strange early this morning."

His eyebrows knit together in a frown. "You did? What was it, love?"

"Since *someone* was snoring," she said, jabbing him lightly in the ribs, "I was wide awake so I got up. I was out on the stern, enjoying the night, when I heard voices about three slips down. I saw Brennan pushing a *wheelbarrow* full of jugs that he and someone else brought back to the yacht."

Max blinked and gave her a smile. "Jugs you say?"

She nodded.

"Were they white?"

"Yes."

He grinned at her. "What a little detective you are! Ah. I believe what you saw was a delivery of hydraulic fluid for the yacht. As you can imagine, we need a great deal of it to run her."

"Yeah, but at *four* in the morning? That's odd, Max."

"It is, but not unusual. People in the delivery business need to get an early start, especially during the season."

Paige pondered this. *That makes sense...I suppose. More importantly, I need to tell him about the cabin.* "There's more, though."

"Yes?" He turned all the way to face her.

She heard the minute shift in his tone; his frown tightened. *He's not going to like this, but he has to know.* After she finished telling him about Brennan's warning and about Stu and Marty counting vast amounts of cash, he looked out over the water.

"I suppose I should have told you sooner, but I didn't think it mattered." He sighed.

"What are talking about?"

"I know Captain Brennan is...shall I say, a bit *odd*. I've known him a long time and part of the reason why I hired him is because he's a true perfectionist—to the point of being strange. That cabin he mentioned is off limits for guests because it *is* only for my personnel—including the crew—not guests."

"But what did he mean by personal reasons?"

Max gazed at her with an eyebrow cocked. "And may I ask why you are *so* interested? Have you *never* needed a spot to conduct personal business?"

He sounds impatient—defensive almost. Her skin pricked

with unexpected goosebumps. She was caught off guard by Max challenging her.

She chose to ignore his question. "Well, thinking back on it, he practically admonished me as you would a child. I suppose it was more his tone of voice than what he said. And frankly, Max, I didn't appreciate the tone."

"I see. Keep in mind, Paige, the man was doing his job. He's a rule follower and a protective sort of individual. He's also keenly aware that I like things just so. And if I have to conduct business, I need a quiet space. Is that *so difficult* to understand?"

She saw how hard his eyes became. *He's defending Brennan! Let it go, Paige.* Changing the conversation to Stu and Marty, she asked, "And Stu and Marty were counting enormous stacks of cash because…?" She gazed at him. "Lots of cash."

She did not imagine the almost undetectable ephemeral stiffening of his body as he quickly replied, "Hydraulic fluid is expensive and our supplier takes *only* cash. A tip is included as well for the delivery. Therefore, it makes sense to keep some cash on board to *pay* our vendor." Turning away from her, he sighed and gazed out at the water. "Are you satisfied *now*, Paige?"

Paige stared at his profile; an unshakable feeling of dread spread throughout her. *What was that all about? Why would he get so defensive about how he pays for hydraulic fluid? It's abnormal. I've never heard him be so angry.*

A few minutes passed as Paige digested what he told her. *I've pushed enough.* She said nothing because there was nothing to say.

As the yacht slowly cruised past the Statue of Liberty, he stared at it and commented, "Isn't she spectacular?"

CHAPTER 22

Paige was crawling out of her skin to call Fina and tell her what she saw and heard on the yacht. All the events of the prior evening bothered her like an unseen gnat buzzing near her ear. *I need to talk to Fina, but I can't. It's not the time*, she thought after listening to Fina's message that Nana Gambone was "slipping quickly." Paige called her back. To her surprise, Fina answered.

"I'm so sorry, Fin. I wish I could do more. When will you be back?"

"Tomorrow. I'll need a drink—or seven." She let out a breath of air. "I'll meet you at Chub's by six. I gotta go."

"Yes. Love you. Call if you need me."

In a tired voice Fina replied, "Love you too and I will."

* * *

At Chub's, Paige made herself comfortable at the bar. Hunger pangs seized her a few minutes later. Earlier in the day, she had eaten a banana, but nothing else. She perused the artery-clogging menu and settled on loaded potato skins. Fina arrived after the potato skins were placed in front of her.

From behind Paige heard, "Those look so good!" Paige shot from her stool and hugged her friend tightly. "I'm so happy you're back! I have so much to tell you. But first, sit down and help me eat these."

Fina fell onto the stool. "I'm so tired and glad to be home." She lugged her bag up and dropped it on the bar.

"Taking care of your grandmother was a lot of work huh?" Paige asked.

"Oh yeah." She chomped on a potato skin. "And Mom is a mess."

"Sorry to hear that. But I've got the perfect fix for you." Paige raised her hand to get the bartender's attention. "Two house whites, and keep them coming."

Paige and Fina chatted about Fina's grandmother and any news from the old neighborhood, work, and eventually the conversation turned to Max. Paige smiled. "Things are okay with him. We were out on the yacht this weekend."

Fina's head snapped around. "Lucky you! But why only okay?" She looked closely at Paige and knew something was not right. "Hey, are you okay?" She touched Paige's arm. "You don't sound too thrilled."

Paige took a deep breath and was about to tell Fina about her conversation with Captain Brennan and what she saw in the cabin, but she was stopped.

"Hey! Fancy meetin' you heah!" Martha clapped Paige on the shoulder.

"Hey Martha!" Paige stood up and gave Martha a warm hug. She turned to Fina. "This is my best friend and roommate, Fina."

"Nice to meet ya. This is my friend Lindsey," Martha gestured to Lindsey.

"We already know each other!" Fina waved her hand between herself and Lindsey. "She helped me with a photoshoot, well two shoots actually. Good to see you again."

"Yeah, you too," Lindsey replied.

"Nice to meet you, Lindsey," Paige said.

"You guys wanna grab a table?" Martha asked.

Paige cut her eyes to Fina, who happily agreed before Paige could reply. *Damn. I really need to talk to Fina.*

Martha motioned to a table by the door where they all took a seat. "It's closah to the outside so we can catch a smoke."

"Sure." Fina and Paige took the potato skins and their drinks to the other table. Once seated, they figured out how they were all connected.

"Crazy how we all know each other," Fina commented.

"That six degrees of separation thing is true," Lindsey agreed. She regaled the table with how she came from a large family and everyone everywhere always seemed to know someone from her family. "Even when I moved heah, people knew relatives ah mine. Crazy shit!" She turned to Martha. "You ready for a smoke?"

"Yeah."

"These guys are so much fun!" Fina exclaimed. "I'll hang out with them any time!"

Paige turned to Fina and grasped her arm. "I need to tell you something about the yacht."

"Okay. First though, I really need to go to the bathroom!" Fina dashed to the back of the bar and into the ladies' room.

Paige shook her head and picked at a potato skin. A waft of air from outside blew in, glancing off Paige's face. Finished with their smoke, Paige saw Martha and Lindsey open the door, laughing about something.

Fina returned and plunked down in her seat. "Okay, what's up with Max's yacht?"

Martha and Lindsey exchanged a wary glance. "Max's yacht?" Lindsey echoed, looking at Paige with trepidation. She leaned forward. "Do you mean *Max Dovic's* yacht?" She narrowed her eyes at Paige.

An unseen void abruptly engulfed the once-cheery

ambiance as all eyes came to rest on Paige. Redness popped on her neck and crept up to her face. "Yes, yeah I do." She downed the rest of her wine and glanced pleadingly at Fina.

"You guys want another drink?" Fina asked. "But hold any discussion about the yacht!"

Eyeballing their drinks, no one said a word.

"I'm buying," Fina tempted.

Paige piped up first. "God yes. I'll have another!"

"I'll take another Jamison on the rocks." Lindsey rattled the ice in her glass.

"Any lite beer for me."

Fina returned. "We're all ears."

"Okay, here's what happened on the yacht." Paige captivated them with everything she saw and heard on the day of Max's birthday and the early morning after.

"At *four* in the morning the captain was getting hydraulic fluid?" Lindsey asked. She pursed her lips and shook her head.

"According to Max, yes. He said that it can be delivered at all hours of the day or night."

Lindsey cut her eyes to Paige over her bottle. "In my thirty-plus years of being on boats, I've never had a delivery at that time of day. That's fuckin' weird."

"I think so too. It also a tad sounds underhanded," Fina added. "And this is what Max told you, right?"

Paige nodded. "I saw the jugs with my own eyes," she added defensively.

Lindsey waved that off. "But four in the morning? Are we sure it's hydraulic fluid?"

Fina chirped in, "More intriguing, though, is why Captain Brennan warned you about that room. And then you see Stu and Marty in there counting stacks of cash in the same place."

Martha piped up, "Yeah, what the hell is that about? And that table?"

Paige shrugged. "As far as the table, Max gets a weekly massage so it would not be out of the realm of possibilities that he has a massage table on the yacht." She added how Max admitted that Brennan was odd and protective. "Brennan admonished me like a kid. He also said that Max, his personnel, and the crew use that room for personal reasons too. Max said he uses it to work."

"Personal reasons? What the hell is that about? Something's wrong with that. To me, it sounds like Brennan is trying to hide something," Martha said. "Especially with that warning."

"Did you ask Max about it?" Lindsey said.

"Yes, and his response was one I wasn't really expecting." Her voice trailed off. She looked down at her lap.

Lindsey, Fina and Martha traded worried glances.

"Which was…?" Fina prodded.

Paige sighed and looked at her friends. "He was pissed. When I asked about the personal reasons, he became defensive and asked why I was so interested."

Silence fell over the table. Paige swallowed the rest of her wine and sat back in her chair.

"I want to hear more about this money. You're tellin' me that you saw stacks and stacks of cash on the boat?" Lindsey asked.

"Yes. I saw Marty and Stu in one of the cabins counting cash. Stacks of it. Max said he keeps it on board to pay for the fluid in cash. Apparently, his vendor takes *only* cash. I wish you guys could have heard his tone of voice."

Martha asked her to try to describe it.

"I'd say angry, impatient, and dismissive. Like it was a normal thing. I also heard snatches of a strange conversation between Stu and Marty." She did her best to retell what she heard.

Fina turned to Lindsey and asked if she knew Captain Brennan. "Yeah, but not well. I know he's been *Baltic Blue*'s captain for a couple of years. Word on the docks is that he does anything Dovic demands."

The women sat for a while and mulled over their discussion. When the server returned, Lindsey ordered another round and commented again on the fluid. "Here's the thing. Since that fluid was delivered in the dead of night, I wonder if Dovic is getting it on the black market?"

"That's a possibility. And as we all know, that's illegal," Martha said. "Sorry, Paige."

Paige let out an audible sigh. "Great."

Fina grabbed Paige's hand. "We don't know *for sure* he's using the black market. Has Max ever given you a reason to not believe him about anything?" Fina asked.

"To this point, no. But the amount of money I saw was shocking. At the time, I didn't ask him where he got all of it. And now I can't help but wonder where he *did* get it."

"Since he's a rich guy, he'd probably have cash all over, right?" Martha put in.

"Yes, but why on board? I don't think he's buying *that* much hydraulic fluid," Lindsey replied. "I still smell bullshit."

Martha sighed, absorbing her friends' theories. "Two things aren't sitting well with me. One, how Brennan warned you," she said, pointing to Paige, "the cabin is off limits because Max does business and personal things in theah. Two, the fact that Max became irritated when you asked about the cash."

Paige piped up, "Maybe he uses some of that cash to pay the crew?"

Fina added with a salacious smile, "Maybe Marty, Stu,

and Brennan are using his boat to do something illegal, like drug dealing! That might explain the cash."

Three pairs of eyes flew at Fina.

"Whoa, I was *kidding*, ladies! Well, kind of."

Lindsey started, "But what—"

Clink! Clink! Crash! The women whipped around, hearts racing at the earth-shattering crash from behind the bar.

"What was that?" Martha yelled as all four popped up from their seats to see a server sprawled on the ground, sitting in a pool of beer, hugging his ankle.

"Hey kid, you okay?" Lindsey asked.

He waved her off. "Yeah, fine. Slipped on something." Another bartender lifted him up and cleaned up the mess. "We're all fine. Sorry about the noise."

Martha picked up a few shards of glass and put them in a napkin. After placing them on the bar, she nudged Lindsey. "You ready for a smoke?"

"Yeah." Turning to Paige and Fina, she said, "Don't go anywhere."

"We won't." Paige pointed at her and Fina's drinks. "We have all this to finish."

* * *

Outside Chub's, the air was heavy with the aroma of years of fried grease and cigarette smoke. Fiery orange dots from others' cigarettes bounced in the dark night. Exhales and laughter from others enjoying a smoke filled the humid evening air.

Lindsey bent over to light her Tiparillo from Martha's antique silver lighter. "Somethin's goin' on with that boat and money," she said and simultaneously blew a stream of smoke from the corner of her mouth. "I know it."

"No doubt. I don't trust fuckin' Dovic as far as I can throw 'im." Martha let loose a trail of smoke into the air.

"I know. I feel bad saying this in front ah Paige, but I don't trust him either."

Martha nodded. "I can find out more about Dovic." She held out her hands as if she was typing on a computer.

"Yes. I'll do some digging at the harbor; there're lots ah ears down there."

CHAPTER 23

Andreas waited for Max and Paige outside Max's building in the early afternoon. On the way to the marina, Max placed a call to the captain of his yacht.

"Captain Brennan, it's Max." He switched the phone to his other ear and continued. "I want your assurance that my yacht is pristine in all ways. I expect to see my reflection in the handrails on deck. There should be enough Dom Perignon and caviar to last the evening as well as all the other food I ordered. If my expectations are not met, there will be consequences." He hung up.

Paige turned and stared at him. "Don't you think you were a little harsh?"

Max threw her a look. "I pay my crew handsomely and I expect to see *my* yacht the way I want it. Is there something *wrong* with that?"

"Of course not. However, there are ways to make your point without sounding like you own them."

"Oh Paige, you are so adorable. There's so much you don't understand. In some ways, as a matter of fact, I *do* own those people. What I pay them allows them to have a life that is only a dream to most." His smug smile made Paige want to smack it from his face.

Whoa. She turned around and faced him. "Where did *that* come from? How patronizing of you to speak to me like that." She slid away from him. "All I'm trying to say is that there's a more human, less demanding way to speak to the people who do so much for you."

Max's eyes went at her like a vulture. "Do you think I've made it this far being *soft*? How dare you question the way *I* speak to *my* employees."

Frigid fingers of fear inched up Paige's spine. An uneasy, suffocating silence hovered in the car. She glanced up to catch Andreas's eye in the rear-view mirror. The faint shake of his head and cautionary expression spoke volumes.

"Why are you so on edge?"

Max said nothing at first. His face warmed; his eyes did not. "You're right. I'm sorry. I'm ah, a bit upset about a business deal that went awry earlier this morning."

Paige rotated around to face him. "While I'm sorry about the deal, I'm not your verbal punching bag, Max. It's the Fourth of July. Why are you doing business today anyway?"

He sighed and took her hand. "Again, I'm sorry." He lifted her hand and kissed it. "As far as business, it's not an international holiday. A deal fell through with a foreign entity. I was counting on a handsome payday."

Several blocks rolled by until Paige spoke. "How about we focus on enjoying the Fourth of July celebration? Forget about this morning."

* * *

Paige took in the gleaming white yacht in the slip. Its beauty never ceased to amaze her. Water lazily lapped at the hull, and thick white mooring lines wrapped around cleats kept her still. Paige blinked twice to make sure it was not a mirage. The afternoon sun bounced from the spotless polished handrails. *I've never noticed how big she is. This has to be at least 110 feet.* She turned to Max, sharing her estimate.

"You do have a wonderful head for numbers. You are correct."

Paige's eye roamed the rest of the yacht. *Baltic Blue* was emblazoned on the bottom half of the stern in bold black letters. A full-size American flag rippled in the gentle breeze at the bow. On deck, the crew of *Baltic Blue* stood at attention, dressed in the customary black and whites. It was not lost on Paige that the three female members of the crew were poured into their short black pencil skirts and breast-hugging white tops. *Typical.*

One of the women, who resembled a Victoria's Secret model, held a gleaming silver tray with two flutes of champagne. The breeze tossed around the ends of her raven hair. Not a line or blemish marred her mocha complexion.

"Champagne?" she asked in an exotic accent Paige could not place.

"Thank you." Paige took the flutes and handed one to Max.

"Welcome aboard, Mr. Dovic and Miss Buckley," the captain greeted them. His close-set eyes lingered on Paige. "You will be pleased to know that the *Baltic Blue* is stocked with everything you requested."

"Excellent. We anticipate the guests to arrive starting at six this evening," Max said, sipping the champagne and eyeing the women. "As the itinerary states, we will have chilled cocktails prepared at that time, with dinner at eight thirty."

"Yes, sir. Chef is preparing an exquisite dinner." The captain turned to Paige. "Miss Buckley, may I show you to your and Mr. Dovic's cabin? It has been redone in the past few weeks."

"Really, Max? It's different?"

Max nodded. "It needed it."

"Yes please. Thank you."

The opulence of the yacht always made Paige feel as if she was in a movie. Gleaming light wood floors shone proudly. Walking past a fitness area, Paige saw two treadmills and three elliptical machines facing the bow. Cutting through the main dining area, Paige stole a glance and marveled at the lustrous cherry table surrounded by ecru leather chairs.

The master suite glowed in warm ambers, comforting creams, and splashes of forest green. A king bed faced the stern. On it were two plush white cashmere robes. Windows allowed for a breathtaking view of the river.

"Sir, I think you will find everything to your satisfaction," the captain said.

Max nodded and dismissed Brennan, who bowed respectfully and left.

"Max, this is beyond beautiful. It's so different from before! I've never seen anything like it." She stood in the middle of the room, turning in small circles to absorb the lavishness. "This rug feels as if I'm walking on a down pillow."

"Anything for you Paige, anything." He took her in his arms and held her tightly. "I'm very sorry about my severe tone earlier. I took my frustrations out on you. You deserve better. I simply want everything to be perfect—especially for you." He stroked her face and kissed her passionately. Pressing himself against her, he rubbed her gently.

Breathless excitement swept over her and she kissed him hungrily. His hair was soft in her fingers. "We have time," she whispered and gently pushed him down on the bed.

"Yes, we do." Desire lit his eyes as he watched her strip off her clothes. She straddled him and undid the silver buckle of his alligator belt and unzipped his shorts.

"Take them off," she ordered before rolling onto her back.

"Yes ma'am, with pleasure." Max stood and dropped his clothing on the floor.

Paige saw he was ready and gave him a sly smile and purred, "I've never had sex on a yacht."

"Allow me to help to welcome you on your maiden voyage."

Kneeling at the foot of the bed, he caressed her smooth calves with his warm hands. Leaning forward, he kissed her tenderly on her inner thighs and gently stroked her. Laying back, she ran her fingers through his hair as he teased her.

"Lie down." Her voice was husky. "Now."

"With pleasure," Max obeyed.

Paige rolled over on top of him and slowly lowered herself, taking him in. Closing her eyes, she tossed her head back and rocked back and forth, fully consumed. Slowly leaning forward, she gripped the pillow Max rested his head on and clutched him tightly between her thighs. The rest of the world fell away as she kept up her rhythm.

"Oh! Oh Paige!" Max's hands were hot on her thighs; his grip left marks in her skin. In perfect sync, he moved with her as they were swept away in a tsunami, pure and primal.

Paige threw her head back, drowning in the passion. She dug her nails into Max's chest until the wave crested and dissipated. Panting, she collapsed onto Max's damp chest. They lay in damp sensual solitude until Paige giggled.

"What's so funny?" Max asked.

She sat up and gazed at him. "We brought the Fourth of July in with a real *bang!*"

"We certainly did." Max laughed and kissed her on the head. "Shall we?" He rose and retrieved his discarded clothing.

* * *

Cocktails flowed. Hors d'oeuvres were passed. Laughter and conversation filled the air. Max's yacht soon filled with guests dressed in the proverbial colors of the nation's 225th birthday.

Fina and Paige stood on the bow of the yacht, absorbing the celebratory ambiance of the evening. Fina, who had arrived after Paige and Max, stood in awe of the boat. "This thing is unbelievable, Paige! And just look at the views of the city! I feel like I'm a princess!"

The lapping of water against the *Baltic Blue* was a steady soft beat. A slight breeze carried the scent of grilling food and rippled the hems of their dresses. Red, white, and blue lights crisscrossed the night sky. They rehashed their plan of getting into the cabin below.

"We'll wait about a half an hour after the fireworks when more drinks will be served. You'll pretend that you've had enough and go to bed. I'll wait until I know Max is well into the sambuca and is a little drunk. I'll say I'm exhausted and come get you."

"And I'll bring my camera. If something is going on, we need to capture it. Especially after what you saw in that room."

"All I can hope is that Stu and Marty are involved in something, but Max doesn't know about it."

"Do you honestly believe that, Paige?" Fina's tone was gentle.

Staring out at the dark water she replied, "I don't know. Over the last couple of months, I've never gotten the impression that Max is a criminal of some kind." She sighed. "God, it feels horrible to say that."

"I'm sure it does. The fact, though, is that you said it, which means you *may* have thought it, right?"

Paige sighed heavily. "I can't lie, Fin. Since we all talked at Chub's that night, I know I have to be honest with myself. Yes, the sex is incredible, but I need to push that aside and think clearly. Plus—"

"And what are you two ladies discussing so seriously?" Max's voice came from behind them.

Paige gasped and felt her body seize in fear.

The lie glided easily from Fina's lips. "I was telling Paige about my mom. I'm worried about her because Nana is really sick and my mom is so depressed."

Max put his hands on Paige's shoulders and pulled her to him. "I'm sorry to hear that, Fina. I hope she is well soon." He kissed Paige's head. "Are we ready for dinner?"

Paige winked at Fina. "I'm starving. Aren't you, Fina?"

"I am."

* * *

On deck, Max and Paige stood with the guests and cheered as red, white, and blue fireworks exploded in the sky. Just as Paige said, after-dinner drinks flowed freely during the fireworks display.

"Where's Fina?" Max slurred, his arm hung loosely around Paige's shoulder.

"She just left to go to bed. Too much champagne and fun!" Paige replied.

"Ah. Time for sambuca. Shall we?" Max clapped his hands and the party followed him inside. After Max drank two overflowing snifters, Paige excused herself to go to bed. She kissed Max on the head and bade goodnight to the handful of inebriated guests. Just as she stepped from the bow, she took out her phone. With her limited vision and the inky darkness, Paige held the phone up and tried to use the dim light for guidance; she did not see Captain Brennan and collided into him.

"Oh! I didn't see you!" Paige said, startled.

"I know. You should be more careful about walking and using that thing." He pointed at her phone. His response dripped with disdain. "Someone with your, ah, *disability* should be more careful."

Paige felt the ire rise in her. *Screw you, asshole. Play the game, Paige.* "Thank you for watching out for me. Goodnight."

He retreated into the shadows of the stairs. When he was out of sight, she hustled to Fina's door.

"Ready?" she asked Fina who stood at the door, camera in hand.

Fina and Paige stole down the tomb-like passageway. Not a sound from above deck was heard. A small light shone down on the floor of the wooden passageway. Light on their feet, they were silent, except for the pounding of their hearts.

At the door of the cabin, Paige inhaled and turned the handle. Locked.

"Shit! Now what?" Fina hissed.

"I'll get it open." Paige took a small screwdriver from her pocket and loosened the lock.

They stepped inside the lightless room and glanced around. The table was fully draped. Fina pulled the drape away and took pictures of the table. "Strange-looking massage table if you ask me." She took some more photos. "This is weird, Paige. I'm getting a bad vibe in here."

"Me too."

Across the cabin, Paige opened the small closet. On the lone shelf was a tall stack of plastic notebooks. Paige counted fifteen. Their naked spines faced her. Looking closer, she realized they were in order of color: black, red, white. The color sequence repeated in all fifteen of them.

Black, red, white.

Curiosity got the best of her. Lifting a red one from the stack, she flipped it open. Written on the lined paper were rows of dates, followed with country names. Staggering amounts of money followed the dates and countries. Underneath the amount of money was a notation, one Paige could not fully comprehend. *What on earth does that mean?*

"Fina! Get over here!"

"What?" Fina shot over.

"Quick. Take pictures of this." Paige held the notebook and flipped through the pages. Fina snapped and snapped.

CHAPTER 24

Paige carefully closed the cabin door behind them. A gentle *click* and it was locked. Paige jiggled the handle as a precaution.

Inside the noiseless passageway, Paige and Fina looked at the pictures on the camera. They leaned forward, heads almost touching as Fina hit the forward button on the digital camera. Images of the metal table and notebooks slid by. The women frowned at each image, trying to identify anything relevant.

"What do you think all this means?" Fina asked. "Those letters and numbers and countries?"

"I really don't know. The only thing coming to mind is Max deals with contacts in those countries." She sighed, "What's written in the notebooks is the most confusing, and possibly concerning. All my opinion, of course."

"It's all strange, and yes, concerning. If they are dealing drugs, they have quite the international network."

Paige exhaled and laid her head back against the wall. "Do you think I should say something to Max?"

Fina's eyes shot at Paige like a missile. "Absolutely *not.* What if he *is* doing something illegal? Who knows what he'd do if he found out we were down there."

Paige nodded her consent. "I was afraid you'd say that. But on the other hand, it was Stu and Marty I saw down there, not Max."

Fina sighed. "I know. I completely understand you

may not want to believe that Max might not be the man you think." She softened her tone when she saw Paige's shoulders slump. "Like I said, Stu and Marty, even revolting Brennan, could be keeping something from Max. But they work for him, remember?"

As they walked back to Fina's cabin, they were completely unaware of the miniature ceiling cameras following their every move for the past fifteen minutes.

"Care to explain what you were doing down here? Specifically in the cabin you were told to stay away from, Miss Buckley? And Miss Manzetti, why do you have a camera?"

Paige and Fina froze at the voice of Captain Brennan slithering down the passageway. Wide-eyed fear splashed across their faces. They felt their hearts pounding through their throats.

"You'd be smart to follow me up to the bow to discuss this." He materialized out of the darkness like a ghostly predator. "I'm sure you do not want Mr. Dovic to know what you were up to, do you?"

Paige and Fina stared at him like terrified schoolchildren caught stealing candy from a teacher's jar.

"Follow me." Captain Brennan turned and walked toward a spiral staircase that led to the bow.

As the women followed him, Paige felt an urgent tug on her dress. She whipped around. Fina whispered, "Here, take this and put it in your pocket." She pressed the SIM card from the camera into Paige's hand. "I don't trust him, especially since he mentioned my camera."

Paige nodded as she stumbled up the last step to the bow. She prayed that Max was not up there any longer. *How would I explain this to him?* Bewilderment clouded her thinking. *What if he's still on deck?*

The walk to the bow seemed interminable. The pounding beat of her heart matched her footsteps. She held her breath until she saw the entire area was empty.

The acrid stench of fireworks filtered through the inky sky. Sounds of celebrations carried over the still water. They stood on the bow, Captain Brennan casually leaning on the brass handrail. His pencil-like, pale arms crossed his chest. A smirk was pasted on his ferret-like face. "All right, ladies. You have two choices. One: I will report to Mr. Dovic your visit to that cabin and you took pictures. Or two: Give me that camera and Mr. Dovic will not know of this."

Fina and Paige exchanged a look. The breeze picked up. A flash of lightning split the sky over Lower Manhattan.

Fina squared her shoulders and stepped forward. Eyes lasered on the captain's gaunt, malevolent face, she asked, "How do we know you aren't lying and will tell him anyway?"

"You don't, Miss Manzetti. However, since you find yourselves in a precarious predicament, I will not make it worse. If you choose option two, I will honor my word and say nothing to Mr. Dovic."

Fina pushed further. "What goes on in that cabin you want to be kept secret?"

The disdain on his face was if he had swallowed rotten meat. His lips curled into themselves. He opened his mouth to respond, but Paige intervened.

"Fina. Stop. Just give him the camera. Obviously, whatever's going on in there—if anything—is none of our business." She took the camera from Fina's hand and handed it to the captain.

"I'm glad one of you has an iota of common sense." He turned and hurled the camera into the river.

Fina gasped. "You fucking idiotic *asshole*! That cost me three months' salary!" She ran to the front of the bow to see her camera sink quickly into the dark water. "Shit!" She pounded the handrail.

A dry high pitched trill escaped from him. "Such language." He pushed himself from the railing. "Another thing. I would not want to upset Mr. Dovic if I don't need to. Understand?"

The wind swirled. Celebrants yelled in the distance. Exploding fireworks popped in the air. No one said a word.

"I'm glad we're in agreement."

The women watched him enter the bridge and slide the glass door shut. They said nothing until they were sure he was gone.

"How do you think he saw us?" Paige wondered. "Do you think he was spying?"

"I'm sure there are cameras all over this boat. Someone with Max's kind of cash would definitely equip a boat like this."

Paige gazed out into the night. She whispered, "Do you think we're being watched now?"

"It's entirely possible. He saw us somehow; I'd say the passageways have cameras, the cabin too. No one else was down there, so that has to be it."

Paige curled her lips in thought. "Yes. But I doubt he will say anything to Max because he would look incompetent and he doesn't want to lose his cushy, high-salaried job."

Fina kept her voice low. "True. And don't forget, we have the SIM card loaded with all the pics I took." She laughed. "And that dick," she added, jutting her chin toward the bridge, "has no idea."

CHAPTER 25

July fifth blew in with whipping wind and torrential rain. The weather matched Paige's mood. She slouched deeply into the couch in the living room, fiddling with the edge of a pillow nestled in her lap. Her eyes were glassy, but her mind raced. Entrenched in thought about Brennan, the cryptic writings in the notebooks, and the cabin, Paige was oblivious to her surroundings. *You have to be honest with yourself. What if Max is involved in something terrible?* she thought and responded to her own questions. *I just don't want to picture it. I'd have to break it off.*

"We lucked out with weather yesterday." Fina stood at the kitchen window and watched the thick gray clouds crash into one another. Rain bounced off the window. "I'm gonna get a snack. Want anything?" she called to Paige.

Not hearing a response, she turned around.

"Hey, are you okay? You look ten thousand miles away."

"Hmm? What?"

Fina came and sat down next to her.

Paige sighed sadly. "I'm not sure how I am, Fin. I was thinking about Max and the cabin." She rested her head back on the couch and stared at the ceiling. "What's driving me crazy is if Max is involved in some kind of crime, even black-market stuff, what am I going to do? I haven't *seen* him doing anything illegal with my own eyes."

Fina rubbed her friend's arm. "I understand. *But*, to play devil's advocate, when you asked him about the cabin and

Brennan, you *did* say he got irritated and defensive."

Paige turned and faced Fina. "I know. Which doesn't sit well with me. Yet it doesn't prove Max is involved in something illegal."

"It doesn't *disprove* anything either," Fina said, carrying a bowl of potato chips and plopping down on the sofa.

Paige dropped her head back and sighed audibly. "So, do I ask him or confront him with what I heard and saw? And that we have pictures?"

"Again, my gut says no, say nothing. Continue seeing him and keep an eye out for any signs of him engaging in weird behavior."

"Such as?"

Fina threw a handful of chips into her mouth. "Phone calls he can't take in front of you. Canceling dates last minute and offering a lame excuse, things like that."

"Sounds like I'm trying to catch him cheating on me!" Paige managed a laugh.

The women sat in contemplative silence until Fina reached for the pictures she developed from the SIM card.

Fina waved the folder with the pictures in it. "You know who I think may be able to really help us here?"

"Who?"

"Lindsey and Martha. Lindsey knows firsthand what goes on around on the docks and Martha works in the same building as you and Max. And because Martha is head of security and a former cop, she knows how to do some digging."

Paige processed the idea. "I like it. I'll call Martha and see if they're around."

* * *

At Fina and Paige's cramped kitchen table, Martha and Lindsey, brows furrowed, flipped through the pictures developed from the SIM card. Martha leaned back in the chair and tossed her glasses on the table.

"No doubt in my mind, something's going on heah," she declared.

Lindsey piped up, "And those weird annotations in the notebooks, especially the countries and money—plus the bullshit four a.m. fluid drops—tells me Dovic's using his yacht for something unlawful." She swigged her beer. "Or if not Dovic, his henchmen—including the captain—are."

Martha shifted her gaze to Paige. "If that's the case, hopefully Max is not part ah whatever may be going on. I can hack into the system and check pretty much whatever I want." She gave a little snicker.

"Thanks Martha. I hope you find nothing, but I need to know. And if there's something there, I'll deal with it. Aside from him getting testy those few times, nothing else stands out to me. Otherwise, I'd tell you guys." Paige's face held a tinge of sadness.

Martha noticed and squeezed her hand. "Hey, like you said, it may be the captain. We don't know. It'll be okay." She turned to Lindsey. "You and your crew can keep an ear and eye out too. You got all kinds of connections."

Lindsey smiled. "Oh yeah. Me and the boys'll definitely keep a look out. I can also talk to my port authority pals."

"Speaking of Max, we're meeting in a little while for drinks and dinner. Which means," she said, consulting her watch, "I need to get going if I'm going to be on time. I'll pack work clothes just in case."

"Do you think you'll sleep at his place?" Fina asked.

"Probably. I'll call you either way."

"Please do, and keep an eye out," Fina asked.

"I will. I promise."

* * *

At dinner, Max and Paige discussed the Fourth of July party. Specifically, he asked Paige if Fina had a fun time.

"She loved it. Thank you for inviting her."

"I'm sure she did. And I was told she drank a lot of champagne. I hope her hangover didn't linger." Over his glass of wine, he stared at her.

What's that look all about? Anger? Disappointment? Fear? Mistrust? Is he challenging me? And who told him about the champagne? Play it off. Focus on him.

"Oh, Fina can still handle her booze like a twenty-one-year-old! She's fine. More importantly, did you have fun?"

"Entertaining is something I enjoy. I think the party went seamlessly. Captain Brennan did a marvelous job of keeping a *very sharp* eye on all the guests, ensuring they were enjoying themselves."

Paige's knee started its nervous bounce. *Not good. Thank God, he can't see it.* She slid her hand down to her leg and calmed it. "Yes, he's very good at his job." *This is weird. Change the direction of conversation.* "I was thinking, maybe we could visit Philadelphia some time? We can take the yacht down! You can meet my parents."

"Something to think about. I'd like that."

For the rest of dinner, the discussed their potential trip to her hometown.

Afterward, they waited curbside for Andreas. Max's arm snaked around her waist as he asked, "Will you spend the night?"

"Would you like me to?"

"What do you think?" Max whispered as Andreas pulled up.

Paige took out her phone and called Fina. Leering at Max, she left a message. "Fin, I'm spending the night at Max's. See you tomorrow. Love you."

* * *

Early the next morning, Paige stepped from the shower onto a plush bathmat and reached for the towel Max put out for after he stepped out. Usually their showers used up all the hot water. Today, though, Max cut it short because he had a breakfast meeting across town. The oversized navy blue towel felt soft and plush against her damp skin. *This is more like a bath sheet, not a towel.* Paige dried herself off and wrapped herself in the luxurious cloth.

Max dashed back into the bathroom, grabbed a hairbrush, and ran it through his still-damp hair. Paige ogled him, admiring the expensive, fitted suit and pink shirt. "Don't you look incredibly handsome this morning. Too bad you have to leave." She dropped the towel.

His eyes slowly roamed her body from head to toe. "Stop. You're *very* bad, you know!" He stepped toward her and kissed her quickly.

"And you like it that way," she whispered.

"You have *no idea* how much." He reached over and stroked her cheek. "I'll call you later."

"After six. Meetings all day."

"Will do. Oh, can you please drop the trash down the chute? I forgot and I'm already late! Thanks love!"

* * *

Paige dressed and wandered into Max's kitchen. She poured herself a cup of coffee and ate an apple. She was due into the office by nine thirty. Glancing at her watch, she thought, *Good, I have almost an hour.*

On the kitchen table sat the unopened *New York Times*. Settling herself at the table, Paige read as much of the paper as time allowed. After another cup of coffee, she glanced at her watch. *I gotta get going.* She pushed the chair under, rinsed her cup, and placed it in the empty dishwasher. From the hook by the front door, she removed her work bag, hefted it over her shoulder, and unlocked the door.

Crap, the trash. I forgot. Pivoting and jogging back to the kitchen, Paige dropped her bag on the counter, opened the trash bin, and removed the overflowing bag. *Gross.* It needed to be tied shut. She glanced around the kitchen, looking for something to tie the trash bag with. She was surrounded by drawers. Nothing in the drawers nearest the trash bin. Sighing, she started to dig through them.

Pulling open a drawer by the fridge, she lifted some papers with one hand and hunted for a rubber band or a twist tie with the other. Nothing. She cursed when several papers scattered on the kitchen floor.

They were letters from various credit card companies. *Why is he saving all these?*

Paige scanned the letters. *What?* She scowled. Her mouth became dry, her hand shot to her lips. "What is this all about?" Her heart pounded in her chest as she read the first one.

Dear Mr. Dovic,

According to our records, you are delinquent in paying the outstanding balance of $25,680.97. According to our records, this balance has been outstanding for six months. We have contacted you by telephone several times to inform you that your account is currently frozen and will not be available for your use until you either contact us or make a partial payment of $5,000.00.

Thank you for your attention in this matter.

Immediately she looked at the date. A blanket of chills encased her when she saw the letter was a year old. *A year?* She shuffled through the others. *All of these were sent at least six months to a year ago!* Paige did not need to read the rest. Instead she scanned each letter for the amount owed. After adding up the outstanding sums, she collapsed into a chair. All the air in the spacious kitchen thickened to where she felt smothered.

My God Max, you owe over a hundred thousand dollars on credit cards! How could you not pay your bills? You're rolling in money! In disbelief at what she saw, she stood and put the letters in order and walked to the still-open drawer. *I know I shouldn't this, but after what I just saw...*

Rummaging further in the drawer, her curiosity exploded. *What else is he hiding?* Buried underneath a pile of unopened envelopes from other credit card companies, insurance companies, and utility companies was a fairly recent bank statement. *I know this is none of my business, but I'm in too deep now.*

Taking a deep breath, Paige seized the statement. Her eyes flew over the columns. She gasped. After reading it again, she gazed around the spacious, well-appointed penthouse. *How can he afford this place? He's broke.*

CHAPTER 26

Aboard the *Boston Babe*, Lindsey and her crew chugged back into the harbor after what seemed like an eternity. Humidity hung like an old overcoat in the air; the day felt like it was drenched in syrup. The *Babe* was one of four tugs to pull fully loaded cargo ships to the Atlantic. By three in the afternoon, they had let loose the last ship to make its way to its European destination.

Up in the wheelhouse, Lindsey radioed the port authority that she was returning. After hanging up, Lindsey admired Lower Manhattan as the vessel slogged through the water. Never tiring of the view ahead of her, she smiled and marveled at the massive, sun-drenched buildings that made that part of New York famous. The magnificence of the Twin Towers always took her breath away. After reading about their construction, she held them in the highest level of reverence. *Gorgeous buildings.*

She removed her hat and dabbed her head and face with a towel. She slid open a few windows, yet the heat won out. *Christ, I feel like I'm in a greenhouse!* Lower Manhattan drew closer as did her thoughts about a cold beer with Martha.

"Hey Marth, I'll be at Chub's by six." Placing her phone down, she stole a glance out the portside window, her attention drawn by an engine's rumble.

At a distance, a yacht slowly glided out of its slip toward the *Boston Babe*. Lindsey took in the gleaming white boat. *Now theah's a super yacht. Damn.* The slick, behemoth vessel inched out into the water. *I wonder what it's like to have that kind ah money.* On its massive deck stood two figures who were blurry from the distance. Lindsey squinted at them. *Can't see for shit anymore.*

From the hook above her desk, she snatched the binoculars and lasered in on the people. *Stu and Marty. What the hell are they doing on Dovic's yacht in the middle of the week? On a joy ride?*

She swept the binoculars over the entire yacht. In the bridge, she saw the captain and no one else. *No sign ah Dovic.*

As she turned her attention back to Stu and Marty, she saw Max appear from below and point at something on the ground. Flipping the binoculars at an angle, Lindsey saw at their feet two medium-size coolers. Stu pointed at one of them and Max nodded. Lindsey watched as Marty opened one. All three men peered inside.

Suddenly, Max reared up and gesticulated wildly at Stu and Marty, his face twisted into a mask of anger. Like two dogs who were being punished, Stu and Marty hurriedly picked up the coolers and disappeared below deck.

On the hull, she saw a row of faded, illegible black numbers. *What the hell? I wonder if Dovic knows his ID numbers are hardly visible. Those things need to be obvious! How did he get by the port authority?* Something stirred in Lindsey's gut. *For a yacht this new, those numbers should leap out.*

Flipping the binoculars back up, she studied indistinct numbers. Listening to her gut, she jotted down whatever was visible. *I wish I had a camera. Martha has one! I'll call her. She'll get down here before I dock* Babe.

Knowing the *Baltic Blue* would dock well before her tug, she called Martha but it went to voicemail. *Shit! I'll try Fina. Might be a crapshoot, but worth it.*

Fina picked up after a few rings. Lindsey told her what she was seeing. "Now's the time to get down to the marina and take pics. Make sure you snap pics of the of the ID numbers on the bow—portside."

"What's portside?" Fina asked.

"Left side ah a boat is portside. The bow is the front—snap those numbers."

"What the hell? Why?"

"I'll tell ya later. Just get your ass down theah. You can shoot from a distance. I'd say they'll be at the cove in under thirty minutes."

Fina checked the time. "I can do that. Thanks Lindsey! I'll call you later."

* * *

With her bag bouncing on her back, Fina raced through her office to the elevator, punched the lower level, and ran out to the street. Her ear-splitting whistle summoned a cab who sped her to North Avenue Marina where Max kept his yacht.

Enough cars were parked in the lot to give her a place to hide. Squatting behind one closest to the slips, Fina searched the river. She did not have to look far as the *Baltic Blue* coasted closer to the dock.

Sweat dampened her scalp under the late afternoon sun and drippy humidity. Wiping her brow with her T-shirt sleeve, she double-checked her camera's battery and saw it had plenty of juice.

The *Baltic Blue* backed slowly into the slip; she saw Captain Brennan nudging her gently toward the dockies waiting to tie her up with thick, ropy lines. Fina held her camera steady and zoomed when the identification numbers revealed themselves. *Click! Click! Click!* She tilted the camera toward her. *Perfect.*

Like two prairie dogs, Stu and Marty suddenly popped up onto the stern from below deck. *No sign of Max.* With her eyes glued on their every move, she continued to photograph them and the numbers on the hull.

Soon, the *Baltic Blue* was securely tied into the slip. She photographed Brennan talking to Stu and Marty, who handed Stu a briefcase. Fina snapped away. Stu placed the briefcase on the deck before shaking Brennan's hand.

Fina's eyes were glued to Stu and Marty. Camera at the ready, she snapped countless pictures until they vanished from sight for a split second. *What the hell?* She soon saw why. They each hefted a medium-size white cooler from the deck and carried it toward the lowered gangplank jutting out from the stern onto the dock. *Click! Click! Click!*

Stu jogged back to the deck and retrieved the briefcase. Glancing in all directions, they took the items from the gangplank, headed to the parking lot toward a dark sedan. *Click! Click! Click!* It was close enough for her to get pictures of the license plate.

"Hmm, and the plot thickens," she murmured as the sedan turned out of the lot.

* * *

Paige fought to concentrate on her work. After realizing she entered four rows of incorrect data into a report, she gave up. *This is absolutely futile. Fuck! Damn him!* She rose and entered the cheerfully colored break room. The light green and white walls, coupled with the spray of purple tulips popping from a red vase, did nothing to alleviate her simmering frustration, anger, and disbelief.

Paige slumped against the window and stared out at the

day rolling by down below. Her stomach hurt. She picked at a cuticle as thoughts zoomed through her crowded head. *What is going on? How could he not pay any of his bills, especially taxes? What else do I not know?*

"Are you okay? Earth to Paige?" Todd asked Paige when he entered the break room and saw her staring out the window.

Paige was as motionless as a statue until he patted her on the shoulder. "Paige?"

"Huh? Oh, Todd. Hi." She turned around to face him. "Yeah, I'm fine. Just a little preoccupied at the moment."

"Anything you want to talk about? I have to say, you look pretty upset."

She managed a half smile. "Thanks, but no. It's something I need to figure out. I appreciate your concern, though."

Back at her cubicle, she flipped open her date book several months back. Running a finger over the square calendar boxes, she counted all the dates she and Max had gone on since they met. Among a smattering of yacht rides and cultural events, most were dinner dates at restaurants whose names Paige had jotted down. After scanning the names of the eateries, she was struck with an epiphany that shook her to the bone. *Cash. He always pays in cash. I now know why. And I now know he's running from creditors. Oh my God. What else do I not know about him?*

She called her friends and asked if they could meet at Chub's that night.

* * *

Paige entered the bustling bar and saw her friends seated a few feet away, laughing and chatting. Staying put for a bit, she observed her friends and was bowled over by an intense wave of affection and gratefulness. Out of nowhere, she felt her eyes prick with tears of gratitude for these women. *I'm so lucky*. Blinking quickly, she dabbed at her eyes and walked over to their table.

"Hi ladies. How was everyone's day?" Paige asked.

"You're here!" Fina exclaimed. "Wait till you hear about my and Lindsey's day! Holy crap!"

"I definitely need a drink first," Paige said as the server came over. "Dirty martini, extra dry."

Three heads whipped around to Paige. Fina remarked, "Damn girl, you must have had a rough day."

"You have *no* idea." *Just wait till I tell them what I found*. Paige threw back half the martini. The frosty gin slid down her throat, calming her nerves.

"What the hell is going on?" Fina prodded.

"I'm not quite ready to tell yet. You two start first." She gestured to Fina and Lindsey.

Martha flagged over their server. "Anothah round please, and bring some snacks—like mozz sticks, skins, and nachos."

Fina opened her bag and handed them the camera. "Take a good look at these."

Once Paige, Lindsey, and Martha finished studying the pictures, a conversation ensued about the coolers, car, and Max.

"Good work, Fin." Paige picked up a mozzarella stick. "Max is nowhere to be found in these pictures though. I guess he wasn't on the boat. I know he said he had a busy day."

Lindsey piped up. "Oh shit, no. He was on the boat too. I forgot to mention this because ah something else I saw."

Three pairs of eyes cut to her; eyebrows raised in anticipation.

"*And?*" Martha said.

"*And* Max freaked out on Stu and Marty after he looked in one of the coolers. He was waving his hands around like a fuckin' crazy person."

Paige responded, "Could you see what was in the coolers?"

Lindsey shook her head. "Whatever it was—or wasn't, judging by Max's reaction—didn't make him happy."

Fina asked, "I wonder what pissed him off so much?"

"Who knows," Martha said. Martha flipped through the pictures again. "What's that?" She pointed to a brownish-burgundy orange-size splotch on the stern deck near Stu's shoe. A few more flecks of it dotted the deck in other spots.

Fina shrugged and added she was not aware of it when she took pictures.

"Gimme the camera." Lindsey studied it. "Looks like the weather-stain used to protect the bows ah super yachts." She handed the camera back to Fina. "Remember, get these developed."

Martha turned to Lindsey. "But you alluded to something else, Linds. What is it?"

Lindsey explained about the row of black numbers on the portside bow. "Numbers must be visible at all times for identification and legal purposes. These are dull and practically illegible. Given the newness of this yacht, it's strange."

"So boats need to be ID'd, like a car license plate?" Fina asked.

"Yes. Boaters technically should *never* be out without visible ID numbers."

Paige sank in her seat. *That sounded ominous.* "If I'm hearing you right, he's violating boating rules when he's out on the waters without visible numbers, correct?"

"Correct."

"And speaking of numbers, I was able to shoot the license plate of the car they left in."

I don't want to ask this, but I have to. Paige puffed out a breath and rubbed her temples. "What kind of car was it, Fin? Do you remember?"

"Um, I know it was dark blue. I think a Mercedes. Why?"

"I was afraid you'd say that." Taking a deep breath, she said, "I'm pretty sure you saw Max's car."

Three heads snapped to attention. No one said a word.

"And there's much more. Here goes." Paige told her friends about what she found in the drawer.

Fina, Lindsey and Martha all sat-slack jawed. No one could say a word. They stared at Paige.

"Yup, my reaction too."

Fina chirped up first. "So he's not nearly as rich as he pretends to be?"

"Evidently not. And he likes to skip out on paying his bills. And now I know why. He has no money."

"But what about the penthouse? Yacht? Trips?" Fina asked. "And you read online he's rich?"

"I thought of that. I'm not sure what happened there. I know WHS Shipping is worth an enormous amount of money, but not Max."

"What the fuck?" Martha said. "This guy is a total fraud."

Lindsey gently placed her sun-dappled hand over Paige's and gave it a squeeze. "Aw lovie, we're so sorry."

Martha glanced at Paige. "You've had a pretty shitty day, honey." Martha gave Paige's shoulder a squeeze.

Paige nodded. "I've been so angry and confused all day. On my way here, the one question that kept surfacing again and again is: Where is he getting *all this cash*?" The question hovered over the table until she eventually continued. "It sure as hell isn't from his salary. Furthermore, we now have a shred of proof—the cash—that there's potentially *something* illegal going on." She raised her glass. "And I'm going to get to the bottom of it. Who's with me?"

The clink of their glasses was all she needed to know.

"Great. We'll call you guys tomorrow."

CHAPTER 27

During the ride back to their apartment, Paige said to Fina, "We need a plan to figure out exactly what the hell is going on. As much as I want to throw all of this in Max's face, I can't. He'll know I snooped and I can't have him lose trust in me at this point."

"I know. I still can't believe what you found in the kitchen drawer. Fraud."

"I'm pissed, frustrated, and shocked. I should have known he was too good to be true."

Fina took hold of Paige's hand. "Paige, you had no way of knowing. There very well could be an explanation, but who knows."

"I'm not feeling that, Fina. Not at all." She rested her head against the darkness of the subway car window.

* * *

Paige and Fina moseyed through the throngs of people enjoying the sun-drenched day at the outdoor farmer's market on their block. Every third Saturday of the summer months, vendors from all over New Jersey set up booths and tables. Ears of yellow and white corn lay in perfect rows, stacked on one another like bricks. Yellow and green peppers shone in the sun. Bright red Jersey tomatoes nestled next to one another in neat, small baskets. The doughy-beefy aroma of pigs in a blanket wafted from the Get Your Piggies booth.

Local artisans, including an author, chatted up would-be buyers about their wares.

Paige and Fina perused the produce stand and eyeballed the corn. Fina suggested they buy a few ears.

"We can try it. But the *really* sweet corn will be here in August."

"You're gonna make me wait two weeks? Oh, the horror!" Fina laughed.

They loaded up their bags with lettuce, zucchini, doughnuts, hamburgers, and wine. They found a vacant table and plopped down. Fina removed her sun hat and waved her hand in front of her face. "Damn, it's hot!"

Lunchtime was prime people-watching time. As they waited for Martha and Lindsey, they observed people buying goods, or not buying goods. Pigs in a blanket being devoured by skinny teenagers. Parents or grandparents wiping the runny noses or ice-cream covered faces of their young ones.

"Hey ladies!"

Paige turned all the way in her seat to fully see, even though she knew the voice. A smile popped when she saw her friends. In their hands were trays loaded with enormous Reuben sandwiches, chips, and pickles. Fina trailed behind with an equally loaded tray.

"Let's eat before we get down to business," Martha suggested.

After tossing away their trash, they discussed their next moves. When they agreed that they needed to take baby steps, Lindsey asked Paige when she was going to see Max again.

"Soon. I'm going to stay the course with him. He's very sharp and will notice if I start to break dates and things like that."

"Smart. No need to raise suspicion," Martha said. "Here's

Snap Decision

what Linds and I came up with last night after you guys left Chub's. I'm going to keep a real close eye on him at work and figure out a way to hack into his computer. Guaranteed I'll find shit on him theah. People think their info is safe. Far from it."

Lindsey added, "I'll do some recon on his yacht. I'll be very surprised if he owns it. I have plenty ah favors to call in at the port authority and even the Coast Guard if that's necessary."

Lindsey turned to Paige. "When you're on the boat again, maybe keep an eye out for any more odd-timed deliveries, stuff like that."

Martha added, "And we've been thinking about those cryptic entries in the notebooks. Any clue as to what they mean?"

Fina and Paige shook their heads. Fina said, "No. The combination of money amounts and countries is very peculiar. All I can think of is drugs."

"Personally, I'd like to decode the notations in those books."

"Makes four of us," Lindsey said. "I'm leaning toward drugs too."

Paige ruminated over everything her friends thought and said, "Truth be told, I'm itching to get back on the yacht. My gut tells me that cabin holds the silver bullet. I need to be discreet and cautious though, given Brennan's weird omnipresence."

"You got that right." Fina stretched her muscled arms overhead. "Enough of boat and notebook talk for a while. Anyone but me up for trying that local brewery's beer?" She pointed to a sign that read BILL'S BORN AND BRED BREWERY.

"Who are we to say no?" Martha laughed and stood. "Let's do it!"

Post beers, the four women strolled through the next block overflowing with antique dealers. Scratched tables, chairs of all sizes, strange lamps, and dusty books covered practically the entire block. Lindsey commented that the vendors looked as worn and haggard as their merchandise. Martha laughed and added she had not seen so much crap since college when she and her friends frequented Happy's Flea Market.

"This thing looks like it was made in a junior high aht class." Martha waved a crooked, thick, ball-like hunk of gray clay with a hole in the top. "What the hell is this supposed to be?"

"Beats me. It's ugly though," Lindsey said. "Put it back."

After thirty minutes of walking in the mid-July sun, the beers took their toll on the women.

"Time for a nap!" Martha laughed.

"It is," Fina yawned. "We'll see you guys later."

"Talk to you soon. Keep us in the loop with anything we discussed," Martha said. She and Lindsey peeled off and headed up the block.

"We will. Thanks," Paige replied.

CHAPTER 28

Fina was putting the finishing touches on a layout when her boss Leigh approached her. "Fina, you have a call. It's your mother; line one."

Oh no, no. Fina thanked her. Placing the roll of tape she held on to her desk, she slid her eyes to the phone. *I never get calls in the middle of the day from Mom. This isn't good.* Hand trembling, she picked up the phone. "Hi Mom."

Fina hung up with her mother. As expected, her grandmother had taken a turn for the worse. She told her mother she would be on a train home later that evening. Fina sat at her desk and wept.

A gentle knock on the door made her look up. It was Leigh.

"Your nana?" Compassion and sorrow crossed Leigh's face.

Fina nodded solemnly.

"You take all the time you need. I understand and so does Peter. Your mother and your family need you." She walked around the desk and hugged Fina. "We will hold down the fort but will miss you. Go home and pack."

"Thank you for being so understanding."

"Of course."

* * *

During a morning coffee break, Paige checked her phone and saw Fina called. She felt a stab of melancholy when she listened to Fina's despondent voice mail. *Oh no, Nana.* She called her friend back and Fina explained she was going home for an indefinite period of time.

"According to what Mom said, I may be home for a week or two. She was not sure."

"I'll miss you. Please keep me updated and send your family all my love."

"I will. I'll call you later."

"Love you, Fin."

"Same. Talk soon."

Sorrow for her friend and her family settled heavily into her bones. Staring at her computer, she realized she was a million miles away. *I wish I could make Fina and her family feel better. But I can't. I can only be there for her.*

* * *

A week had passed and Fina was still back home in Philadelphia. She and Paige talked every other day. She informed Paige she most likely would be there for a stretch more.

"Hospice is here and Nana is comfortable. Mom is *really* down, so it's good I can be here for another week."

"I'm glad for your mom you're there. But I miss you. The apartment is way too quiet!" Paige told her. "How are *you* holding up?"

"I'm tired, but okay. I miss you too and our apartment. I'll get through this. But..." Fina said she needed to change the subject and asked about Max and if Paige had seen him.

"He's been out of town for a few days. He's coming back tomorrow night and we're going to have dinner."

"Where'd he go?" Fina asked.

Paige realized she did not know. "Good question. I didn't even think to ask him. I've been preoccupied."

"I understand the preoccupation, trust me." Fina sneezed and continued. "Ask him where he went. I'm curious. Thinking about him and what we discussed with Lindsey and Martha is a much-needed diversion right now."

"I'm sure it is. I'm curious too, so I'll find out tonight."

* * *

That evening, Max gazed at Paige over the table and commented, "You've barely touched your dinner. What's wrong, love?"

Paige smiled. *Where to start? Why you have boatload of cash on the yacht? What really goes on in that cabin? Who the hell are you anyway?* Paige realized Max was unaware of Fina's situation with her grandmother. Through the candlelight, Paige studied his expression. Concern, worry, and care crisscrossed his face. She sighed. "She's really close to her nana and her mother is not handling this well. Nana Gambone is in hospice; it won't be long."

Max took her hand and told her how sorry he was for Fina. "Paige, you are a kind, compassionate, and caring friend. I wish I had someone like you in my life when I was younger. Fina is lucky to have you in her life, as am I."

Are you lying about that too? "Thanks. And I'm lucky to have her."

He finished his wine. Nothing more was said about Fina. "I was thinking that maybe you and I could escape for a weekend in a few weeks, perhaps in early September? There are several beautiful resorts upstate from here. Spa, wine, sumptuous cuisine, you, me, and lots of, ah, *play* time?" He caressed the inside of her palm.

She cocked her head and gazed at him, her emotions a swirling, confusing hurricane. *He's so smooth and convincing.* As much as she wanted to punch him in the face, she stayed calm. *How are you going to pay for that? How can you so calmly live a double life? You're obviously used to it.* Giving him a sweet, indulgent smile, she replied, "Max, a weekend away sounds wonderful. I'd love to."

"Perfect. I'll arrange it."

"Speaking of travel, how was your business trip? I forget where you said you were."

Flipping his eyes at her, he snapped, "I don't recall telling you." He folded his napkin and tossed it on the table. "That aside though, I traveled to South Korea to inspect the construction of a new container ship. Fascinating country." Cool eyes gazed at her. "Satisfied?" He stood, picked up the plates, and headed to the kitchen.

Watching him stalk into the kitchen, the few pieces of filet Paige had eaten flipped over in her stomach. *Whoa, I struck a nerve. He actually remembered he didn't tell me where he was going.* She rose from the table, salad bowls and utensils in hand.

Paige watched as Max stood at the sink, angrily scraping any remnants of dinner before rinsing each plate, the jamming of the utensils into the dishwasher conveying his anger. *This needs to change. Do something, even if you don't want to. You can't risk him becoming suspicious.*

She placed the salad bowl on the counter and embraced him from behind. She felt his muscles melt and his hunched shoulders relax. *That was easy.*

Max shook excess water from his hands, grabbed a dishtowel and dried them. He turned around and gazed down at her. "I'm sorry I snapped. I've been under immense pressure and I didn't mean to take it out on you." He pulled her in and kissed her.

"I've missed you," he whispered. His still-damp fingers hastily unbuttoned her blouse. It fell to the floor.

"I know." She tugged his shirt from his pants. It joined her blouse.

Grasping his hand, she led him to his bedroom where they fell onto the bed, a heated twist of arms and legs and sweat. Max rolled over on top of Paige and slid his way down her body. His tongue traced the insides of her thighs. She gripped his head and floated into another world. Waves rippled through her body, carrying her away. Beads of perspiration pricked her breastbone. Her heart banged against her ribcage. *Oh. My. God.* Paige inhaled deeply and pulled Max toward her.

A small intake of breath slid to the back of Paige's throat when Max entered her. He rocked them gently at first until Paige held him forcefully with her legs. Gently, she purred, "Your turn."

"Oh Paige." He slid his arms around her back and pulled her closer. Each thrust became more powerful. She tilted her hips back and moved with him in heated rhythm. Deeper he went. Only the two of them existed in this sensual, carnal, warm world.

Max's body quaked. He rested his chin on the top of Paige's head and was silent aside from his panting.

"I think I'm addicted to you, Paige Buckley." He kissed her and rolled over on his back. "That's one way to be welcomed home."

Look who's leading a double life now. "Happy to oblige." She rose and entered the bathroom.

CHAPTER 29

Paige was dozing on the couch when she heard the key in the door. She leaped from the couch when she heard the door open. *Yay! Finally, Fina's back!* She hurried to the kitchen to welcome her friend. "Hi Fin! I'm so happy you're home!" She threw her arms around her. "And I'm so very sorry about Nana."

Fina nestled in the warmth of Paige's arms. "Thanks, so am I. It was peaceful and she's with Poppop now." She pulled away and wiped her eyes. "We're going to have a service later, probably October. Too hot now."

"Good idea." Paige took Fina's bag and put it on a kitchen chair.

"I'm so glad to be home. What an exhausting two weeks."

Dark bags under her friend's eyes coupled with the heavy fatigue in her voice pulled at Paige's heart strings. "I can imagine. Do you want anything to eat or drink?"

"I had some snacks on the train. I think I may just take a hot shower and a nap. I'll rebound afterward."

Fina fell dead asleep for two hours and roused by six that evening. Rumple-haired, sleepy eyed, she joined Paige in the living room.

"Morning, sunshine. How're you feeling?" Paige asked.

"Better. Still tired, but that's more mental fatigue." Fina yawned. "But a beer would taste really good."

"I thought you may say that. I'll get some." Paige returned with a few beers and a bowl of pretzels and peanuts. "Cheers."

Late into the evening, Paige and Fina talked, ate, cried, and laughed. Stories Paige shared about Nana Gambone brought more smiles to Fina's sad face. "I loved her like she was my own nana."

"Thanks, Paige. I'm so glad you have these stories." She yawned and rose from the couch. "Everything is tired. I need sleep."

* * *

Fina sat alone on the couch the next evening. Paige was out with Max at a concert. Nothing on television held her attention. "Television sucks." She tossed the remote onto the table. Staring at the darkened screen, she thought about Max, his yacht, and the pictures. Doubts about Max swirled in her head, specifically after she interviewed him. *The guy's a slimy, broke prick. But like Paige said, where is he getting all that cash?* She thought about the yacht and how Paige said she believed it held many secrets. *She's my best friend. I need to find out what's going on.*

From the table drawer, she took the folder of pictures. For an hour, she painstakingly scrutinized them all. Turning one sideways, she focused on the package Stu was handing to the captain. *Money? Too big to be a normal envelope—large enough to hold cash, though.* Turning her attention to the coolers Stu and Marty hefted from the *Baltic Blue* to the car, she wondered about their contents. *What's in there that needs to be taken from the yacht to the waiting car? And where are they going from there?* Goosebumps pricked her petite body. *It's drugs or money in the coolers. What else could it be?* She leaped from the couch, ran to her bedroom, and changed into all black.

I can't sit here. Time to find out.

***

Armed with her phone, her camera, a flashlight, and a screwdriver, Fina skulked through the marina parking lot. Positioning herself behind a car closest to *Baltic Blue's* slip, she took out her phone and called Paige. She left a message about where she was. *I better send a text too, just to be safe.*

Fina peered over the hood of the car. The vessel's bow and stern lights glowed in the pitch-black night. A yellow light cast a buttery shade in the bridge. Seeing no one on deck, Fina crept down the ramp to the dock where other fancy yachts were moored.

Clouds walled off any light from the moon. Fina pulled the small flashlight from her pocket. On catlike feet, she stole toward the *Baltic Blue*. Taking a deep breath to steady her pounding heart, Fina leaped over the handrail and landed on light feet. *Please God, let the captain be asleep.* She waited. Hearing nothing, she crept over the deck to the staircase that led to the passageway of cabins.

Certain there was a camera somewhere in the passageway, Fina took no chances. She yanked the ski mask over her face. From her bag, she took the can of spray tan and aimed it at the light above her. *Screw you Brennan!* The brown mist covered the light. *Perfect.*

On trembling legs, she sped down the passageway to the door, ignoring her palpitating heart. At the cabin she placed her hand on the handle and turned. *Click.*

Thank God.

Once inside, the smell hit her immediately. Her stomach clenched as she fought back a wet gag. Rotting egg smell hung in the air. *What the hell is that? Block it out or breathe from your mouth.*

Fina flicked on the flashlight and glanced around.

Nothing looks out of place.

She pointed the flashlight under the draped table. Fina's eyes widened. *Bingo.* Under it sat the two coolers. *Jackpot! Time to catch this slimy son of a bitch!*

She reached down to open one. Her hand shook slightly when she gripped the edge of the lid. She cracked it open a hair and was about to remove the lid when she heard voices.

Shit! Fina froze. Her bowels loosened. Her skin tingled, eyes watered. *Hide!*

The draped table was closest. She darted around it and crouched behind the sheet. Squeezed between the wall and table, Fina hardly dared to breathe.

Outside the door, the voices grew louder. The click of the door handle made Fina's throat constrict. Any saliva in her mouth evaporated. *No! Stay calm.* Her heart slammed against her ribs as the door opened. A lightswitch was flipped on. She could see two pairs of shoes under the edge of the sheet.

"They expect delivery in three days. As usual, everything you need is right here."

Fina recognized Captain Brennan's voice. The next voice was unfamiliar.

"The package will be here tomorrow evening?" asked a woman.

"Yes."

"What's the time frame? I have rounds until three."

"Seven p.m. is delivery."

"I will be here at six to prep. You understand that the cost of this part is fifty thousand, of which I will receive twenty-five percent."

"We understand and you will be paid accordingly, like all the other times."

What are they talking about? Fina committed everything

to memory.

"Do you need anything else?" Captain Brennan asked.

"Do you have pictures? I like to see what I'm dealing with before I work."

"The folder on the desk has the information."

Fina stopped breathing. She was convinced the jackhammering of her heart would give away her presence. The woman's feet came closer. Sweat trickled down Fina's spine. She knew the cabinet was right next to the table. She squeezed herself closer to the cover of the sheet. *Please don't let her see me. Oh my God.*

The woman leaned over the edge of the table, inches from Fina. Fina cast her eyes to the right and caught a glimpse of a tanned calf, dotted with sunspots. On the woman's feet were light blue sneakers, no socks.

"I will bring my own instruments," she commented, and stepped back toward the open cabin door.

"As you wish," Captain Brennan said and the two of them exited. The door clicked after them.

Instruments? What the hell? Fina counted to ten and expelled the breath she held. *Phew, that was terrifying.*

On all fours, she crawled to the front of the table where the coolers sat. She jimmied the lid open and peered inside. Nothing. *Shit!* She inspected both of them. All she saw was flecks of brown on the inside of one of them. *What is that?* From her pocket, she took her camera and snapped a close-up picture. *I better get outta here soon.* Her muscles uncoiled when she stood up and stretched.

Nerves still crackling, Fina ran to the desk and grabbed the folder. *This wasn't here before.* She opened it. Inside were grainy pictures of people, young women and men, of all ethnic backgrounds. Scowling, she studied them. *Who are these people?*

Written in black marker at the bottom of each picture were capital letters: L, K, C, LV. *What are these?* Fina guessed names of places. A handful of the shots were marred with a red X scrawled through the young faces. *An X? Are they dead? What the hell?* Skimming through the rest, Fina gasped when her eyes came to rest on two of the photos.

Her jaw tumbled open. She stopped breathing. *Oh my God.*

* * *

Slipping out into the passageway, Fina fought to keep her wits about her. *Holy shit! I need to tell Paige what I saw! I need to get the hell off this boat.* Knowing the captain was aboard made a ball of panic bounce around in her chest.

Listening for any noise, Fina crept up the last step of the spiral staircase. She pressed herself against the side of the yacht as she inched toward the bow, grateful for the coolness of the it. Keeping her voice low, she called Paige. Frustration bubbled when it went to voice mail. *Damnit!* Fina gave Paige an abbreviated version of what she saw below deck.

Fifteen feet stood between her and the dock. Scampering across the stern to the handrailing, she gripped it tightly. Before she could propel herself from the yacht, Fina was violently grabbed from behind.

Fina kicked and screamed and flailed. Powerful arms crushed her ribcage. Hot breath hissed against her ear. "You don't listen very well."

Those were the last words Fina would ever hear.

CHAPTER 30

The gold-trimmed, red-velvet curtain dropped after the bespectacled, beloved singer bowed, waved, and disappeared into the darkness of backstage. Fans had leaped to their feet, whistling, and applauding the sold-out performance by one of the world's most influential and important guitarists of all times: Eric Clapton.

"I'm blown away. That man is a true genius," Max exclaimed to an applauding Paige. "Wow!"

She turned to him. "I'm glad you enjoyed it. He's always been one of my favorites."

"I can see why. He's a brilliant guitarist and legend, and always will be. Thank you so much for this." He leaned over and kissed her. "Are you up for a drink?" He consulted his watch. "The night is young."

Smiling brightly, she replied, "Of course." She sat back down and waited for the row to clear.

After other concertgoers filed out, Paige and Max walked hand in hand to the front of the concert hall. Bright yellow taxis idled outside. At the end of the yellow line, Andreas waved at them.

How can he afford a driver and a nice car?

"Where to, sir?" Andreas asked and then smiled at Paige. "Hello, Miss Buckley."

"Hi Andreas."

"The Baccarat."

"Of course."

Andreas pulled the car out and drove to one of Max's favorite bars. Paige put the window down, closed her eyes, and absorbed the warm, humid-free air coming through the window. *I can't go home with him tonight. I need to think of an excuse.*

Max's hand covered hers on the back seat. "What are you thinking about, beautiful?"

Max's voice broke her concentration. "Oh, just absorbing the greatness of the concert. What a gift," she lied.

"Yes, and so are you." He removed his hand and began to caress her exposed, tanned thigh, inching closer and closer to the pink lace panties she wore.

Oh boy. Paige glanced down at his hand and then back up at him. "Drink first, remember?"

"I know, I know." His hand stayed on her thigh.

* * *

Inside the Baccarat, Paige ogled the exquisitely crafted chandeliers hanging from the ceiling, reflecting shards of glittery light. Red velvet barstools with white leather backs lined the black granite bar. A huge rectangular mirror reflected the well-dressed crowd of slick-haired men and botoxed women drinking and trying to outdo one another. Bartenders dressed in traditional wear chatted up guests and stirred chilled, colorful creations.

"Angel's Envy, neat. Manhattan, three cherries please," Paige ordered. She sat back, gazing around. "Seems this is the place to go to be seen."

The bartender brought their drinks. "You're right, lots of beautiful people. Cheers." Max lifted his glass.

Paige took a deep sip. "That's delicious." She glanced up at Max to see him staring at a dark-haired woman at the bar. The woman glanced up, saw Max staring, and abruptly turned away. "Do you know her?" Paige gestured with her head.

Max slid his eyes back to Paige. "Ah, no. She reminded me a bit of your friend, Fina. How is she by the way?"

"She's fine." Paige savored her drink. "She misses her grandmother though. I'm glad she's home." Paige opened her clutch for her lip gloss. Her phone lit up. Glancing at it, she saw she had two missed calls and a text.

Max sipped his drink and noticed Paige frowning at her phone. "Is everything okay?"

Paige shrugged. "I guess. I have two calls and a text."

Max drained his drink and said he needed to use the bathroom. As he sauntered to the back of the bar, Paige chuckled as she watched Max turn the heads of women as he walked by. *If you ladies only knew.* She picked up her phone and listened to her messages.

"It's me." Fina's voice, a hushed, urgent whisper. "Don't get mad, but I'm at the marina where the *Baltic Blue* is. I had to go try to see what's going on. Especially after what you saw in Max's apartment and being threatened by that asshole Brennan. I'll call you later."

Paige saw that call came in after eight. *Holy crap, Fina! What're you doing?* With her left hand, she blocked her ear and closed her eyes to concentrate. *Max'll be back any minute.* She listened to the next message. Again, Fina's voice was low, and urgent and hurried, matching her audible footsteps.

"Oh my God Paige! I was almost caught! I hid under the weird metal table...it kind of reminded me of a doctor's table... Brennan and some woman came in...and said something about doing rounds...and a lot of money and a folder? This folder...it had effin' pictures of *people* in it. I took pictures of them..."

Paige opened her eyes and saw Max heading in her direction. *Oh no. Hurry up, Fina!* Her brain split. Pasting on a fake smile, she listened to the rest of the message.

"And the last two photos were of...*you and me!* What the *eff?* I gotta get off this boat!" *Click.*

Paige felt a bubble of fear lodge in her throat as Max sat back down and gazed at her. *Keep smiling. Breathe. Smile. Breathe. Smile.*

He rubbed her knee. "Everything okay, love?"

Lie convincingly, Paige. Stay the course. "Yup. Just my mom."

"You look startled. Are you sure?"

I have to listen to her message again before we leave. Think, Paige! Under the bar, her knee began to bounce. *Stay calm.* "Yes. She's upset that, um, our dog is sick."

"I'm sorry to hear that." His eyes cut into hers. "Dog?" he questioned. "I don't remember you mentioning a dog."

That's because we don't have one. Think, Paige. She met his gaze. "Oh, I thought I did. Her name is Sadie and she's an old Lab. Mom's worried." Paige fiddled with a cocktail napkin. "I'll call her back tomorrow." Reaching for her drink, she saw Max's attention was diverted by an enormous, sparkler-filled birthday cake carried by singing servers.

"Damn!" Paige exclaimed after purposely letting the glass slip between her fingers. A deep brown stain defiled her dress. "I love this dress and I just ruined it!"

"Oh no! Hang on!" Max snapped his fingers and asked the bartender for a towel. "Here." He handed her a rag.

"I just bought this dress! I'm going to go to the ladies' room to see if I can blot this out. Be right back."

Inside the bathroom, Paige locked herself in a stall and listened to Fina's message again. *This is bad.* She called Fina back. It just rang and rang. A brick of fear crushed her chest. *Where are you, Fina? Damnit! Answer!*

She dialed again. Nothing.

At the marble sink, Paige raised her eyes to meet her blurry reflection. Taking a deep breath, she gave herself a mini pep talk. *You can do this. You need to do this. Act like nothing happened. Fina needs you. I have to get home.* A quick blot of lipstick and she was out the door.

Max sighed when he looked at her dress. "Oh no, I guess nothing helped. We can head back to my place."

No we can't. Ratcheting up the sadness in her voice, she said, "I'm sorry Max, I just want to go home. This is a brand-new dress and I should try to soak the whiskey out. I'm sorry."

"I see. Let's get you home then."

* * *

After calling Fina again on the way home—with no answer—Paige urged the cab driver to drive as fast as possible. *Please be home. Please be home.* Paige tore at a cuticle as the cab raced through the streets in the black night.

Paige burst through the door, throwing everything on the floor. "Fina! Fina!" She ran through the apartment. "Fina!" She panicked at the choking stillness. "*Fina!*"

Racing down the hallway, she saw Fina's bedroom door was cracked a few inches. *Oh God! Please be in bed!* Paige peeked around the corner. Her throbbing heart was the only noise she heard. Slowly she pushed Fina's door open. The bed was perfectly made. *Oh no! No!* On the night table she saw Fina's night retainer. *Fina always puts the case in the bathroom at night.*

Running down the hall to the bathroom, Paige glanced

in, praying to see some sign that Fina had been there. A wet towel, toothpaste cap left off, something to indicate her friend had been home. Nothing.

Alarm bells clamored throughout Paige. Her heart raced and her mouth was a desert. She hustled to the kitchen to find her phone. She fell into a chair and called Fina. It rang and rang.

Paige ended the call and tried again. Queasiness swept through her. *Please Fina, answer!*

She tried one more time with the same result. Her hand shook when she put the phone to her ear and listened to Fina's messages again. She checked the time they came in: 8:24 and 9:03. It was now close to eleven.

Where are you, Fina? Paige battled to keep dreadful thoughts from entering her mind. Pacing around the kitchen, her breath was ragged as the terrible thoughts won. *Oh my God, something has happened to her. I know it. She said there were pictures of us! What if she...*

Her phone leaped from the table, vibrating with an incoming call. *Please let it be her.* Paige snatched it up. "Fina?" she yelled.

"No, sorry. It's Max."

Oh shit! What does he want? Be cool. "Oh, hi Max."

"You don't sound very happy to hear it's me. Are you okay?"

He can't know Fina was on his yacht. Paige felt as if she was a tight-rope walker, five hundred feet above ground. Her heart knocked in her chest. Each word a step, carrying the weight of truth.

"Hello? Paige?"

She swallowed. "Sorry. I'm here. I was dozing off."

"Oh, I'm sorry. Were you able to clean your dress?"

My dress! I totally forgot. Glancing down at it, she lied,

"It's soaking, so fingers crossed."

"Good."

"Max, I'm sorry to cut this short. I'm really not feeling too well. My stomach is upset." *Not a complete lie.*

"I'm sorry to hear it. Is Fina there to help take care of you?"

A crackling in Paige's brain momentarily turned her into a frozen statue. Everything suddenly stopped. *Why would he ask that? He rarely asks about her.* His question caught her off guard.

Teetering on the tight-rope, Paige answered, "I can take care of myself. I'll call you later. I really need to lie down."

"I understand. I'm sure Fina will be happy to help. If she can't, call me."

"Thanks, I will. Talk to you later."

CHAPTER 31

Rolling the dart between her thumb and pointer finger, Lindsey stared at her opponent. "Last toss, Ed. Double or nothin'?"

The man nodded. "You're on."

Lindsey placed her left foot behind the throwing line and balanced herself in a split stance. Swigging from the beer she held in her left hand, she cocked her right elbow, narrowed her eyes on the bullseye, and tossed the dart. The tiny missile spiraled through the air. *Thwack!* It hit dead center.

"Yes!" Lindsey raised her hands in the air and did a little victory dance. "Pay up!"

Her opponent shook her hand and pressed several bills into her palm.

"Thanks Ed!"

"Great shot, Linds!" Martha clinked her beer bottle against Lindsey's.

"I love takin' that guy's money!"

Lindsey and Martha returned to their seats at the bar and chatted up the regulars. As Martha was entertaining the group with a story, she felt her phone buzz. Pausing midway, she reached into her pocket and answered it.

Lindsey grew concerned when she saw the color drain from Martha's face.

"Sit tight honey, we're on our way." Martha hung up

and looked at Lindsey. "We gotta go. It's Paige and she's hysterical."

* * *

One look at Paige's tear-stained face, Martha and Lindsey knew something horrible happened. Black mascara lay in the tiny lines around Paige's sorrowful eyes. Her red nose stood out against her wan complexion.

"Oh honey, what's going on? Is it Dovic? That prick hurt you?"

"No." At the kitchen table, between sobs in a raspy, strained voice, Paige told them all about Fina's messages. "She never came home and the yacht is the last place I know she was. I've tried calling and calling and no answer. I'm so worried I can't think straight! Oh my God... What if...what if she's..." She dropped her head on the table and sobbed.

Martha and Lindsey exchanged a look before Martha reached over and rubbed Paige's shaking shoulders.

"Let's not jump to conclusions. Start again, from the beginning."

Lifting her head and dragging the back of her hand across her nose, Paige breathed deeply and told them everything. She played the voice mail messages from Fina.

"And you had no idea she was going to go rogue?"

"No. I wasn't home. Once Fina sets her mind on something, there's no stopping her." She rubbed her face. Through her fingers, she whispered, "Fina said there're pictures of *us* in one of those notebooks in the cabin! What is *going on*?" Slumped in the chair, Paige bit back more tears.

"We need to figure that out." Martha eyeballed the coffee maker. "It could be a long night. Mind if I make some coffee?"

"I'll do it. I need the distraction." Paige dragged herself

from the chair and shuffled toward the coffee maker. She stopped halfway and whirled around. "Wait! The *yacht*! We need to go there! What if Fina's still there? What if she fell and hit her head?" Her voice grew shriller and more urgent as she went on. "Oh my God, what if she's floating unconscious in the water?! We have to do something! *Please!* We have to go to the yacht! *Please!*"

Lindsey and Martha placed their cups on the table and looked at Paige. Her frantic, anxious tone sliced through the gloomy room and right into their hearts. The desperation and fear carved into Paige's pale face sealed the deal.

"Good thing we didn't already have plans tonight. Let's go," Martha said.

* * *

Underneath the soft white moonlight and through the nearly empty streets, the women sped to the marina. Paige sat silently in the back seat, her only movement the bouncing of her left knee.

Martha killed the headlights and had barely parked the car before Paige leaped out in a desperate search for her friend.

"Fina! Fina!" Paige yelled into the blackness of the night as she raced toward the gates of the marina. "Fina! Where are you?" Paige yanked at the gate, but it did not budge. She pulled harder and harder. "Fina! No! It can't be locked! No! No!" Paige grasped both gates and shook them as if they were ragdolls. "We have to get in here!" Her hair whipped around her face. Her hands were claws on the metal. "Fina!" The rattling echoed across the still water and bounced off the sides of the yachts.

Martha and Lindsey trotted up behind Paige.

Martha reached out and put her hands on Paige's quaking shoulders. "Look honey, let's focus. It doesn't seem like anyone is here." She glanced around. "Hey, how about we walk down the side of the water, along that wall." She pointed to a cement wall that buttressed the water. "We can try to see if the yacht is even here."

Lindsey added, "Yeah, we may be able to see across the water. It's a clear night."

Through the dampening grass they walked. Crickets and cicadas sang their evening songs. Orange and yellow blinks from the tail of lightning bugs dotted the darkness.

Please God, let the boat be here. Paige peered across the marina, through the darkness at the row of slips. She stared. The *Baltic Blue* was nowhere to be seen. "It's gone," Paige whispered. "And so is Fina." Tears rolled down her cheeks. "Oh my God, what do we do?"

Lindsey spoke up. "All right, let's stay calm, lovie. Getting upset won't help. Since we can't go out on the dock to look around and we know the boat isn't theah, we should head back home and figure out our next move."

Paige slowly shuffled toward Martha and Lindsey who led Paige back to the car.

From a distance behind, they heard a man's voice call out to them. "Hey, what're you doin' here?"

They spun around and saw a light beam bouncing in the darkness. "Who's there?" The unfamiliar thin voice came from the darkness.

Lindsey whispered, "It's probably a security guard."

The person stopped about five feet from them. Flipping the light in their faces, he asked, "Help you ladies?"

"Hey! Easy with the light!" Martha yelled. "Ya tryin' to blind us?"

The man lowered the flashlight and clicked it off.

"What're you all doin' here?"

Paige glanced at her friends and spun a half-truth. "We ah, were supposed to meet my friend here earlier tonight. But we got the time mixed up. Have you seen anyone around here in the past few hours?" *Please let him say he saw Fina.*

"I only got on shift about an hour ago. But no, I've not seen anyone."

"Was another guard here before you?" Paige asked.

"No. Not during the week."

"Okay, well maybe we're at the wrong place. Thank you, sir," Martha replied. "Let's go girls."

Back in the car, Paige sank in the back seat, staring out the window, the blackness of the night matching her state of mind.

CHAPTER 32

Two powerful pots of coffee later, Paige, Martha, and Lindsey decided upon a plan. As they agreed, Paige would call in sick the next day from work. They decided it was best for her to stay at the apartment in case Fina called or returned home. "And I could file a missing person's report too, right?"

"We can discuss that. Why don't you go call Todd? Take care of that first, lovie," Lindsey encouraged. When she was sure Paige was out of earshot, she said to Martha, " I don't think we should put out a missing person's report. If we did and Dovic caught wind of it, he'll know we're sniffing around, agreed? I'm sure he has people everywhere."

"Oh yes. Scumbags like him use people like toilet paper."

Paige returned and continued talking about Fina. She told them Max asked if Fina was there to take care of her hours after she called from the yacht. "He *rarely* asks about her either. Don't you think that's odd?"

"That's fuckin' weird," Martha commented.

"Which begs the question: Why would he ask about her?"

"I don't know," Paige sighed and melted deeper into the couch. "But my instincts are telling me he knows something."

They rehashed their plan, and by the time they were finished, Paige had fallen asleep on the couch.

"I'll stay with her. It doesn't matter when I get to the office," Martha whispered.

"Sounds good. See you tomorrow," Lindsey replied.

Snap Decision

***

Paige woke to the sharp, welcoming aroma of coffee. *Why do I smell coffee?* Sitting up, she turned and saw Martha bustling about in the kitchen. Love and gratitude overwhelmed her. *She must have stayed with me. What would I do without her and Lindsey?* She sat up and reached for her phone, praying a message from Fina would be there. Paige wanted to ignore her instincts; sadly, they were accurate. Nothing. Tears sprang to her eyes. Her stomach was in knots. *She's dead, I know it.*

"Morning honey how did..." Martha began. "Oh Paige." She placed the coffee cups on the table and sat down. In Martha's arms, Paige sobbed. In between hiccups and nose blows, Paige shared her thoughts of Fina being dead.

"Hey, hey, don't go down that street. We don't know anything for sure, right? And I can guarantee we're gonna work like hell to find out what the hell's going on." She stroked Paige's hair and patted her back. "Okay?"

Paige nodded and reached for the coffee. "Thanks for making coffee, it's exactly what I need." She took a long, grateful slurp. "Do you think I need to file a missing persons report?"

Martha regarded Paige before answering. "To be perfectly candid, no I don't."

Perplexity and sorrow stood out on Paige's face. "Why not?"

"First, two days have to pass to report one, and second, someone like Dovic has people *everywhere*. Which means odds are he has connections in the police department. If he found out we suspect she's missing, we could jeopardize everything."

Paige's face crumpled like an airless balloon. "Damn

him. You're probably correct. I didn't think about that. This is so frustrating, Martha! I want to kill him!"

"I understand. Staying home today will be a positive thing. Do your best to relax. When I get to the office, I'll hop on my computer and do some hacking into Dovic's computer and see what I unearth."

Paige pivoted to Max. "What do I say to Max when he calls? I know he's going to call."

"Act like nothing happened and that you've been puking all night, or have horrible cramps, something like that."

"Something like that. He doesn't need to know about Fina if he doesn't already. My instincts are telling me he knows something."

Martha said, "Then you need to listen to them. Stay put here today, watch TV, whatever you want. If he calls, sound really sick, okay?"

Paige grasped Martha's hands. "I don't know what I'd do without you and Lindsey. Thank you so much."

"We got your back." Martha squeezed her hands.

***

Inside her compact office, Martha started pecking the keyboard. *Time to do some checking up on Max.*

She studied Max's email account history of his inbox and outbox. No red flags showed themselves there. In the junk box lay unopened messages, consisting mostly of the unsavory types. Her attention then turned to the folders on his desktop. Most contained data about shipping, costs, spreadsheets, personnel, and clients. Under Personnel was another folder. Clicking it, she scowled as her eyes raced from left to right. *What the hell is this? Some kinda spreadsheet?* Sliding her glasses up her nose, she continued to read.

Locations, dates, times, and a notation of *F/M* filled the screen. Each entry was numbered. She scrolled down. More of the same filled the screen. She counted over fifty lines. *This has nothing to do with what's in the other folders.* Martha noticed that all the locations were within a twenty-mile radius of Lower Manhattan; many were near the Hudson River.

Page two yielded the same results. Line after line of the same data. Guessing the *F/M* meant female or male, she jumped to the third page. *I was right.* Next to each *F/M* notation was a thumbnail picture of a person. Despite their graininess, Martha distinguished a common denominator—every person was in their late teens to late twenties. *What's going on here?* She sipped her coffee and squinted at the pictures. *What's that?* Tiny, almost illegible letters to the right of each picture caught her eye: *LV, C, L, K.*

Martha took her mug from the desk and leaned back in the chair. She stared at the opposite wall, contemplating what she saw in Max's files. A tinge of frustration nibbled at the fringes. *I need to figure this out.* She sat up and called Lindsey and asked her if she was available to meet her.

"Gimme an hour or two. I'm just gettin' back to the dock and I got a call from Nate, the harbor master. Seems he has some info on Dovic's yacht."

"Oh really? I can't wait to hear. See you soon."

* * *

Lindsey bid her crew goodbye and headed to the port authority office. Her friend and harbor master, Nate Elliott, sat behind a paper-piled desk.

"Hey Linds, have a seat," he said after she knocked.

"How are ya, Nate?" She lowered herself in a threadbare corduroy chair.

"Not bad, thanks. Anyway, I did some digging and I have to thank you for tipping us off on that yacht. You won't believe what I found out." He took a long drag from the straw sticking out of a thirty-two-ounce cup of something.

Lindsey drummed her fingers on the armrests of the chair. "Yeah?"

"It's not his yacht."

She stopped drumming. A frown accompanied a smack of disbelief. Lindsey gaped at Nate. "*What?* It's not Dovic's? Who the hell owns it then?"

"Seems it's owned by a mega-rich woman who lives in Sweden, right on the Baltic. According to my source, she's a higher-up at a shipping company over there. I'm assuming she and Dovic know each other through business."

Lindsey nodded and asked if he had a name.

Nate rattled off a name that was not familiar to Lindsey. "I wonder if she knows he uses the yacht?"

"Who knows. Those ID numbers? Seems as if they've been taken care of. I had one of our guys check them out."

Lindsey gazed at her friend. "Interesting. Thanks for all this, Nate. I owe ya a beer."

"Sure. Let me know if you need anything else."

Lindsey rose. "Will do. Thanks again. See ya around."

She called Martha outside. "Marth, you won't believe what I just learned. I'll see you in a bit."

* * *

"You gotta be fuckin' kiddin' me. The boat's *not his*?"

"Swear to Christ I ain't shittin' ya. Belongs to some woman in Sweden."

Martha leaned back in her chair and laced her fingers together. "Linds, all this is beyond whacko. Take a look at what I found."

The two women sat at the desk, scrutinizing the data Martha uncovered in Max's folder.

"Do you think these people worked on the yacht?" Lindsey asked, pointing at the photographs. "As crew?"

"Maybe, but wouldn't he have written their names somewhere near the picture?"

Lindsey agreed. She ran a thin finger along the line of the letters. "Is it some kind of code?" She glanced at Martha.

"I don't know. But they stand for something or else they wouldn't be written down."

Lindsey pointed out the peculiarity of all the locations being near the Hudson River. "Dovic's yacht, or whoever the hell owns it, isn't far from here. I wonder if that's coincidental?"

"Not sure." Martha opened a pack of crackers and handed Lindsey some.

"Thanks."

Martha studied the data in the folder again. Squinting, she leaned in closer. She saw there was another page in the spreadsheet.

"Linds, there's another page."

Two pairs of eyes scanned the next page. One read-through was not enough. The same thumbnail shots stared back at them, only larger. Martha and Lindsey sat in taut silence, scanning each picture. Along with a date, they noticed a new notation under the pictures, one not notated on page three: *Delivery approved by MPD.*

"What the hell?" Martha whispered. "They're Dovic's initials, right?"

"Yep. What do you think he's approving for delivery?"

"I don't know. But it's gotta be listed somewhere."

"Keep scrolling down."

Martha scrolled. More thumbnail faces stared back at them. All had the same notation underneath: *Delivery approved by MPD.*

Lindsey tore her eyes from the screen and slouched back in her chair. She stared at the ceiling. "Sweet Mother of God," she whispered. "Marth, do you think this SOB is *sex trafficking* these kids?"

Martha did not respond. She was a statue, hands resting on the keyboard, eyes locked on the screen.

"Martha?" Lindsey sat up. "What is it?"

Martha raised a shaky finger to the screen. She pointed at the last two thumbnails.

"Oh no," Lindsey gasped. "No."

Gazing back at them were pictures of Fina and Paige. Under Fina's picture: *Pending.* Beneath Paige: *Pending.*

Invisible fists squeezed the air out of their lungs. The women sat, unblinking, their minds not processing what they saw. Frozen to their seats, Martha and Lindsey gaped at the photographs on the screen. Martha ran her finger over the images. "They're our girls." It came out as a horrified whisper.

Lindsey could not tear her eyes away. "Yeah, this is bad, Marth."

At last Martha spoke. "I feel sick, Linds." Pointing at the screen, she continued. "Fina and Paige are in real trouble. If he's trafficking, they're next." She finished the crackers. "I need a beer."

Lindsey rose and opened the mini fridge. The bottles clinked in her hand. "Opener?"

"It's above the cookies."

Popping open the beers. Lindsey tossed out a suggestion. "Hey, check out those two shitheads, Stu and Marty."

"Good call." *Click click click.*

"Truth be told Marth, I'm a little afraid of what else we may find heah." Lindsey slid into her seat and handed Martha her beer.

"Yeah. Me too."

After a fruitless search into Stu and Marty, Lindsey suggested Martha check in on Paige.

"Yeah, I will. She was so upset this morning. I'm afraid she's convinced Fina's dead."

Lindsey gazed grimly at Martha. "Let's hope she's wrong. But considering no one has heard a word from her, I can't rule it out. On the other hand, if Dovic is sex trafficking these kids, there's the potential that Fina *is* being held somewhere—and that she's alive. Which means we could rescue her."

"Correct." Martha's lips formed a firm line. Shaking her head, she said, "Plus, I can't go down the street of Fina being dead."

"Same here. We don't know for sure."

"I think we should tell Paige about all this in person. I'll call her and tell her we'll come by later on today or tonight."

"Okay." Lindsey reread the info on the computer. *Considering the yacht is docked near these locations and it's not Dovic's, what's he doing acting like it's his? He's gotta be trafficking these kids. And he's using the yacht to transport them. Possibly drugging them first.* Her mind drifted to Paige. *We can't let that happen to her. It may be too late for Fina.*

Martha returned. "She sounded better than last night, but I'm still worried about her. We'll bring her some food or something when we go over."

"Perfect. First thing though, we need to go to the marina and scope out the yacht."

CHAPTER 33

Martha shut off her computer and said to Lindsey, "Yes, we do. I'm starting to agree with Paige about the yacht being the nucleus of everything going on. It was the last place Fina went and she hasn't been seen since. What Fina saw on it that night—and with Brennan warning Paige, Max's caginess about answering questions, and other crap—it's hard to disagree with Paige," Martha said. "Do you have the time to go?"

Lindsey nodded. "I'm scheduled to pull a tanker in tomorrow afternoon. I don't need to be onboard *Babe* till nine or so tomorrow morning." She stood and scanned the three shelves mounted on the wall. "Do you have a camera?"

"Whatta you need a camera for?"

"To take some pictures in case we see something strange at the marina."

Martha smiled and replied, "I knew there was a reason why we get along so good." She winked and pointed at her head. "Great minds..." From her desk, she removed an instant camera. "Ready?"

They grabbed their bags and headed out to the parking garage where Lindsey had parked her car.

"Traffic can be a bitch at this time. What's the fastest way to the marina?" Martha asked.

"How am I supposed to know? I work at the docks on the othah side of the river." She popped open the glove compartment and pulled out an old city map.

"Well shit, it's only two blocks away," Martha said, pointing to the map. "Go north on West Avenue to Vesey Street. Left on Vesey and another left onto North End Avenue."

"Luckily it's close."

Six traffic lights later they pulled into the parking lot of the marina. Lindsey killed the engine and gazed at the super yachts tied in their slips. Each yacht sparkled in the bright late-morning sunshine.

"Wow, those are some impressive yachts," Martha commented. "Must be nice."

"I'll stick with my little tug," Lindsey said.

Several minutes later, a black Cadillac Escalade crept through the parking lot and maneuvered down the wide dock to the stern of the farthest yacht—the *Baltic Blue*.

"Check that out." Martha nudged Lindsey. "Looks like some kind of government car."

"I can't see shit. The trees are blocking my view. I'm gettin' out."

They shut the doors quietly and walked toward the black car. Pretending to be tourists, they oohed and aahed over the yachts. An audible conversation floated toward them from the *Baltic Blue*. Lindsey grabbed Martha's arm and ducked behind the yacht adjacent to the car.

"Everything ready to go?" a voice called. "Are the coolers sealed properly?"

"Yes sir, all packed and ready."

"I'll send the confirmation as soon as you leave."

"What's all that mean?" Martha whispered.

The yacht sat at least fifty yards away. "We gotta get closer than here," Lindsey said. "Come on!" She grabbed Martha's arm and they skittered nearer to the Escalade and hid among a grove of trees. They peered through and clearly saw a man appear on the stern. In each hand was a small, white cooler.

"Hey, there's shithead number one—Stu," Lindsey whispered. "And they look like the exact same coolers from Fina's pictures."

"I think they are. Take a picture of him," Martha whispered.

She retrieved the camera from her bag and snapped several pictures, including Stu carrying the coolers and placing them in the back of the Escalade. "Hopefully these won't be blurry. I think we're close enough."

"We should get back to the car in case they leave soon and we can follow," Martha said.

"I have enough pictures, so yeah, let's go wait."

They did not have to wait long as the Escalade drove off the dock, turned left, and disappeared into traffic.

"Shit! We have to see where they're taking those coolers!" Lindsey said.

"What do you think are in those things?"

"Like the girls said, I'd say cash or drugs—or both, wouldn't you?"

Martha nodded and followed the Escalade. The vehicle headed north on West Avenue, then merged on the Hudson River Greenway. Martha and Lindsey trailed at a safe distance. Eventually the car reached 87 eastbound. For close to an hour, the women followed the Escalade. At last, it exited onto 684 northbound.

"Where the hell are we going? We've been following forever!" Martha's frustration bubbled over.

"Easy. We don't know. I don't like this anymore than you do, but we've come this far," Lindsey said, patting Martha's leg.

Up ahead they saw the Escalade had moved to the right lane and exited in the direction of Westchester Airport.

Martha and Lindsey did not let up.

"Think they're going to the airport?"

"Look, look they turned off the road onto that access road!" Martha yelled.

"I am! I can't run up their backs. Let's take our time," Lindsey barked back.

The Escalade pulled onto a small runway and stopped next to one of the smaller jets that were lined up like toy planes.

They watched as Stu exited the vehicle and retrieved the two coolers from the back. A well-dressed female appeared on the steps to the plane. One by one, Stu carried the coolers up the steps and placed them at her high-heeled feet.

Bending over, she opened up both coolers and smiled broadly. She held up her pointer finger to Stu and disappeared into the jet. A few seconds later, she reappeared and placed a large, thick envelope in Stu's hand.

"What's she so happy about?" Martha mumbled. "Well, they wouldn't be swapping cash for cash, so there's got to be drugs in those coolers, right?"

"No idea. Unless they *are* trafficking kids and knockin' 'em out with drugs they keep in those coolers. If so, Stu and Marty are the mules."

They watched Stu peer into the envelope, grin, and shake the woman's hand.

"And there's shithead number two," Martha exclaimed, pointing at Marty who appeared from inside the jet and hoisted the coolers into the jet where he stayed.

Stu gave a brief wave, jogged down the steps, and returned to the car. The steps retracted into the jet that turned and taxied down the runway. Within seconds, it was a tiny, white dot in the blue sky.

Scouting out his surroundings, Stu slid into the car. It

drove off in the opposite direction of the jet.

"What in *the hell* do you think is goin' on? A private jet? Coolers inside? I think this is worse than we ever expected. Let's see where he's going. Obviously, something *very* important is in those coolers."

"Agreed. Some kind ah drop with a transfer ah cash." Lindsey pulled a quick U-turn.

"What, you got eagle eyes? How do you know it's cash in the envelope?"

"Isn't it always?"

Racing down the highway, they caught up to the Escalade that was traveling back down route 684 in the direction of New York City. Without warning, the Escalade exited quickly, catching Lindsey by surprise.

"Oh shit, hang on!" she cried out as she snapped the wheel and cut across three lanes of traffic for the exit.

Horns blared. Middle fingers popped up.

"Holy crap, Linds! Pay attention!"

At the bottom of the exit they observed the Escalade was parked at a gas station across the street. Lindsey pulled in and backed into a spot far enough away to be inconspicuous, yet close enough to watch. She killed the engine.

"Are you crazy? Keep it on. It's hot as balls!" Martha complained.

"Fine."

"What do ya think they're doin'?"

Soon the driver and Stu exited the store. Stu wiped his forehead as he stood outside the car, eating with his mouth wide open. After stuffing the rest of the food in his mouth, he walked to the back of the vehicle, popped open the rear hatch, and reached inside. In his hands were two large white jugs. He walked to the dumpster by the side of the store, put one jug down, and opened the lid. He tossed both into the mouth of the vile dumpster. Martha snapped pictures of every one of his movements.

She turned to Lindsey, frowning. "What would he need to throw away jugs here?"

"I don't know, but once they leave, I think we go and see."

To be safe, the women sat for five minutes after Stu left. They jogged from the car and approached the dumpster. Martha opened the lid and promptly slammed it shut.

"Oh my gawd. I may puke!" She bent at the waist and gagged.

"That bad?"

"Yeah. See for yourself."

Lindsey lifted the lid and quickly shut it. "Bad news. We need to get those jugs, Marth. But neither one of us is crawlin' in that dump. No fuckin' way." She took out a Tiparillo and lit it. Through a puff she asked how much cash Martha had.

"Cash? Why?"

She nodded at the dumpster. "I'll bet you we can talk some kid to jump in there for us if we offer money."

Martha stared at her. "You wanna stand out in this heat and wait for a kid? How do you know a kid's gonna come by here?"

Lindsey pointed down the road. A pack of kids on bikes pedaled in their direction.

Martha snorted. "You actually think some *kid*'s gonna talk to us? What about stranger danger?"

"Just tell me how much cash you have!" She held out her hand.

Martha placed two folded twenties into it. "Happy?"

Lindsey inhaled. "Now we just wait till some kid comes by and we make the deal." She puffed out a cloud.

From a distance, Lindsey and Martha heard the high-pitched voices, the same group of kids—boys and girls—on bikes. Into the lot station they rode, simultaneously hopping off and tossing their bikes on the cement. They raced one another into the store. Several minutes later they exited with ice cream cones.

"Hey kid!"

Five heads swiveled. One of the boys, who looked to be the older ones, pointed to his chest in a *who me?* gesture.

Lindsey barked, "Yeah, you. Want to make an easy twenty bucks?"

The four others frowned at the women. Rumblings of "stranger danger" rippled among the group.

"Stranger danger my ass. Look kids, we need your help. Do we look like weirdos?" Martha said.

One of them replied, "Usually weirdos are men, not women."

Martha and Lindsey nodded and chuckled.

Emboldened by his friends' trust, he asked, "What do I have to do? Nothing creepy right? Like getting into a van?"

"Kid, do you see a damn van anywhere?" Martha asked. "Nah, nothing creepy or weird. We want you to climb in this dumpster"—she pointed—"and grab the two empty jugs at the bottom."

The boy shot them a perplexed look and glanced at his friends. Shrugging, he and the group ambled over to the dumpster. Two of the kids interlocked their hands, forming a human step. The boy hoisted himself onto the hands and leaped in.

"Oh my God! It smells like total shit in here!" He tossed the jugs tossed out like grenades, plucked from the ground by two girls. "Get me outta here!"

"Here ya go, lady," one said.

"Thanks honey."

The one boy hoisted himself out of the dumpster. He

held out his hand. "Easy twenty bucks."

"Here you go young man, thanks for your help." Lindsey handed over the twenty bucks. "Here's a little extra for your friends." She handed a girl a twenty. "Thanks again."

The kids beamed. "Thanks lady!"

They returned to their car and headed back home. On the way, Martha reached into the back seat and hauled one of the jugs into her lap. She looked at the label and read the bold letters aloud. "HTK. HTK? What the is that?"

"How in the hell do I know?"

Martha unscrewed the lid and took a sniff. "Holy crap that stinks!" she yelped. "Like a thousand rotten eggs! Gross!" She quickly replaced the lid and put the jug on the back seat.

"Oh man, I can smell it too! Gross! Open the windows!"

During the rest of the ride, they tried to put the pieces of the fragmented puzzle together: the pictures Fina took, odd notations in notebooks, the empty jugs of HTK, Fina's disappearance, and the jet taking the coolers. They landed on the same potential theory that Max and his crew were sex trafficking.

Lindsey theorized that HTK was a drug that knocked people out. "What else could it be?" When they were several blocks away from home, she said, "You're the computer expert and as soon as we get home, you're going to look up this HTK shit and find out what it is."

Martha smiled as she was thinking the same thing. "We're gonna shower first, though, before we do anything else. I'm feeling a little ripe."

Lindsey chuckled. "Damn right."

CHAPTER 34

Paige immersed herself in work. Numbers demanded her attention and she was appreciative that Todd put her in charge of several small audits; her days were long yet she was grateful, as work kept her mind off the impenetrable sadness she felt about Fina. Going home every night to a quiet apartment tore at Paige, so she stayed late at the office.

Her concentration was interrupted by Millie's voice barking through the speaker on her phone. "Paige, Max Dovic is on line one. Do you want to take it?"

God no. "I can't talk right now. Please have him leave a message. Thanks Millie."

"Fine."

During lunch, Paige listened to his message. "Hello Paige, I'm off to South Korea for a brief trip. It's last minute. I was hoping to see you before I left. Anyway, something went awry with the construction of that container ship. I'll call when I return, which will be tomorrow night. Looking forward to seeing you. Miss you."

I'm so glad you're far away, Paige thought.

The rest of the day flew by and by six thirty, Paige was done. *I need to get out of here and stare at a wall at home.* As she was packing up her things, her cell phone rang. *Oh shit, don't be Max.*

"Hello?"

"Hey it's Martha. How are you?"

Paige instantly felt comforted at the sound of Martha's

voice. *Phew.* "I'm okay. I'm really tired and starving."

"Oh sweetie, I'm sure. If it makes you feel any better, we got some good stuff to tell you. We'll get some pizzas and come over, okay?"

"Please do. I have beer."

"Say no more."

* * *

Three pizzas and two six packs later, the women sat in Paige's kitchen and discussed everything that had transpired in the last thirty-six hours.

Rapt, Paige did move a muscle as she listened to her friends' adventures of snapping pictures of the yacht, following Stu to the airport, the coolers, and dumpster diving.

An enormous smile spread across Paige's face when she heard they paid a kid to jump into a dumpster. "You *paid* a kid to get the jugs from the dumpster?" Paige laughed. "That's brilliant!"

"Yep. We sure as shit weren't gonna get in theah!" Martha laughed.

"It gets better," Lindsey said, tossing a pizza crust onto her plate. "You ready for this?"

Paige nodded.

"The yacht? It isn't Dovic's. It belongs to some woman who lives in *Sweden.*"

Everything stopped. Shock paralyzed Paige's brain and it raced through her entire body. She flicked her eyes between the two women. *Not his yacht? Sweden? What on earth is happening?* Once she processed what Lindsey said, her questions were machine gun fire. "*What?* Not his? How's this possible? And you said *Sweden?*"

"Apparently, the owner is a bigwig in shipping, so the

yacht could be part of an LLC. But we think Dovic is trafficking and using the yacht."

Paige cocked her head at the word. "Trafficking? Do you mean like human sex trafficking?"

"Yeah, we do. And you and Fina were next. Those pictures of young people—your age—we think they're victims. Our theory is Dovic finds them probably on the streets, and lures them to the yacht under the guise of hiring them as crew."

Apprehension filled Paige. "Then what?"

"We're not sure, but we think he drugs them and has them taken away by whoever he's workin' for. From there, these poor kids are never heard from again. That would definitely help to explain all the cash on board."

Paige felt the pizza roll up in her stomach into a heavy ball. "Oh my God! Do you think that's what happened to Fina?"

Martha sighed, "It's possible, honey."

"How do we find out for sure? I can't just ask him." Paige leaned heavily against the back of the chair. She closed her eyes. *I don't know how much more shock I can take.* "So there's a chance Fina *is* alive, but we have no idea where she is."

"It's possible."

"I need to know. We can't let Max get away with this; *I* can't let him get away with this. I have to do this for Fina. I'm going to confront him and see how he lies his way out of this one."

"Whoa! Paige, you could be putting yourself in danger. He's a *very bad* person. Confronting him may backfire. We all need to put our heads togethah and figure out a way to nail this guy."

"I've already *been* putting myself in danger for months—naively, of course. I'm such an *idiot*."

"Stop. Don't you dare blame yourself for any of this. Understand?" Lindsey ordered. "You're not a mind reader."

Paige remained silent yet nodded at Lindsey. "What do you suggest I do?"

"Don't change anything you've done. Keep acting like everything is great. Snoop when you can. Martha and I will work on our end to help you. Okay?"

"I will. He needs to go to prison."

CHAPTER 35

Inside Alfredo's Max sat at the table, waiting for Paige. He thought about the conversation they had earlier in the day. *Did I imagine a certain frosty tone in her voice? If so, why? She didn't seem too enthusiastic to have dinner tonight. I'll see how she is tonight.*

Max jumped to his feet when Paige entered Alfredo's and wrapped her in a tight embrace. He held her at arm's length and commented on her beauty. "I never tire of looking at you, especially your perfectly exquisite eyes. People would kill to have eyes like yours."

Play along, Paige. Act. "How was your trip?" She hugged him back. His cologne was intoxicating; to the point of slipping for a split second into another world, one in which there was no suspicion cast upon Max. *Pull yourself back!*

"Successful. We fixed a glitch in the ship's electrical system."

"Good news, right?"

"Yes."

"I'm glad to hear it. Do you think you'll have to return any time soon?" she asked after ordering.

"Why? Are you trying to get rid of me, Paige?" Max pushed out a laugh.

I wish. "Don't be silly. Since you like things perfect, that's a reasonable question to ask, right?"

"I can't disagree with you there."

Oscar asked if they cared for anything else.

"A check will suffice. Thank you, Oscar."

After a quick scrutiny of the check Oscar brought, Max laid a stack of cash on the table. Paige stared at it. *I don't want to imagine where he got that.*

"Are you all right, love? You're staring at the table." He reached over and caressed her cheek.

Paige inwardly winced at his touch. "I'm fine. Tired, but fine."

"Shall we?" He stood and helped her from her chair. Hearing a buzz, he took his phone from his pocket. "Who might this be?"

Paige saw his eyes widen when he saw the number. "Go ahead, answer it."

He nodded and stepped away. "Dovic." For several seconds, he listened until he placed his hand over it and told Paige he needed to take the call. "Sorry love, I'll only be a few minutes." He walked toward the other side of Alfredo's, near the bathrooms.

Perfect. Paige pounced on the opportunity to use the bathroom. She waited a few seconds for Max to settle into the call until she wound her way through the tables to the restroom.

Slipping by him unseen, she loitered outside the women's bathroom door. Above the clanking of silverware, chefs shouting, and people laughing, she was able to hear snatches of Max's conversation: "I'm glad she is no longer a problem... Are you sure you were thorough? ...No, nothing here...but it's only a matter of time with her... I'm not doing the grunt work, that's your job..."

His tone became laced with aggravation and menace. "Yes! That was the price we agreed on... Stu, I will not negotiate with that son of a bitch...too much cash is tied up... I'm running the operation and I will not...the price for her...it is...*set*. I have to go."

Paige heard Max snap shut his phone. *Oh no!* She quickly dashed into the bathroom, lunged into a stall, and collapsed onto the toilet lid. Resting her head against the stall wall, she felt her throat close. *Who is 'she'? Fina? And the price for her? Is he a pimp? Or worse?*

She knew Max would wonder where she went. Exiting the stall, she glanced in the mirror and reapplied her lipstick. Arranging her face with a bright, convincing smile, Paige took a deep breath and stared at herself. *Be strong.*

* * *

Back at Max's house, Max poured them a nightcap. Paige made her way into the living room and settled onto the couch. Music from his favorite playlist drifted in from the kitchen.

"Here you are. Cheers." He joined her on the couch, clinked her glass and took a deep drag of the chilled sambuca. "Delicious. Just like you." He leaned over and kissed her.

"Mmm, it is good." She sipped a tiny amount. "It's nice to be sitting here with you."

Stevie Nicks's sultry voice flowed from the kitchen. The sambuca danced in Paige's stomach and calmed her. She felt Max nestle back on the couch. He rested his hand on her thigh as he stretched out his long legs.

"I agree."

Several more songs played until Max rose and took Paige's hand. "Time to get more comfortable."

"Yes, it is. I need to use the bathroom first." Once inside, Paige took several deep breaths to help shift her mindset and detach herself from her feelings. *Time to go to that other world. Do it for Fina.*

Paige came out of the bathroom to see Max lying naked on his back, a smile spread across his face. "Hope you don't mind that I got more comfortable quicker than you."

Paige snickered. "Of course not." *Well done.* She dropped her bra on the floor and crawled between Max's thighs, onto the bed. She lay on top of him and kissed him, grateful that his eyes were closed. *It's just sex.*

Max started to gently move his hips under Paige, who matched his movements. He moaned lightly and gripped her backside forcibly. "I've missed this," he whispered. He looped one finger into the hem of her panties and gently tugged them halfway down. Until he stopped.

"Oh no." Gently, he nudged Paige from him. "I think my sugar is going low. Will you hand me my lancet and tester please?"

She obliged.

He pricked his finger and the bright red drop of blood stained the test strip. Max inserted it into the reader. It blinked *88.* "I'm okay." Relief was heavy in his voice. "Now where were we?" He pulled her onto him. "About here, as I recall." Their bodies meshed together in perfect, sensual sync.

It's just sex.

* * *

Paige lay awake and stared at the ceiling. She turned her head and gazed at a sleeping Max. Sadness and anger overcame her as she watched him sleep. The curl of his mouth, his dark lashes which curtained his eyes; she loved all that about him. *But not anymore. You're a fraud and a liar.*

Like a cat, she slid out of bed and spied his phone on the dresser. Lifting it carefully, she scrolled through recent calls;

nothing seemed unusual. His texts told a different story. Several were from Captain Brennan. Paige read them. Two of the three contained Fina's name. *Oh my God, no.*

A sudden snort made Paige's heart stop. *Oh no, he's awake!* Whipping around, she saw Max lying with his mouth hanging open like a car door, his face white as paste. Tossing the phone aside, she ran to the bed.

Sweat covered him. "Max!" She tapped his cheeks. "Max!"

His eyes were vacant and he began mumbling. Paige understood the words *doctor* and *yacht*. "Max!" Touching his clammy chest, she watched in horror as his eyes slowly rolled back. "No! You're not allowed to die!" *Not until you tell me where Fina is*, her mind added.

She dashed into the kitchen, yanked open the refrigerator, and took the orange juice.

Tilting his head back, she poured some of the juice into his mouth. He continued mumbling. "Fina...gone."

Mid pour, she stopped. *What did he just say? Fina? Gone? I know what I heard.*

Something inside her snapped. She waved the juice bottle in front of his pallid face. "You want more of this? Is that it? You're not gonna get it." She was possessed by a darkness; her hand crept up his neck to his sweaty throat. Looking down at his pale face, she squeezed.

"Where's Fina? You said her name! Where is she?"

Without warning, Martha's voice came to her. *"Yeah, I know he likes the girls. I've seen him with lots of them. You just need to be careful honey. Just cause he's hot as hell doesn't mean he can walk all over people. Guys like him think their shit don't stink. Who needs 'em?"*

Adrenaline pounded in her veins. *Martha's right. Who needs you?* She applied more pressure on his throat; his pulse raced. She squeezed harder until his tongue lolled out of his mouth and he began gasping. She felt sucked into a void as she slowly pressed even harder until the gasps turned to gurgles. Paige stopped for a split second and looked down at his pale, waxy face. *Damn you Max! I know you know where she is! I should kill you right now!* She continued squeezing.

Paige's heart sped into a full sprint when she heard Fina. *"Oh my God! Paige, stop! What are you doing? What's going on in your head? You need him alive! He's your link! If you kill him, you won't be able to help find me! Stop Paige! Stop!"*

Tears dampened her eyes at the sound of Fina's voice. Unexpectedly, Paige felt her hand release itself from Max. Her body shook as if she was sitting naked in a snowstorm.

"Oh my God! What *am I* doing?" she whispered. She stared at her hand, horrified that she almost killed him. Dizziness overcame her when she stood and reached for the orange juice.

Staring down at Max, she tilted his head back and poured more life-saving orange juice into his mouth. *You're not allowed to die.* "Swallow it." Over the throbbing of her heart, she heard his breathing level off. Perspiration poured down her back.

After what seemed an interminable wait, Max returned. Blinking widely, he looked at Paige. "What happened?"

Incredulous, Paige replied, "You don't remember?" *I almost killed you.*

Shaking his head, he replied, "I remember the sex and I remember falling asleep." He patted the mattress. "It's soaking wet. My sugars got too low."

"Yes, dangerously low, I'd say, based on how much you were sweating. I gave you juice to bring you back. Do you remember mumbling? You said some pretty strange things." *Let's see what he says.*

Max blanched. "I did? Such as?"

"Words—like *doctor* and *yacht*." Paige studied his reaction. "Oh and you also mentioned Fina's name and something about 'gone.'"

A flash of unease crossed over his face. He shifted position in the bed.

He knows something. She felt it in her bones. "Why do you think you said Fina's name?"

Max remained silent for a beat. Staring ahead, he gathered himself. "Interesting. I ah, don't know why her name came out. Hypoglycemia has a mind of its own and can reduce a person to a blathering fool." He took her hand, kissed it, and pressed it to his cheek. "What matters is that you helped bring my sugars back up. Thank you, love."

Paige took the juice and went into the kitchen.

Max dropped his head back into the pillow. A worried sweat pricked his scalp.

CHAPTER 36

At home, Martha and Lindsey each took an empty jug from the back of the car and headed to the elevator.

Martha turned to Lindsey. "For the love of God, don't open that jug again. The smell almost killed me."

"I won't. I hope it's not some toxic chemical we inhaled."

"Nah. Plus, we smoke, so what's the difference?" Martha laughed.

"True!" Lindsey cackled.

Lindsey showered first while Martha rummaged in the fridge for the leftover spaghetti and meatballs to heat up for dinner. Lindsey appeared twenty minutes later and offered to make a salad while Martha showered.

Her eye caught sight of the two jugs sitting on the floor by the front door. *What is this HTK?* she wondered. *Aside from smelling like friggin' dog shit.* She knew that Martha was the computer whiz so she called out, "Hurry up! I wanna know what this stuff is!"

Martha materialized several minutes later, towel wrapped around her head. A frown formed between her eyebrows. "What's the big rush?"

"I want you to check out this stuff on the computer." She pointed at the empty jugs.

"Fine, but gimme a minute to get dressed."

Martha reappeared and plopped down on her office desk chair. Several minutes passed until the computer booted up for her to get online. An unexpected whiff of rotten eggs snuck up her nose. She turned to see Lindsey sniffing an open jug.

She whipped around in her seat. "Ah crap Linds, what're ya doing? That stuff smells so bad! Why are you sniffing it?"

"I was looking in to see the color of the liquid. It's clear."

"Great, now put the top on it before I friggin' puke!"

The computer buzzed and the screen turned from dark green to blue.

"Here we go." Martha typed in the three letters. The rainbow icon swirled around like a stickless lollipop until the result popped up.

HKT is a synthetic fluid for hydraulic brakes based on polyglycols and corrosion additives. Martha reread the words aloud as Lindsey leaned over her shoulder.

"What the fuck? That stuff is *hydraulic* fluid?" Lindsey echoed. "Weird smell for hydraulic fluid. I've never smelled this kind before."

"What do they use it for?" Martha asked.

"It's used for steering wheels, motors, cylinders, all that kind ah stuff."

"Like all the stuff needed to run a super yacht?"

"Yeah, so I guess. I know I don't use it on my tug. Two totally different boats though." Lindsey frowned. "But why were they tossed miles away?"

"That's the million-dollar question. Something is way off." Martha leaned back in the chair, her mind racing. "Like you said before, black market?"

"That's the first thing that comes to mind. We can talk about it over dinner. First though, I'll toss these out." Lindsey grabbed the two jugs, walked out to the hallway, and threw them into the garbage chute and slammed the door shut.

* * *

The sound of wailing siren in the distance woke Martha up from a deep sleep. She looked at the clock and saw it was five thirty. She knew she had to get up for work around seven.

Ah man. That siren is so loud. I hope I can get back to sleep before my alarm goes off.

She closed her eyes, rolled over, and tried to fall back asleep. The whirring sound of her small fan, coupled with the siren, denied her wish. She lay there staring at the ceiling when it hit her: *Did I type in correct letters from those jugs? Hydraulic fluid should not have a rotten egg smell. Lindsey even said that.*

Martha rose and put on her Bruins sweatshirt and pants. She headed out the apartment and took the elevator to the basement. *I gotta check the trash to try and retrieve a jug.* Good luck was on her side as the trash bin was still full. She heard the truck rumble her way.

The trash truck is here. I've got to get those jugs. She waved at the driver who brought the truck to a halt. "I need your help. I accidently threw two white jugs in the trash and I need to get them back."

"Really, lady?" His dark eyes bore into hers.

"Please? It's really important!"

The driver stared at her for a second then threw the truck in park. He put on his safety glasses and exited the truck's cab.

"I really appreciate this," Martha said.

He chuckled. "Believe it or not, this kinda thing happens all the time. Give me a second to sort through this stuff." He grabbed the bags sitting bunched on the curb and hurled them into the back of the truck. Within minutes he had the two jugs and handed them to Martha.

"I figured since they weren't bagged, they'd be easy to find."

She beamed. "Thank you very much. I feel bad I slowed you down this morning."

"No worries, happy to help."

She returned to the apartment and made coffee and jumped in the shower. Once she was dressed for work, she sat down at her computer and typed in the correct letters, *HTK*.

Her mouth fell open. She double-checked the letters on the jug. *What? Shit! Damn dyslexia screwed it up the first time!* "It's HTK! Not the other way around! Oh my gawd!" Her eyes, wide as frisbees, raced down the screen. *This is very, very bad.* She picked up her phone and called Lindsey.

"Yo what's up?"

"My dyslexia screwed me up last night! I typed in the letters in the wrong *friggin' order* from those jugs we found! And after you mentioned hydraulic fluid shouldn't smell that way, I got those jugs from the trash and I typed in the letters the *right way* this time. It's *HTK* and you won't believe what this shit is used for."

"I can hardly hear you; I'm about to head out to pick up a tanker. I won't be available till late. I'll call you later. Sorry."

Martha stared at the screen sipping her coffee, rereading the information on HTK. *I can't believe what I'm reading.*

* * *

On the subway ride to work, Martha almost missed her stop. She was consumed with what she read about HTK. Upon arriving, her supervisor informed her that the afternoon guard, Barry, was sick and she needed Martha to pull a double, which meant her workday would end at eight that night.

Fuck you, Barry you aren't sick—you're probably playing golf. Bastard. Rather than wasting time thinking of Barry, Martha decided the best course of action would be to show Lindsey the search results of HTK. *Plus, I can't remember all those technical words. I want her to read it to confirm.* After she unlocked her office door, she called Lindsey and left her a message about dinner.

* * *

Martha sat at Chub's sipping a beer. Her mind galloped like a racehorse with thoughts and theories about HTK and why it would be on Max's yacht. She looked at her watch, she thought, *Linds should be here soon.*

"This seat taken?" She chuckled as Martha turned to her.

"Yea, I'm waiting for a rich millionaire to sit there and ask to marry me!"

Lindsey snickered. "Yeah, right."

The bartender brought over Lindsey's whiskey. She took a long sip and smiled. "Ah, that is what I needed."

"You can say that again." Martha clinked her beer against Lindsey's glass.

"So tell me about those jugs. What is HTK?"

"It's a chemical, but not what I thought earlier. It's too nuts to try to explain. I know I'll screw it up because all ah the technical language. I want you to read it for yourself before we can talk about why it's on that yacht."

"Sounds kind of serious."

Martha cast her eyes at her friend. "Lindsey, this is a whole other level of bad. Worse than what we thought earlier."

Lindsey asked if she told Paige. Martha replied Paige left

her a message that she was with Max and would call in the morning.

"Wait till she hears all of this," Lindsey said and ordered another drink.

CHAPTER 37

Before showering, Max sat on his bed and checked the units of insulin in his pen. With his fist balled, he punched his thigh three times when he realized he injected too many units before dinner at Alfredo's. *Idiot! Pay attention! You could have ruined everything! Or killed yourself! How could I be so damn careless?*

He could have easily incriminated himself because of his diabetes. *You need to be more careful, Max. She's a smart woman and can't know about Fina.*

Max relished in the hot water gushing over his tired body. Rubbing his sore neck, he closed his eyes to try to replay the previous night's events. He failed. He continued to verbally punch himself for allowing his sugars to plummet. *You must control this better.* As far as he could remember, he did not feel as if he babbled about his "side business" to Paige. *But she said I mentioned Fina's name. That may tip her off. I'll play dumb if she asks about it again.*

He stepped from the shower and dried off. Towel wrapped around his waist, he sauntered to his bedroom and chose casual clothes. Clanging and banging coming from the kitchen made him smile. *Oh good, she's still here and she's cooking breakfast.* A sharp crack on a glass bowl was followed by four more cracks. Max then heard metal knocking at a brisk pace against the glass, followed by a sharp sizzle of a pan. *Eggs. Good, I'm starving.* Smoky, fatty bacon popped and sizzled, and its mouth-watering aroma danced into the air.

Crossing through the living room, he heard Paige whispering in a low, urgent voice. He padded over to the door leading into the kitchen. Ducking his head around the corner, he saw that Paige clutched her phone, her right hand waved anxiously, matching the tone of her voice.

"What are you *talking about?* Seriously? The *yacht?* I think..." Instinctively she glanced toward the bedroom; just in time Max ducked his head to the side. "Yeah, he's still in the shower...okay...yes, I believe you... *What? Body parts? Fina's name?* Oh my God, Martha...what're you *talking* about? I need to tell you guys about last night too... He was babbling about the yacht and he said Fina's name... Why would he say that? I'll call back in a little while..."

When she jammed the phone in her pocket, he scampered to the other side of the door, to be on her "blind side," as she called it. He felt the sweat under his arms. His heartbeat ramped up. *Who's Martha?* Max spun through his mental rolodex. Digging deep, he could not put a face to the name. *Never mind that. She heard something last night, but what and how much?*

"Good morning, Paige," Max said as he entered the kitchen.

Paige set her eyes on him, her smile cheerful and saccharine. "Good morning to you. How're you feeling?"

She looks fine to me, but you heard her. Max searched her face for a sign of alarm or fear. He saw nothing but radiant beauty. *Did I imagine what I heard? No. No I didn't.*

"I'm feeling good, thanks to you. I'm starving though."

"Good. Sit down then." Paige set a plate piled high with scrambled eggs and three slices of bacon. She poured him a cup of coffee. "Bon appetite!" She turned and went back to the sink to wash the pans.

"Who *does* this kind of thing? Who thinks to *murder* people and *sell* their organs as a cash commodity?" Paige snuffled and wiped her puffy eyes with her sleeve. "All those people in the notebooks..." A wistful, despondent look lay on her face.

"Sick, heinous people who make a lot of money doing this, that's who."

Paige drummed her fingers on the table. Quietly, she added, "This explains *so* much—the cash on the boat, him paying cash for everything." Her hand flew to her mouth; a horrifying epiphany crackled through her. "Oh no, oh God no! All the times we went out, he paid with the cash from..."

"Honey, *if* it was blood money, how could you know?" Martha said.

"I need a drink," Paige said. "My head is about to explode."

"Help yourself." Lindsey pointed to the fridge.

Paige rose and opened the fridge and gaped. "You're well stocked. Thank God." Bottles and cans of all varieties stared back at her.

She filled them in on what happened to Max and his odd ramblings.

"He's a diabetic? No shit!" Lindsey exclaimed.

"Yes, and when he went into hypoglycemia, he blathered and sort of passed out. And then..." She trailed off.

"Then what?" Martha pushed.

Paige took a gulp. "I...I...put my hand around his throat... and squeezed until he gasped."

Martha and Lindsey were still as tombstones. Finally, Martha broke the silence. "You wanted to kill him, didn't you?"

Paige did not respond.

"You look a little pale, honey," Lindsey remarked.

"I've never felt a feeling like that before. I felt like I was outside my own body." Paige sipped her beer and gazed at the wall. She told them Max uttered Fina's name and the word *gone*. "I'm shell-shocked, and I need some time to digest this. I'm having a really hard time believing Max actually killed Fina."

Lindsey and Martha exchanged a look that Paige did not like.

"What?" Paige uttered.

Martha did not hold back. "Paige, the date next to Fina is August 15–30. We think that means that she was gonna be taken somewhere between those dates. And since her last message came in after she went to the boat, we assume she's been snatched. We're hoping she..." Martha swallowed and cleared her throat. "...may still be alive."

"What are we going to do? *If* she's alive, we have to find her, wherever she may be." Paige fought back tears. "He could be holding her captive on the yacht, right?"

Martha spoke up. "Anything is possible. Speaking of the yacht, we agree with you about it being the hub of operations. I think we need to go back."

"When?" Paige asked.

"Tonight. The sooner the better."

"Okay, but I need to go home for a bit. I need to sort all of this. I'll call later."

Paige was grateful for the clear afternoon air. Walking down the sidewalk, she stopped and sat down on a bench. *How has all this happened? I can't believe I've been sleeping with someone who has been selling organs. And most likely, murdering people.*

Across the street, she watched a young couple walking hand in hand, laughing at something. *Must be nice to be oblivious to the horrors of the world.* She sat for a little while longer before hefting herself from the bench.

***

Stu and Marty watched her exit Martha's building.

"I wonder what all that was about," Stu said.

"I'll call Dovic and ask what he wants us to do," Marty said.

The call did not last long.

"He doesn't want us to do anything. He wants her alive. Time to go back to the office. He wants us there."

Stu put the car in drive and headed back to Lower Manhattan.

CHAPTER 39

Feeling the beers she tossed down earlier, Paige lay down on her bed in the soundless apartment. *I hate how quiet it is here. I miss Fina's awful singing. I miss her arrabiata sauce.* Thinking about Fina made her body ache with sadness. *Close your eyes, you need some sleep before tonight.*

A few hours later she woke and lay still. Her head spun like an agitator in a washing machine with all she had learned. Her thoughts turned to Max. *That son of a bitch. He's a liar, a criminal, and a possible murderer. Someone has to stop him. And that someone is me.*

She reached for her phone and called Martha. "I think we need to go late tonight. Sound okay? Meet me downstairs here at eleven."

* * *

Into the dark night went the women to the marina. Darkness swallowed up the practically empty parking lot. No light shone from the guard's booth. The dock stood lifeless and empty. A smattering of tall, skinny lights cast dull light down on the worn, damp concrete. Gentle lapping water played its rhythmic beat against the sides of the yachts. Night lights situated at the top of the bridges and masts on some of the yachts popped in the dark. It felt strangely peaceful and looked eerily beautiful. Arriving at the stern of the *Baltic Blue* they saw one light on in the lower deck.

"Shit!" Lindsey whispered and pointed at the light.

"Doesn't mean anyone is here," Paige said.

"Hope not," Martha whispered as she and Lindsey took steps forward.

Paige grabbed both by an arm and said, "No, just me. I know the inside of this yacht and what room to look for. Plus, I need lookouts."

Lindsey and Martha reluctantly agreed. "You sure?"

Paige nodded. She tiptoed to the gangplank that led to the sprawling stern deck. As she boarded, Lindsey and Martha ducked into the grove of trees across from the yacht. They shot Paige a thumb's up.

Crouching down, she stayed beneath any windows leading into the living areas. Like a cat, she crept to the steps leading down to the passageway. Her heart pounded and her mouth felt like a desert as she felt her way along the wall, counting the door handles until she arrived at the cabin. Inhaling deeply, she prayed the door was unlocked. Reaching out, she slowly turned the handle. *Brace yourself.* The door opened.

Stepping in, a waft of rotten egg aroma hit her. She gagged and forced herself to breathe from her mouth. What Martha said about the odor of HTK came back to her. *Oh no, it must have been used in here recently.*

She turned on her flashlight. The beam glanced off something shiny laid out on the desk. Peering closer, she recognized a scalpel. Surgical scissors, a suction cup with a hose, and gauze pads were laid out as well. Tendrils of fear crept up Paige's back. Her stomach was sour. *Surgical tools.*

Turning full circle, she spotted the coolers across the room. *I have to see what's in them.* She reached out a trembling hand, grasped the lid of one, and removed it. She shrank back at the smell. *HTK. Oh no.* Her skin tingled with fear. Peering in, she was both relieved and dismayed it was empty. *I wonder if the other one is empty too.* She pulled off the lid. Nothing, aside from a brownish smudge on one side.

Next to the coolers was a notebook, one that looked exactly like the others she had discovered earlier in the summer. Flipping through, she saw on each line was written a name, an organ, and a date. *Oh my God. This goes back to over a year.* Flipping through the pages as quickly as possible, she turned to the most recent entry: *Fina Manzetti – Cornea and kidney, 8/15 – 8/30.* Next to the date was an asterisk with *MPD* initialed.

She struggled to breathe as the cabin shrunk in on her, her brain spinning like a merry-go-round. Her knees buckled and she collapsed onto the floor. Paige lay still, sweating profusely. Her pulse throbbed in her ears; her chest heaved. She knew she couldn't stay here.

Get control of yourself. Count to ten. Sitting up against the coolness of the wall helped control her breathing. *Stay clear-headed.*

It took several minutes, but she regained her composure. Rising from the floor, she looked at the notebook again. What she didn't notice the first time was an entry several lines down from Fina's. It read: *Paige Buckley – Liver and heart: 9/12.* Again, the asterisk and *MPD* initialed.

Oh God! I'm next. I'm in a nightmare and—

A thump from the floor above paralyzed her. She muffled her gasp. Tearing the page from the notebook, she stuffed it in her pocket and flicked off the flashlight. The darkness of the passageway felt like a tomb. As she crept toward the staircase, the cool night air floating in was a perfect head-clearing elixir. Up the steps she went. Scampering toward the stern, she heard it.

"Now what do we have here?" the voice asked.

Captain Brennan. Paige spun around, her heart raced. *Don't let him see your fear.* She met his eyes.

"I know what's going on here, you sicko. Or more accurately, you're a murderer!"

"Oh dear. I don't like to be called *names.*" The last word twisted his face into a mask of hatred. He took a step toward her, pushing Paige toward the side of the bridge.

Paige stared him down. "Where is she?"

He pointed at the dark water. "Your stupid little friend is fish bait. Just like you're going to be!"

Paige leapt forward toward the gangplank, but Brennan was too quick. He lunged and grabbed her sleeve. Paige screamed and kicked him in the crotch. It did not stop him. Raging, he grabbed her and threw her against the stern wall. Stars danced in her eyes and she felt dizzy as she slid down to the carpet.

"You nosy little bitch. I should have killed you earlier!" he screamed as he gripped Paige's throat.

Paige tried to yank away his hand, but he was so strong. She panicked like a trapped animal.

He leaned in and hissed, "It's going to be fun watching them cut you up too! If I had my way, I would've done it sooner, but Dovic liked having you around as his toy."

Paige's horror ratcheted up a notch as she struggled to breathe. Mustering her strength, she spat in his face.

Glaring at her with hot-white hatred, he squeezed harder. The sky over his head spun like a wound-up top. Dizziness did not stop Paige from groping the wall in desperation for anything to fight. Something cold was under her right hand.

"Oh no you don't!" He threw the object into the water.

Her esophagus was being crushed. She felt life slipping out of her. *It can't end like this! Fight, Paige!* The deck started to spin. The dark abyss opened and began to pull her in.

More pressure on her throat. *Oh God no!*
"Take that mutha fucka!" *Crack!*
Paige did not see Brennan crumple. On the deck she lay unconscious, like a broken doll.

CHAPTER 40

Opening her eyes, Paige studied the walls of the room bathed in early-morning light. The striped wallpaper was fuzzy at first. Blinking her eyes, things came into view. A portrait of a woman with a stern face stared at her from the wall opposite the bed. Sitting up, she glanced at the bedside table. On it was a picture of four smiling people in a wooden frame. Picking it up, she recognized a young Martha. *How did I get here? And why does my neck...* She suddenly remembered what occurred. *The yacht. Brennan. I almost died.*

Voices floated underneath the door. *I'm at Martha's.* After a few minutes, Paige slung her feet onto the carpeted floor, rubbed her face, and joined Martha and Lindsey in the kitchen.

"There she is! How're you feeling, lovie?" Lindsey asked.

Paige slid into a chair. "Beaten up, but glad to be alive."

Martha poured her a cup of coffee. "Heah, this'll give ya that much-needed jolt."

The scalding rich coffee hit the back of her throat. "Thanks, this is good."

Martha asked what she remembered from earlier.

"Just about everything until I blacked out. What else happened?"

Martha filled her in. "And then I smashed the captain over the head with a pole! Whacked that MF'er! He crumpled like a sack ah potatoes."

"Is he dead?"

"We don't think so. We heard him whimpering when we

stepped over him and carried you off the yacht. But I bloodied him pretty good!"

"He's the least of our concerns."

Paige took another sip and digested everything from earlier that morning. "I need to show you guys something." She returned to the bedroom where her jacket was. Retrieving the ripped page from the notebook, and her phone, she returned to the kitchen and put it on the table.

"What's this?" Martha asked and put on her reading glasses.

"Just read it."

Martha's eyes grew wide. She then handed it to Lindsey whose mouth fell open as she read it.

"Holy shit. This is bad," Lindsey said.

"Yes, it is." Paige sighed. She dropped her head in her hands. "I don't know what I'm going to do. My name is on that list. Which means..." She could not stomach the thought.

"Honey, this is the proof you need. Dovic is in on this—if not leading it," Martha finished.

"You're right. I didn't want to believe it, but his initials are there in *his* writing." Paige rubbed her temples. "What a nightmare."

"We don't know if Dovic knows about earlier today. We should be smart and go on the assumption that he will find out. Brennan may tell him."

Paige pondered this. "Unless Brennan does *not* tell him which he may not do because Max detests failures of any kind. Brennan may not have the balls to tell him. But that aside, what do I do?"

"We—" Martha was cut off by the bouncing and vibrating of Paige's phone.

She recognized Max's number. "Oh no. It's Max. What do I do?"

"Don't answer it. Let's see if he leaves a message," Lindsey suggested.

Soon, the phone registered one voice mail. "I'll play it."

Max's smooth, silky voice filled the room. "Hello love, I thought I'd call to check on you. You seemed flustered when you left the other morning. Perhaps we can have lunch sometime next week. Please call me."

"He sounded normal to me," Lindsey observed. "Then again, most psychos do."

Paige nodded absentmindedly. Her thoughts switched to the date she saw with her name next to it: September 12, only a few days away. "This is so much to take in. I don't want to see him, but I know I have to in order to catch him." She rose from the table and paced the living room.

The women glanced at one another. "Yes, you do," Lindsey said. "This guy can't do this to anyone else."

"We know you love Max and we're so sorry. He's a sick son of a bitch and we need to keep you safe and protected. We could not do that for Fina," Martha added.

"Love him? I want to kill him!" Paige returned to the table and dropped solemnly into the chair; her top lip quivered as white hot anger burned inside. *He killed my best friend.* We need to nail his ass sooner than later, for me and for Fina."

"Good. We are working on a plan to keep you safe," Martha said. "But there are things about it you may like."

Paige scowled at her. "Really? Like what?"

Martha sighed. "Until everything is finalized, I don't want to tell just yet. Plus, before we tell you, you need to deal with him."

"Yes." She sighed. "I guess I need to call him back. He'll be very persistent and mistrustful if I don't."

Lindsey rose from the table and returned with a plate of doughnuts. Paige helped herself to a jelly one, covered in powdered sugar. "What do I tell him? My head is spinning so much it's a fight to think clearly."

"When you call him back, tell him you misplaced your phone. Suggest meeting for lunch. Safer during the day than the night."

Paige nodded and swallowed the rest of the doughnut. "Right. I'll call him later."

"Okay then. Lindsey and I will put the final touches on the plan. I need some time to take care of a couple ah things over the next two days."

"Okay. Can you at least give me a hint as to what your plan is all about? Remember, I have a job and things like that."

Lindsey responded, "Before too long, you will need to give your boss the notice that you're leaving."

Paige was caught off guard. "You're serious, aren't you?"

"Oh yes."

CHAPTER 41

Paige and Martha boarded the subway together and discussed the week. Paige explained she was involved in a weighty and important project that would be very time consuming.

"That's a good thing, even though you're going to be giving notice. Before we part ways today, I need you to follow me to my office for that thing we talked about."

They entered Tower Two together and headed to Martha's office. From her desk drawer, she took a small microphone.

"As nuts as this sounds, you need to tape this to your bra when you know you're gonna see Dovic. I can record everything you say, provided you stay within a hundred or so yards."

Scowling, Paige asked, "What if he sees it? I'll be in real trouble."

"Unless you plan on doing a strip tease or having sex, he won't see it." Martha chuckled.

"Hard no on both of those." Paige dangled the small microphone and inspected it. "I feel like I'm in a spy movie." She laughed quietly. "After I talk to him, I'll call you. Thanks Martha."

* * *

Thankful for the detailed and time-consuming audit she was overseeing, Paige was able to concentrate mostly on work and not Max. Around midmorning, she returned his call, saying she'd like to meet for lunch and to call her back later.

Paige, unaware of the world around her, was knee-deep in running columns of numbers and comparing spreadsheets. She practically leaped from chair when she heard his voice.

"Busy, I see."

Snapping her head up, she saw she had company. "Oh, Max! Hi! I didn't know you were going to stop by." Her heart triggered into a fast, unwelcome beat. *Stay calm.*

"No you didn't. I wanted to see your beautiful face in person," he purred. "I've missed it."

She stood and cleared her throat. "I ah, left you a message about lunch. Are you free today?"

"As a matter of fact, I am. Shall we go now?" He pulled back the cuff of his monogrammed shirt and consulted the enormous wristwatch. "It's nearly twelve."

Think. Don't answer too quickly. "Shoot. I can't quite yet because of all this." She gestured toward her desk. "Meet you down on Liberty around twelve thirty?"

He leaned against her cubicle wall, gazing at her. "Fine." Pushing himself from the wall, he sauntered around her desk. Bending down, he whispered, "Don't be late. You know I don't like that." He stood and left.

Fear flashed through her for a split second before anger stomped it out. *Screw you.* Watching him disappear to the elevator, one thought crossed her mind: *You're going down, you sick son of a bitch.* She waited until he stepped into the elevator to call Martha. "We're having lunch in thirty minutes on Liberty."

"Great. I'll come up and help you get wired."

* * *

Back in his office, Max called Brennan. "Get the yacht and the cabin ready. We'll be there by one."

* * *

Paige stepped out in the glorious late summer September afternoon. Blue sky stretched for miles, giving the day a pure clarity. As Paige glanced around for Max, she admired how the Twin Towers stood out majestically against the sharp blue sky. *What beautiful buildings.*

Aromas from the food trucks mingled in the air. People sat on benches, enjoying lunch in the sun; one of those people was Martha. Paige gave her a small wave. From the small distance, Paige saw her put in the earpiece and sit back on the bench. Tapping the wire, Martha flipped her a thumbs up.

"There you are." Max surprised her from her blind side. "Are you ready, love?" He kissed her cheek.

Oh no, did he see me wave at Martha? Paige smiled at him. "Yes. I'm starving."

"Good." He firmly took her arm and led her to the sidewalk, past the food trucks.

"Aren't we eating down here? You like the food trucks." She felt unnerved at his firm grip.

"Since we've been apart, I thought I'd take you on the yacht for lunch; you work hard and you deserve only the best." He waved at someone. "Andreas is right there. He will take us." He steered her toward the waiting car.

Oh no, oh shit! Paige fought back the panic, fought the

desire to turn and run. Instead she replied loudly, "We're going to *the yacht* for lunch? What a nice and thoughtful surprise." *Oh my God.*

Fingers of fear curled around Paige's heart. As she slid into the car, she saw Martha shoot from the bench and look wildly around. Fighting every instinct to scream and wave, she could only pray Martha heard where she was going.

* * *

Martha's earpiece crackled and she could hear snippets of the conversation. *The yacht! They're going to the yacht! I gotta get to her!*

Martha felt her heart was on the verge of exploding when she saw Paige's blond head slide into the car and pull away. *Oh shit! No! This was not in the plan. Fuck!*

She hurried to the garage and found her car. Throwing it in drive, she peeled out into the midday traffic, only to get stuck in a row of cars.

"*Shit!* What the hell's going on?" Up ahead, she saw a mammoth, diesel flatbed truck; half of it straddled the sidewalk. A car with a flat tire sat in the middle of the street. "*Son of a bitch!* Move that piece ah shit!" Honking horns and screaming drivers added to her frustration.

Sweat ran down her face and back as she sat in the traffic. The sun beat through the windshield. Seconds turned into minutes. *I gotta get there!* Finally, the flatbed moved all four wheels to the sidewalk, allowing the traffic to flow again. Martha punched the gas with enough ferocity to jolt her spine.

* * *

Snap Decision

Aboard the stern deck on the *Baltic Blue*, Paige saw a table set with cut crystal, glass plates, and silverware, the sun's rays glinting from each heavy piece. A vase of flowers complemented the green of the plates. Max pulled out a chair for Paige. "Sit, please." It was more of a command than a request.

He's all business—not a good sign. "Thank you. The table is lovely." *Keep him talking. Stall.* She prayed he did not pick up on the slight quaver in her voice. "You did not have to do this."

He smiled, but it did not fill his face. "I felt as if I did. Shall we eat before it gets cold?"

He knows something. Paige gazed down at the plate loaded with lobster tail, asparagus drizzled with Hollandaise, and tomato salad. A bowl of drawn butter sat to the left. Any appetite she had vanished on the car ride to the yacht.

She watched Max stab a chunk of lobster and dip it into the butter. He chewed slowly and asked why she was not eating.

Birds circled above, eyeballing the deck for a fallen scrap. "I guess I'm not used to such rich food at lunch, but I am hungry." She pierced a piece of asparagus and ate it.

"But this is your favorite."

A few quiet, stilted minutes dragged by. The clanking of their cutlery was the only sound to be heard. Paige remarked on the weather and how perfect a day it was to dine outside.

"Yes. I know how much you enjoy spending time on the boat. It's been awhile since you've been on board, say four nights?"

Paige stopped mid-chew. *Uh oh. What do I say? He definitely knows.*

It was in that moment Paige knew she may never be seen again.

* * *

Martha sped to the marina. She had lost contact with Paige but soon heard voices in her ear. It was Max and he was saying something about taking a pleasure cruise after lunch. Whatever Paige's response, she did not hear it; it was carried away on the breeze.

"Come on Paige, stall! Stall!"

* * *

"I'll notify Captain Brennan we're almost finished and to get her ready for the pleasure cruise. How does that sound, Paige, hmm?" He fiddled with the heavy silver knife, turning it over in his hand. His light, airy tone did not fool her for a second.

She felt like she was a mouse being batted around by a huge, fat cat. "I didn't see him when we boarded." *This has to stop.*

"He's here. I'm sure he'd love to say hello."

"Oh, that's not necessary. We can enjoy our lunch, just the two of us."

An invisible, vast gulf popped up between them.

Please let Martha be nearby.

She rolled the dice. *I need more wine.* She sipped a mouthful. *Now or never.*

Leaning as far forward as possible without exposing the wire, eyes locked on Max, she said, "I know you took Fina and killed her—and many others. I know you're selling organs. That explains *all the cash*. You have no money. You're nothing but a liar and a murderer," she hissed. "You're a piece of shit."

Max stopped playing with the knife. He tilted his head to

the right and nonchalantly said, "Oh Paige, I was wondering when you were going to figure that out. Your little friend Serafina made me a *great deal* of money. But she didn't go down without a fight. You on the other hand...well, you will simply just disappear." His eyes glittered like a cobra's.

Springing from his seat, he lunged over the table for her.

Paige was quicker. She threw her glass of wine into Max's face. Anger and adrenaline possessed her entire body. Vaulting from the table, she heaved it over onto a stunned, partially blind Max who screamed and rubbed his eyes. She ran for her life.

Trapped under the table, Max screamed and shoved the table aside. He tried to stand, but slipped on the butter and fell to his knees, tearing his pants. A red bloom pushed through the fine linen, staining it in a dark, angry red patch. Roaring in pain and anger, he shot up from the floor and raced after Paige.

"You bitch! You won't escape! You'll *never* be free of me!" he screamed as he hobbled after her. He was consumed by the vile feeling of helplessness as he watched Paige race toward the gangplank leading to the stern onto the cement dock. "Brennan! Raise the gangplank!"

* * *

On two wheels, Martha tore in the marina. The clatter of dishes and Paige's scream reverberated in her ear. "Oh my God!"

As rapidly as her arthritic knees could, she left the car and jogged toward the slip where the *Baltic Blue* was moored. So caught up in saving Paige, she did not see the rope carelessly strewn on the dock. Her ankle twisted; she fell hard on the cement, tearing up one knee. Cursing in pain, she heard the engines come to life on the *Baltic Blue*.

No! Paige!

She crawled to a light post and hoisted herself up then hobbled farther up the dock.

* * *

Paige dashed toward the gangplank at the other end of the stern deck. "NO!" she screamed when she saw it slowly lifting from the cement dock. The sounds of the engines growling to life made her push harder.

Water churned, creating swirling eddies around the hull. From the bow she heard the metallic grinding of the gears lifting the anchor from the silt below. *Go!*

Closing in on the gangplank, she almost threw up when it freed itself from the dock and folded on the back of the boat. "No!"

Behind her, she heard footsteps.

"You're trapped now!" Max yelled. "You'll never escape me."

Paige raced to the edge, put one foot on the railing, and catapulted herself onto the cement dock. Her shin slammed into the bottom of the metal. Layers of skin were scratched off her hands and elbows as she crashed onto the cement, hands first. She rolled onto her back, grimacing in pain. *Get up!*

"Paige! Paige!" Martha called from a distance.

The abrasive, loud grinding of the yacht's gears being thrust into reverse filled her ears. The engines grinded their protestation at the sudden change of direction. She looked up to see Max and Brennan gesticulating and pointing at her. The *Baltic Blue* slowly began to go backward toward the slip. *Oh God no!* Ignoring the pain in her shin, Paige got on all fours and turned to run.

Seeing Martha limping toward her made her eyes fill with tears. "Martha! You found me!" Her strangled cry filled the marina. "Thank God! We need to leave now!"

Arms wrapped around one another; the two women staggered to the safety of Martha's car.

Panting for breath, Paige could not speak. Blood trickled from the gashes on her hands and leg. She leaned her head against the window and felt the tears prick her eyes. "Oh my God Martha, he was going to kill me."

Her eyes locked on the road, Martha reached for Paige's hand. "It's okay. You're safe—for now." Stomping on the gas, she sped away from the horror Paige left behind.

* * *

Think Max, think. He pulled out his phone and barked into the mouthpiece at Stu.

"Drop whatever the hell you're doing. You two need to get to the boat instantly! We have a serious problem which is getting worse as we speak!" He clicked the phone shut. *Damnit to hell! She knows everything! Son of a bitch.*

Inhaling deeply, Max centered himself and reined in his anger and panic. *Stay calm. Focus on what you need to do. And that is finding Paige. Think!*

He called his source at the police station. He was put through right away. "I need you to come to this address and look for a white four-door Kia SUV with two women. It went west out of the parking lot. I don't care if you need to sit there all day and night. We need to find these women. Call me back with anything you find."

Max glanced out at the parking lot. A car came speeding into the lot, kicking up stones and dust. Doors opened and slammed shut. He waved at Stu and Marty, who sprinted to the dock.

"We got here as fast as possible. What the hell is going on?" Stu asked.

Max motioned to the steps leading below deck. "Brennan, get over here. We need to figure out how to save our asses."

* * *

"Get me the goddamned first-aid kit!" Max barked at Brennan when they went below. He rolled up his pant leg to reveal an angry scrape, raw as uncooked hamburger. "Fuck!" Max yanked the first-aid kit from Brennan. Rummaging through it, he found a large band-aid and slapped it on his knee.

Marty spoke first. "Max, what happened and what do we need to do?"

In a voice tight with anger, he told Stu and Marty what had happened on the deck of the stern. "She knows everything. And obviously the woman who was with her knows too."

Marty cut his eyes to Stu and asked, "Who was the other woman?"

Max sat back in his chair and squeezed his eyes closed in concentration. "I didn't recognize her face at first, but I remember now." He sat up and leveled the three men with his gaze. "She works in Tower Two. She runs security."

An uncomfortable silence filled the area as Max's words settled.

"*Security?*" Marty asked. "Problematic."

"It certainly has that potential."

"We need to assume Paige and that other woman are going to the police."

"Correct assumption. However, we"—he gestured at all four of them—"don't know what, if any, proof she has. I did tell her that I had Fina eliminated. She—"

Brennan interrupted, "Sir, I think I may know if she has any proof. I'll be right back." He rose and exited.

"We need to find Paige and the woman who was with her. I have a car headed to her apartment." Max snapped his fingers at Marty. "Call the office and ask Franklin for the names of the people in security."

Brennan returned, grim-faced. In his hand was the notebook. "Sir, a page is missing."

Max, Marty, and Stu gazed at Brennan.

"And?" Marty asked.

"The page with the two women who were next on our list—Manzetti and Buckley—is gone. Buckley must have torn it out."

"Which means she has it," Marty said. "What if she shows the police?"

Max stood and paced the room. "I'll take care of that."

CHAPTER 42

Frozen peas and icebags were strapped to Martha's ankle and Paige's shin. Both women sat with their limbs elevated in Martha's living room. Lindsey joined them a few minutes later and dropped a six pack on the table. She cracked open three beers and handed one each to her friends. In astonished disbelief, she listened to what befell Paige and Martha.

"Holy shit! Thanks to the man above that you're okay!" she exclaimed when they finished. "But still, way too close for comfort."

"Ya got that right. Damn this is cold! It's turning my skin blue!" Martha said.

"Stop complaining! You both could be dead!" Lindsey admonished.

"True. But we're not." Martha threw a glance to Paige, who sat silently, her head resting on the back of the chair. "Paige honey, are you okay?"

At first, she did not answer. The ordeal of the afternoon hit her like a freight train. Her mind was reeling with what she just experienced and how close she came to never being seen again. *I wish I could crawl into a shell like a snail and hide.* Leaning forward, she was overcome with emotion. The dam broke and the tears flowed. Sobs shook her body; the icebag plunked to the floor. She held her head in her hands and sobbed.

Lindsey stood and wrapped her arms around her. Gingerly, she dabbed Paige's eye with a tissue. "It's okay lovie, we're here." She gave Paige another tissue and rubbed her back.

"I don't know how I am. I thought I was going to die, like Fina. I wish I could turn back the clock. I wish I could change everything. If it weren't for me dating Max, Fina would be alive."

Lindsey and Martha exchanged a sorrowful look; each woman thought her heart would break. Martha spoke softly and tenderly. "No, honey, no. You had no way of knowing Fina was going to go back to that yacht. This is *not* your fault. Banish that thought from your mind."

Intellectually, Paige knew Martha was right. Emotionally, though, it was another story. Emotionally, she knew she would struggle.

"How could I have fallen for a guy like him?" she asked aloud. "I should have listened to you guys. But I didn't, and now Fina's dead." Tears welled again in her eyes. "And I'm really afraid he's going to find me—or his henchmen will."

"We agree with you. And we need to do something about that."

Paige pleaded, "I don't want to put you two in any more danger than I already have. Please. You've done enough for me."

"Don't you worry about us," Martha said and tossed a look at Lindsey. "Thanks to you being wired up, we have concrete evidence against him. But your safety comes first."

Paige stood and walked over to the window. Fixating on a mother bird feeding her hatchlings, she reasoned, "Well, I could go back to Philly, right? My brothers and sister are there. And then come back after he's in jail."

"We thought of that. Guaranteed, a guy like him has two-legged rats crawling all over the place. And he knows you'd probably go back to Philly. He'd send someone to follow you or worse. We can't put your family in danger either."

"Okay, so what do you think I should do?" Paige turned back around and gazed at her friends. "Vanish into thin air or something? Just go 'poof' and disappear?" Paige gave a wan smile. "I wish I could."

Lindsey and Martha gave a small chuckle. "Well lovie, that's exactly what we have planned."

"What are you talking about?"

Lindsey began but was interrupted by Martha. "Hold that thought. I gotta hit the head and get more beer," Martha said.

* * *

Martha dropped back into her seat and cracked open a beer. Handing one to Paige, she said, "We're not going to sugar-coat anything, honey. What you are going to do tomorrow is not gonna be easy. We know you have more than enough strength to go through with this. Right, Linds?"

Lindsey nodded and added, "Paige, we love ya like a daughter and because of that, you need to be safe. The only way for that to happen is for you to disappear—just like that." She snapped her fingers.

Like a kid on a trampoline, Paige's knee bounced in response to the overbearing angst coursing through her. Brows knitted together, she gazed at her friends. "Please tell me. I'm not sure I need to be stressed out any more than I already am! Plus, my curiosity is piqued, to say the least."

"Go ahead Marth, tell her."

Martha nodded. "Paige, we believe you are in mortal danger. Dovic proved that with what we uncovered about his sicko side business. Two days from now is the twelfth;

the day you are—or shall I say *were*—going to be his next victim. Instead, you're going to seemingly disappear off the face of the earth. Poof! Just like you said earlier."

Paige frowned in confusion. "How?"

"At the crack of dawn tomorrow, we're going to take you to Newark Airport where you will board a flight to a city far away from here. From there, you—"

"Hang on." Paige raised her hand. "Airport? Where am I going?"

"Like I said, somewhere far away from here—and Dovic."

What? How far away? "Will I still be in the United States?"

Lindsey replied, "Of course."

Phew. Paige absorbed the first part of the plan. *A far-away city? What about going to Philly?*

"Wait. Why can't I just stay here and hide? New York is a huge city." Nerves buzzed throughout Paige. "Or I can go to Philly and stay there somewhere. I have tons of family and friends there!"

Lindsey continued, "Knowing the kind of *scum* we now know Dovic to be, he'll be looking for you. He's the type who does not work alone either. And if you're in danger, I can guarantee he'll go to Philly to try to find you."

Paige digested the part about Philadelphia. *If he hurt Fina and others, my family could be in danger.* "You're right. As difficult as this is to admit, Philly is out of the question." Wiping her eyes, she continued. "But you guys have the proof necessary for his arrest. Take it to the cops today," Paige protested. "Please!"

"Correct, we do, but we need to take care of you first. We must assume Dovic has a vast web of people—and because of that, honey, you have to begin a new life in a new city." Martha sipped her beer. She covered Paige's hand. "And Paige honey, you must assume a new identity."

A weighty stillness fell over the women. Staring at her friends, Paige spoke. "*What?* A new identity? How..."

"Please listen." Martha cleared her throat and continued. "Yes, and we took care of that as well. We will talk about the identity piece in a little while. Lastly, honey, you cannot contact your family, friends, or us for a year. Dovic is a sick SOB who will stop at nothing to find you to take out his revenge. He probably figured out who we are"—she nodded at Lindsey—"so we figured no contact would keep you and your family safe."

Paige's slowly leaned back in the chair; her head swam in a pool of confusion, her stomach knotted like a ball of string. The muscles in her back were taut. She swallowed the lump in her throat, the questions zipping through her mind. *A new life? New identity? No contact with anyone?*

"Oh my God. I don't know if I can do that! My parents will *go crazy* with worry and my sister just told me she's pregnant with her first baby! She needs me there!"

"Lovie, we know how difficult this is, but your family would rather have you alive than dead. I know we would," Lindsey added.

Paige sighed. *I didn't think about that.* "Very true. My parents don't need to lose a child."

"I'm glad you see it that way. Anyway, here's the rest."

I can't believe what I'm hearing, Paige thought. In awe, she listened to the plan Lindsey and Martha concocted to help her disappear.

"I'm blown away you would do this for me. But you realize that I need stuff from my apartment, right?" *I have a job, bills, an apartment! Oh my God, this is a lot.* Paige rubbed her temples in an attempt to ward off a stress headache. "What about my job? I have bills to pay. My rent is due, plus I have about four months left on my lease!"

"We know, but you don't have a choice. We can help with money and the apartment, right Linds?" Martha turned to Lindsey.

"Yeah, I can take care of those details."

Martha's voice was stern. "You will stay here tonight. Your apartment is off limits. For all we know, Max probably has surveillance on your building."

They're right. I can't go back to my apartment, but I need some necessities. "If I'm going to be leaving so soon, I need some clothes. I can't wear these stained things." Blood caked her shirt and shorts.

Lindsey looked her up and down. "Yeah, you're right. I'll go and get what you need."

Paige rattled off where to find clothes and other necessities. "My backpack is in the closet. Please bring that and obviously my wallet and driver's license."

A coy smile crept across Martha's face. "Actually you don't. Linds, in the kitchen drawer by the fridge," she said, pointing to the kitchen, "is the folder."

Lindsey placed a folder in front of Paige. As Paige opened it, her jaw fell open as her eyes flew over the documents. "I'm stunned. You did all this for me?"

"Yeah, I got people in high places. But Paige, you have to promise you won't contact anyone for a very long time," Martha said.

Paige studied her friend. Something in her tone captivated her. "I promise."

Grasping the seriousness of what was going to transpire in the next twenty-four hours rocked Paige to her core. A hole exploded in her heart. "You *have* to contact my mom and tell her. Please? I'll figure out a way for you to convince her that this whole fiasco is real."

"Fair enough," Lindsey said.

"People like Dovic work and move quickly. Chances are he has had someone watching our apartment buildings."

Paige released a long breath. "I agree. If disappearing keeps you and my family safe, I trust your judgment."

"There's one moah thing you need to trust us with too," Martha said.

Now what? "And what may that be?" Paige asked.

"This!" Martha giggled as she held up a box of hair color in one hand and a pair of scissors in the other.

Paige could not help but laugh. "This is something out of a Jason Bourne movie! You really thought of everything, didn't you?" She looked at her friends and slugged down half of her beer. "Okay, let's do it."

CHAPTER 43

Five a.m. rolled around quickly. Soft music floated through the air, waking Paige. She rolled over and fumbled for the mute button. She lay in bed thinking about the day ahead and the anticipation of escaping New York, her heart and head embroiled in an emotional versus intellectual battle. *I'm leaving this city forever. It's not real yet. I know I need to be safe, but how am I going to survive not seeing my family and friends for who knows how long?* Her thoughts turned to Fina. *God I miss you Fina. I promise I'll get him busted for you.*

"Hey, you awake in there honey?" Martha called through the door, accompanied by a light rap.

"Yup, just rolling out of bed," Paige responded. "I'll be out in five."

"Good, the traffic should be light at this hour. We need to leave heah in thirty minutes. That'll give you plenty ah time to find your gate and get settled."

* * *

Chirps and calls from feathered early risers floated through the pre-dawn air. The sun had not yet cracked the horizon on this late summer morning. Dew, thick, wet, and bubbly, clung to the green grass.

In contented silence, Paige, Lindsey, and Martha rode to the airport, until one of Paige's favorite songs sang from the speakers. Tears filled her eyes and melancholy filled her soul as she listened to the male singer sing the two lines about leaving loved ones and remembering them after they have gone.

"Turn it up, I love this song!" Paige requested when the song began to build. Martha obliged and cranked up the volume. The trio sang along and waited for the powerful instrumentals to kick in. Lindsey played air guitar as Paige pounded the seat as if were a bass drum. At the end of the song, the women laughed at how one song exhausted them.

"One of the best songs ever effin' written!" Martha said.

"Agreed. You know something? Hearing this song is an omen; I'm gonna be a free bird in a few hours, right?"

Martha and Lindsey agreed. "Good call, lovie."

From the back seat, Paige gazed at Martha and Lindsey, her heart swelling with love and at the same time aching with pain.

Paige remembered feeling this awful conflicting storm of emotions when she left for college her freshman year. Excitement crackled through her at the idea of being independent. Yet, when she pulled out of the driveway, her heart lurched at the vision of her parents waving—and disappearing—in the rearview mirror. The saving grace was that she knew she would see them again during school breaks. Today was different because she knew that she would not, could not see her family for almost a year. At a red light, she gazed out the window. Few people were out and about at that hour. To her right, Paige noticed one person, a young woman roughly her age, lacing up running shoes and stretching her legs.

God, I'd give anything to be going for a run, even though I hate running. She observed the young woman place earphones on top of her ears, stretch her arms over her head, and jog away down the darkened sidewalk. *She has all the freedom she wants. I will soon too, even though I'm terrified.*

As they drove to the airport, Paige attempted to tamp down the tangible fear and angst creeping through her. It was futile. *Let yourself feel them briefly but compartmentalize them into your mental file folders. Close your eyes, breathe, and put those feelings in the folders.* Within a few minutes, Paige felt more peaceful and calmer, particularly when she heard the not-so-distant roar of incoming red-eye flights. She smiled. *Oh that sound!* Paige welcomed the tranquility which settled over her. *I forgot how comforted the powerful sound of planes makes me feel.* Tilting her good eye toward the still-dark sky, she saw the blinking red lights above of a jet on its descent. Grinning broadly she asked Martha and Lindsey, "Did I ever tell you guys I wanted to be a pilot when I was a kid?"

"No, you didn't," Lindsey replied, the surprise obvious in her voice. "You did?"

"Really? No shit!" Martha added.

"I sure did. I loved *everything* about aviation. I read every book I could about Amelia Earhart, the Wright brothers, you name it. To this day when I see planes streaking across the sky, I marvel at how an ocean of air supports an aircraft weighing over 220 tons. And when you count the souls on board, it's nothing short of miraculous." She sighed heavily. "But after losing most of my vision, my dream was no longer a reality."

Martha and Lindsey said nothing.

"And now, I'm escaping this nightmare on one of those huge, beautiful planes. Who would have thought, right?" She chuckled.

"Can't argue with you theah," Lindsey said.

Martha pushed out a laugh. "Not me."

Paige gazed at the back of her friends' heads. A surge of genuine affection overcame her. *I feel like I've known them forever. I'm going to miss them so much. It kills me to think I won't see them for a year. If ever again for that matter.*

Martha drove up behind the two other cars in the curbside queue. "Seems like United is a popular airline today."

From the window, Paige set eyes on several travelers clustered around the United Airlines entrance into the airport. *This is real. I'm leaving.* A sudden, sharp terror filled her chest. *Can I actually go through with this?* Panic accompanied the terror. *Just breathe and think about your safety, as well as your loved ones' safety. You have no choice.*

Martha inched the car closer and put it in park. She cast her eyes in the rearview mirror at Paige. "Okay honey, you ready?"

She did not trust her voice. Nodding slowly, Paige took hold of her only piece of luggage: her backpack. Paige watched Martha and Lindsey exit the car first and stand by the curb. Looking through the window at them, her heart clenched. *This is going to be so hard. Fina, give me strength.*

Drawing in a deep breath, she exited the car. An impatient driver behind them honked his horn wanting to get into their parking spot.

"All right! Hold your horses, for Christ's sake!" Martha replied, lifting a single finger at the driver. "Impatient asshole." From her jacket pocket, she took out two envelopes which she held out to Paige. In red pen, each envelope was marked—one with an A, the other with a B.

Paige asked what they were.

"We're not going to tell you. When you're situated inside, you will open them then. Linds, you have the other one?"

Lindsey nodded. "Here." She placed a third envelope in Paige's hand. "This should help with basic expenses."

"What's this?"

"Something you will need. Go ahead, peek inside."

Paige sucked in a sharp breath. *Oh my. Wow. So much money.* "I can't take this." She glanced back down at the envelope full of cash. "It's too much." She slid her eyes between her friends.

"Yes, you can and yes you will." Martha's tone was firm. "Put it in your bag with the other two envelopes."

Paige knew protesting was pointless. "I'm speechless. I hope I can repay you someday."

"Not necessary," Martha replied. "Just be safe for a while."

Paige shook her head, trying to stop her tears.

"Okay lovie, bring it in." Lindsey extended her arms for Paige. "I'm gonna miss you very much. You'll be okay. I promise. Love you," she whispered into Paige's ear.

Paige's eyes welled up and she did not want to let go. Lindsey slowly released her. Paige turned to Martha. "Oh Martha."

"You're a good-lookin' babe with your new 'do and all." Martha's voice cracked as she stroked Paige's short auburn hair. "Come here, honey. Everything will work out, I promise." Martha embraced Paige, who held on as long as she could.

Paige let out a whimper. She did not want to let go, but she knew it was time. "I'm so *afraid.*"

Martha squeezed her. "We understand, but don't be afraid. You're strong and can do this," she said. "Everything is going to work out. I know it."

How I hope you're right. "I love you so much. I'll never forget what you've done for me," she whispered, hugging both of them again. Her eyes stung with tears.

"Time for you to go. Remember, no contact," Martha ordered and wiped her eyes.

Paige whispered, "I know."

Martha flipped her wrist and glanced at her watch. " I gotta go to work. I need to be theah at eight," she said.

"Work this early?" Paige chuckled.

"Yeah, asshole Barry called in sick again so I have to cover."

Paige stepped back, straightened her posture, and blotted her eyes one last time. "It's time. I'll never be able to thank you enough. I love you guys." Her heart fractured into a thousand irreparable pieces. As she entered the airport, she turned for one final wave; she lowered her hand. Lindsey and Martha were already gone.

* * *

Paige weaved her way through people waiting outside to check their suitcases. She entered the airport and was thankful when she spotted a coffee kiosk. *I'm dragging. Before I open those envelopes, I need the caffeine to work its magic.*

Paige sat down with her hot coffee, donut, and newspaper and took a small sip. *So good. Just what I need. My head has to be clear.*

She savored her sips and watched the sun peek above the horizon and turn the sky a sharp, deep shade of blue, clear and full of promise for a beautiful day. Rays reflected off the glass windows and illuminated the waiting area. Travelers hustled through the airport, paper coffee cups in hand, newspapers folded under their arms. Paige laughed when she saw a little boy gleefully riding on his mother's wheeled suitcase. A little girl lollygagged between her parents; a stuffed giraffe dangled from her tiny hand.

Paige snapped open the front page of the paper and

scanned the headlines under the date. *How is it almost mid-September? This nightmare seems like it dragged on for a long time.* She perused the articles for a minute more before she quit. *I can't concentrate on reading this right now. I'll save it for the flight.* Paige folded the paper in half, unzipped her backpack, and placed it inside next to the envelopes Martha gave her. *These are more important anyway.*

Paige laid the sealed envelopes on the tabletop. She took notice that both were identical in size and weight. *Here goes.*

Opening the one with a red A, Paige saw a lined piece of paper folded over something thicker. Extracting it, she saw a ticket and boarding pass for a flight to Chicago. *Chicago. Why Chicago? Hmm. Do they know people there?*

Placing it down, she shifted her gaze to the other envelope. *I wonder if this is another destination.* Tearing it open, she saw it was a flight to San Francisco. *San Francisco. Maybe Lindsey and Martha know people there too.*

Laying both tickets on the table, she read both flights were scheduled to depart at approximately eight o'clock. *Martha and Lindsey gave me two options. Brilliant. It all makes sense now. I get to choose where to start over. But how? Which city? I know nothing about either place. And I don't know anyone in either place.*

Entrenched in thinking about the cities, she went to take a sip of her coffee, but spilled some. A few drops soiled the lined paper. *Crap!* Blotting it with a napkin, she saw some words written in the middle. "What's this?" Notes were scrawled on each piece of paper.

Wow, they thought of everything. Based on what was written on the paper—*Tilden House, Winston Court,* and *Boulevard West Condominiums*—she concluded they were names of places to live in either city. *Martha and Lindsey thought of everything. They're the best.*

She turned her attention back to the boarding passes. *San Francisco or Chicago? How do I begin to even think about choosing? This is so overwhelming. How am I going to decide? Flip a coin?* She laughed. *But at least I'll be far away from here and Max won't know where I am.*

Lastly, she gazed at her new driver's license picture and identity: Samantha Lewis. *I like that name. And I look pretty damn good as a redhead.*

Paige shook her head and reflected on the insanity of the last several months. *Everything was so normal eight months ago and now I have to start over in a new city as a new person. This still feels like I'm in a movie; one in which I don't know the ending.*

Coffee cup empty, Paige stuffed the stained napkins into the paper cup. *Since I'm already anxious enough, I need to go and see if these flights are on time.* She rose, tossed out her trash, and found the board with all the flight information. *Must be my lucky day. One flight leaves from gate 17, the other 19. Good sign.*

Making herself comfortable in seating area 18, Paige heard an announcement float through the half-full seating area.

"Good morning. This morning's flight to San Francisco is fully booked. We have several passengers on standby. If there are any travelers who have the flexibility to fly out this afternoon in order to accommodate a traveler on standby, please approach the check-in desk. We will get you on the next flight and reward you with a five-hundred-dollar flight voucher. Thank you."

I could give up the flight to San Francisco, go to Chicago, and get a five-hundred-dollar voucher, Paige thought. *But San Francisco is so far away from everything I know.*

Another announcement was made regarding a thirty-minute boarding time until the flight to Chicago departed. *Chicago is at least a little closer to Philadelphia, even though I can't go home for a bit.*

The coffee had filled her bladder. *Thirty minutes? I better go to the bathroom before we leave.* Paige stood, lifted her backpack, and wandered to the bathroom roughly two gates away.

As she was washing her hands, she thought of the opportunity Martha and Lindsey gave her to begin a new life. *What would I have done without them? I already miss them. Who knows if I'll ever see them again?* Tears welled in her eyes. She looked up to see a drawn, tired face staring back at her from the mirror. *I look like I rose from the dead.* Smoothing her hair, she admonished herself. *Get it together Paige. You don't have a choice.* A shredded roll of brown paper towels hung like dead leaves from the dispenser. She yanked a few and dried her hands.

Paige stepped out into the crowded concourse and automatically glanced in both directions. No one looked familiar. At first. Her head snapped back to the left. Her blood suddenly turned to ice. She squinted. Her breath left her. *No! This can't be happening!*

Walking her way was Brennan. Like a rabbit, she ducked back into the restroom and sank into the wall. Panting, heart racing with her thoughts. *Max must have sent him. Stay calm. Freaking out will get you nowhere.* Peeling herself from the wall, she peered out the entrance of the bathroom and observed Brennan look to his right and nod. Stu stood outside the men's restroom across the concourse. Brennan nodded to Stu who sauntered over to him. *Oh no! They're both here. No.*

In each seating area, the men stopped and studied the waiting passengers. They approached an airport policeman who took something from Stu. It was a picture.

Oh my God! They're looking for me! How did they know I'm here? How did they know? Max! I know he found out. What am I going to do? Shit, shit, shit! I'm gonna miss the flight if I'm trapped in here. That can't happen!

Paige paced the floor of the bathroom trying to create a plan. *I have to get out of here somehow.* Stopping, she peered at her reflection in the mirror. *Wait a minute! If they see me, they won't recognize me. They're looking for blonde, blue-eyed Paige and I'm not her anymore. Get out of here, Paige. You need to go. The planes leave soon!*

Pulling her hood up, Paige peered out of the bathroom and scanned the area for Brennan and Stu. She spotted them only a few gates over—still too close for comfort. Yanking paper towels from the dispenser, she ran cold water, soaked them, and dabbed her sweating face. *Remember, you look different now. Trust that. You have to get there ASAP without running like a fool.*

Glancing at her watch, she realized time was not on her side. *I gotta get back! I won't make it!*

The bathroom speaker crackled. Paige leaped and clutched her chest.

"Good morning once again. This is the final call for United Flight 93 bound for San Francisco. Boarding is at gate 17." *Oh no, I may not make either flight, but I have to! I can't stay here with Max's people crawling around.*

Another voice filled the bathroom.

"Once again, good morning to passengers headed to Chicago. This is the final boarding call for United Flight 1164 to Chicago. Please proceed to gate 19."

A sea of donut and coffee sloshed around in Paige's stomach. *I may puke.* Her heart knocked against her ribs. Under the hood, perspiration covered her scalp. *It's now or never, Paige. You gotta go!*

Casting an eye across the concourse, she saw gates 17 and 19 were still open for boarding. *Thank God.* Nowhere did she see Stu and Brennan near those gates. Turning to one side, she swore when she did spot them standing between gates 18 and 20. *Fuck! Even with new hair, I still don't want to attract attention by running, but I need to get over there.*

They stood at the last row of seats studying the people seated. Stu stood shrugging his shoulders, palms facing the ceiling. Brennan was tapping his watch, then flicked his thumb in a *Let's go* gesture. Both men turned around so that the backs of their heads faced Paige.

Thank God, they're leaving. Go, Paige! Now! Go! Please be with me, Fina!

Paige made sure her backpack was secured tightly. She stepped from the bathroom and onto the shiny floor of the concourse. Threading through other travelers, Paige tried to hurry. With each step, it seemed the gates moved farther away from her.

A prickle of fear ran up her spine. Listening to her instincts, she lifted her eyes and saw both men were walking in her direction.

Her bowels felt like pudding, her mouth felt like a desert. *Keep moving, keep moving. Don't look over there! Do not change your speed.* Desperately wanting to sprint, Paige strode with long steps and kept her eyes locked on the prize.

Stu and Brennan were heading in her direction.

Steady steps. Confident steps. Breathe. Breathe.

Time seemed to stand still for a split second. A slow-motion movie played in Paige's head as the two men passed within fifteen yards of her. Turning away from them, she stopped briefly and pretended to rummage in her bag. *Do not look yet. Give it time.* Fearing her heart was going to explode, Paige held her breath until she noticed the two men were well past her, lost in the ocean of travelers.

Thank you, Lord. Hustle, Paige. The gates will close soon! Relief flooded her when she realized most travelers had boarded. *No line, thank God.*

Paige's brain raced like a Formula One car. *Make a decision! Make it quick! You're running out of time! Gate 17 or 19?*

Her heart pounded in rhythm to her footsteps. Her head spun as the gates drew nearer. *Only a few more steps and I'm free. Please, Fina! Show me some kind of sign! Chicago or San Francisco?*

Both gates beckoned her to freedom. Both flights would carry her to a new life.

Flicking her eyes back and forth between 17 and 19, Paige came to a fork in the road. *Decide now! Do it!* Saying a silent prayer, Paige veered sharply through one of the gates and onto the jetway.

As she slowed to a walk, Paige felt lighter. Warm sunshine shone on her through the small windows above. Stepping through the door into the magnificent aircraft, Paige immediately became aware of a joyful serenity, one that wrapped itself around her. Soon, Paige and all the other souls would be soaring through the picture-perfect clear blue sky.

Buckling her seatbelt, she laid her head back and closed her eyes. *I did it.*

Author's note: United Flight 93 was scheduled to depart at 8:00 on the morning of September 11, 2001. It was forty-two minutes late in leaving. At 10:03 that morning, the flight crashed into a field in Shanksville, Pennsylvania. You know the rest.

Holly Spofford

Acknowledgments

Thank you to my love, my partner in crime, my husband John. Without your interest and patience as I chatted about, fretted about, laughed about this new "family" and their lives, I'm not sure this story would have gelled as powerfully as it did. Your creativity is beyond measure. I love being witness to how this writing journey has awakened the ingenuity which had been asleep deep inside you for a long time. I love you with all my heart. Thank you.

Thank you to another very important man in my life, my dad. I'm not sure you will ever know the depth of appreciation I feel for your unwavering support since I started this new career. My entire life you've been there as a father and a friend. I'm the luckiest daughter on the planet. I look forward to sharing many more events with you. Thanks Dad, I love you.

Where would this book be without Kristen, my wonderful editor? Your eagle eye, honest words, excellent suggestions, and heartfelt zeal for helping me create engaging, well-written stories is only the tip of the iceberg of your talent. I look forward to you editing many more of my books. Thank you for everything.

Thank you as always to my beta readers: Cheryl, Ed, and Nancy. I can't thank you enough for your suggestions, candor, and willingness to help me out. Thank you.

I am grateful to all my friends and family who support me by helping spread the word about my work. Keep doing it! Thank you.

Thank you to Kingsman Formatters. You always do a great job.

Lastly, to all my readers. You guys are the ones who buy my books, attend my events, and push me to produce a better book than the one before. You make writing fun. Thank you for everything.

About the Author

Snap Decision is Holly Spofford's fourth novel. She is the author of the Taylor-Tyson: A Decade of Danger trilogy. A native Philadelphian, Holly lives outside of the city with her husband John.

www.HollySpofford.com

Made in the USA
Middletown, DE
11 May 2024